THE TRAGEDY OF DANE RILEY

ALSO BY
KAT SPEARS

The Boy Who Killed Grant Parker

Breakaway

Sway

THE TRAGEDY OF DANE RILEY

KAT SPEARS

W

WEDNESDAY
BOOKS
NEW YORK

First published in the United States by Wednesday Books, a division of St. Martin's Publishing Group

THE TRAGEDY OF DANE RILEY. Copyright © 2021 by Kat Spears. All rights reserved. Printed in the United States of America. For information, address St. Martin's Publishing Group, 120 Broadway, New York, NY 10271.

www.wednesdaybooks.com

Library of Congress Cataloging-in-Publication Data

Names: Spears, Katarina M., author.
Title: The tragedy of Dane Riley / Kat Spears.
Description: First Edition. | New York : Wednesday Books, 2021.
Identifiers: LCCN 2020056432 | ISBN 9781250124807 (hardcover) | ISBN 9781250124814 (ebook)
Classification: LCC PS3619.P4343 T73 2021 | DDC 813/.6—dc23
LC record available at https://lccn.loc.gov/2020056432

Our books may be purchased in bulk for promotional, educational, or business use. Please contact your local bookseller or the Macmillan Corporate and Premium Sales Department at 1-800-221-7945, extension 5442, or by email at MacmillanSpecialMarkets@macmillan.com.

First Edition: 2021

10 9 8 7 6 5 4 3 2 1

For George,
for saving my life

ACKNOWLEDGMENTS

The biggest thanks I have to give goes to Sara Goodman, the amazing woman who edited this labor of love. It took the process of writing and publishing three books to learn that the only person who really needs to love my writing, is me . . . and a really great editor. Sara consistently pushes me to not only write the best story possible, but to really think about who my characters are and what they need to bring to the world. Kind, patient, thoughtful—Sara Goodman is an important name in YA publishing for all of the right reasons.

Thanks also to Brenna Franzitta, who copyedited this book. The attention to detail was so critical because of timeline changes made during the story editing process, and she caught all of them.

And thanks to my agent, Moe Ferrara, for waiting patiently for two years, understanding that I needed to love this book.

Miles of gratitude to my writing community at James River Writers and to Greg Andree and Andrew Rossi for reading early versions of this manuscript to give me feedback. #YNWA. A very special thanks to dear friend and uniquely challenging person to love, Stockport Steve, for providing some critical content for this book. I am forever grateful that you choose to share all of your best stories with me, though I know the fact that I hand you beers and am standing next to a screen with a soccer match on it has a lot to do with it. Thanks to Dave Gershman for enjoying this book, even an early draft of it, and making me feel like the story will be appreciated by at least one person, which is all that really matters.

I spent a long time working on this manuscript while the main character and I struggled with questions of life and death and the space in between. My dear friend Sarah Grigsby-Reiser was a cheerleader through all of it and she truly appreciated everything there is to celebrate during our short time on this planet. Sarah did not live to see this book become a bound, printed reality, and that is sad for me. At a launch event for this book, I know I would have seen Sarah's beaming smile enter the room, and she would have stayed to the end of the night to sit with me and rehash all of the excitement and exhaustion. In the midst of a pandemic and the world gone mad, Sarah left us quietly, but her life is a reminder to me that whatever burdens I carry, I don't carry them alone.

Thanks to David Avila, dear old friend, for the cultural sensitivity feedback he provided on the Filipino and other characters of Asian descent in this book. Horns up, man. And thanks to David's daughter, Erin, for giving me insight into the long-forgotten celebrity crushes of a thirteen-year-old girl.

Thanks to Margaret Woody, for giving me cultural sensitivity feedback on my characters of Korean descent, and for being an amazing character in her own right.

I am grateful and give thanks for Dane Carberry—a most darling friend, who I always forget is young enough to be my son—for giving me the perfect name to use for a main character. I'm sorry those of you reading this don't know Dane personally, because he's one of those unapologetically honest people who can make me laugh aloud just by recalling something funny he once said. He is a character in the book of my life whom I will always treasure.

Thanks to Aaron Holmes, my BFF, for consistently and unintentionally giving me the most amazing quotes to use in my books. "Her confidence bothers me" is still one of the best things anyone has ever said to me, in or out of context. I love you to the moon and back, my friend.

Thanks also, in no particular order, to my daughter Josie for inspiring Ophelia's character—it's hard to always be the smartest person in the room—you've got an uphill battle ahead, and I'm looking forward to watching every minute of it; Ingrid, for being hilarious and generally making life worth living; Jack, for being my rock, and a reminder that I have done a few great things in my life; my mom, for always supporting me, even when I don't make sensible choices; Caio, dear friend, for giving me some great ideas about Dane's taste in music; Andrea, for giving me a great idea to use her name in a book, though it wasn't how she intended it; Jerry, for giving me a great quote to use (go average early);

Joel and Sarah, for always being interested in talking about my latest manuscript, even when I've been working on it for so long that they are the only people still interested in talking about it; Lydia, for being the best cheerleading squad a girl could ask for; Jason, for introducing me to Aaron, because without him I'd be lost; Burhan, for making me crazy, because life wouldn't be nearly as interesting without him in it, and because he's the only person who ever brings me bagels and croissants; Chernes, for being consistently hilarious, and kind, and supportive; Jill, for giving me great story ideas that I am not up to the task of writing; the real-life Extreme Sports Asians who inspired Dane's friends in this book; Jina, for being a great advocate, friend, and listener; Sara K., for reminding me that you can be smart and angry while also kind; Adilio, Eddie, and Oyuka, for giving me a place to write where I always feel welcome and appreciated.

XOXO, Kat

It is not the psychologist's job to understand things that he in fact does not understand. . . . Let us state openly that you can't figure out anything in this world. Only fools and charlatans know and understand everything.

—ANTON CHEKHOV

If you knew you were going to die at the age of seventeen, it would impact every decision you made—who you dated, how much time you spent in school or worrying about grades, what risks you would take. Most likely you would take a pass on school altogether, spend all your time partying. Your tombstone would read something like, HE DIDN'T SLEEP WITH EVERY GIRL HE WANTED, BUT HE SLEPT WITH EVERY GIRL WHO WANTED HIM.

If you knew you were going to die at seventeen you wouldn't have to worry about career goals, or finding the love of your life, or whether you'd vote Democrat or Republican.

There would be no anxiety about your endgame: car accident at twenty, colon cancer at forty-eight, a slip in the shower at sixty-five. You'd never have to worry about the biggest worry in life—the worry that eclipses all other worries.

In some ways, it would mean freedom—absolute freedom.

This whole idea, knowing the moment of your own death, came from a sci-fi movie I saw once. In the movie, the moment of every person's death was predetermined, and they all wore countdown timers so they knew exactly how long they had left before the big guy in the sky took them to their final reward. I can't remember the name of the movie, but the idea has stuck with me.

I don't think I spent so much time thinking about death before my dad died. Maybe a long time ago I thought about it, when I was a little kid. Back then sometimes I would lie awake at night, thinking about the death of my parents. Not their actual deaths, because that would be super twisted, but lying there in the dark I would get an image in my mind of a coffin sitting next to a hole in the ground, a group of people gathered around it. At that age I had never been to an actual funeral, so the scene I could picture was what a funeral looks like in a movie.

In my imagined funeral, the cemetery is green and bright, sunlight filtering through leafy trees. The mourners, all dressed in nice clothes, stand around a coffin of dark wood. The priest—also an image I only know from movies—is an older guy wearing all black, holding a book and standing at the head of the casket.

My view in my imagination, as it is in my dreams, is from above, like the perspective of a bird, or a cloud. I am not an actor in my dreams, just a helpless observer. And in that way, my dreams are just like life.

Those thoughts, about the premature death of my parents, haunted me as a kid, lying awake in bed at night in my Teenage Mutant Ninja Turtles pajamas—purple ones, with Donatello on the shirt. He's the only Ninja Turtle who isn't a total washout.

I would squeeze my eyes shut and try to wipe my mind clean, erase the image of the funeral, like scrubbing a whiteboard with a rag. I would try to think of nothing, just blackness, but even blackness is something, and the image of the funeral would creep back in at the edge of my mental vision.

And then, one day, those fears went away, and they were replaced by other fears. Fears about whether kids at school would like me. Or that someone else wouldn't be liked and they would open fire with an assault rifle in the school lunchroom. I had fears about whether I was growing body hair in places that other people weren't, and that my dick might never grow to a normal adult size. There are so many things to fear, I went years without remembering that my parents might die.

And then all of my other fears didn't come true, but the one about my dad dying did. Bam. Out of nowhere. When I hadn't even worried about it in ages.

ACT I

CONSCIENCE MAKES COWARDS OF US ALL

When I wake, the house feels empty, so I think it's safe to get out of bed. I try not to interact with other people because interacting with people makes me question who I am and if I'm wrong to be that person. The fear of interacting with the people in my own house makes my room solitary confinement, though not literally, because my room includes a forty-two-inch television and a PlayStation, which I'm pretty sure inmates don't get in prison.

Usually it takes a while to work up the courage to leave my room-slash-cell. A pill helps push the worry to the back of my mind. Regular people can do it without the pill. They just think, *I'm not going to worry about this right now,* and the worry sits obediently in the corner of their mind on time-out.

My worries are not obedient.

I think about staying in bed for the rest of the day, but then I think about coffee and whether there are any Toaster Strudels in the freezer. Mom keeps things like Toaster Strudels in the house now because Eric likes them. Mom says sugar is poison, which I think is a bit of an overstatement. She likes to say things like that—that sugar is poison—right as you are trying to enjoy a slice of cake or something. In any case, she never kept sugary snacks in the house until Chuck and Eric inserted themselves into our lives.

It's Saturday so, after a quick sniff at my armpits, I head downstairs in the same clothes I wore to school the day before.

Our house is an epic architectural achievement of glass and stucco, boxy in a way that tells you it is intentionally ugly, set back in a deep lot of carefully arranged trees. Despite the trees, during the day sunlight intrudes from all angles because the house has floor-to-ceiling windows in almost every room on the first floor—acres of glass that are a magnet for birds that have lost the will to live. It's like living on a stage, or a movie screen, with a higher than average bird mortality rate.

All of the surfaces in the house are cold—glass and granite and stainless steel—and kept shiny by an ever-changing cleaning person. The fireplace burns gas and has fake logs that have to be dusted during warmer months. The fireplace gives the appearance of warmth, but casts none.

I open the refrigerator, which doesn't have any photos or report cards or certificates of achievements on it. As I'm surveying my choices, Mom walks into the kitchen.

Mom has superpowers. She can hear me opening a can of soda (also poison) from another floor of the house and knows exactly when I don't want her to knock on my bedroom door. Whenever I come downstairs, I do it with a certain amount of fear, as I know she is just waiting to pounce on me. She still sleeps in the master bedroom on the first floor where Dad died. These days she often sleeps there with Chuck.

Obviously Mom and Chuck don't believe in ghosts.

Even though it's early on a Saturday, Mom's hair and makeup are perfect. When Dad was alive she had her morning coffee at the kitchen counter before she brushed her hair or got dressed or put on any makeup. I kind of miss that version of my mom. Now that Chuck is around, she never comes out of her room without looking like she's ready to pose for a Burberry catalog. The Botox started shortly after Dad died, too. Death is coming for all of us, but for some people, looking good is still important.

"You're here," Mom says.

"I'm here," I agree.

"You're up."

"I'm up."

Though we have been distant from each other these past few months, we have reached a new low.

"Get dressed," she says. "We have an appointment to see your new therapist today."

"Absolutely not." I help myself to a cup of coffee and add fake sugar, the kind that gives rats cancer.

"Get dressed," Mom says again, "or I'll report the credit card you have linked to every app on your phone as stolen."

"I am dressed," I say. "This is what dressed looks like."

Mom suppresses a weary sigh as she eyes my vintage Pink Floyd T-shirt and Adidas sweatpants—neck to ankles, and back again—not even attempting to disguise her judgment of me. My Pink Floyd shirt is real vintage, once my dad's, which he wore when he was young and still close to the size I am now, the size he only became again when he was close to the end.

"It wouldn't kill you to try to be a bit more agreeable, Dane," she says.

"I don't know," I say as I lean one hip against the counter. "It might."

"Well, you'd better pull it together before the party tonight. There will be a lot of important people there and I expect you to at least make the effort."

"The effort at what?" I ask.

"At being a normal, polite person," Mom says, her voice rising with exasperation. "I don't want people to think I'm a shitty parent."

My pause before replying is just long enough to convey my thoughts on how shitty her parenting is. "I don't understand why you care so much about what anyone thinks," I say. "I don't worry about what other people think." This is a lie, but I'm an above-average liar.

"Yeah," Mom says with a nod. "Your definition of 'dressed' makes that obvious."

"Very funny." And, truly, Mom can be kind of funny. She's very sarcastic. Dad loved that about her, but not everybody does.

"It's not as if I enjoy this, either," Mom says, and it isn't clear if she's referring to going to therapy, or being a mother. Possibly both. "This Dr. Lineberger is supposed to be absolutely the best family therapist in town. She helped the Landers with their daughter. You remember the Landers?" Mom says, dropping her voice conspiratorially in that way that parents do when they are getting ready to pass judgment on someone else's kid. "Their daughter has a lot of problems."

"Their daughter has a problem with vomiting," I say, because Suzie Landers is bulimic and she's never made a secret of it. I don't see how Suzie's bulimia is relevant because vomiting isn't my problem. I've never once vomited on purpose. I'm just sad, which seems like a completely sane response to the world if you ask me, which Mom doesn't. She never asks me anything, because she thinks she already knows everything.

The warning look Mom gives me doesn't even sting. I have been a disappointment to her for my entire adolescence. It is nothing new to me. But I don't experience the feelings of guilt and shame about it like I used to. The medications help with the worries, and the guilt and shame.

"I heard that Suzie was only eighty-nine pounds when they finally had to put her in residential treatment," Mom continues, as if I care. "She looks better now."

"Well, as long as she looks better."

Mom's eyes go hard as she simmers, but she doesn't take the bait. "I know you don't believe me when I say this, but I'm doing this for your own good. You need help, Dane."

"I'm going to make a Klonopin smoothie for the road," I say. "You want one?"

Mom sighs. I get her sense of humor, but she never seems to get mine.

It turns out that Dr. Lineberger's office is in the McLean Professional Park off of Old Dominion, the same place my last therapist had an office. It's just a townhouse complex, and the buildings all have brick facades that make it look old, established, and respectable. The townhouse complex is called a "professional park" because that is code for mental health offices in wealthy neighborhoods.

The parking lot is discreetly tucked within the courtyard, not visible from the central crossroads of McLean. We all know our neighbors are visiting their own therapists once a week, too, but polite society demands we pretend as if none of us have problems. Feelings are messy things, and McLean is clean. Free of poverty. And litter. And feelings.

The door to Dr. Lineberger's townhome office is un-locked. The weather stripping around the outer office door makes a *whoosh*-scrape noise as we enter the carpeted stair-well, and I wish now that I really had made a Klonopin smoothie before we left the house. Visiting a new therapist means new judgment, new diagnoses.

As we climb the stairs to the second floor, the smell of plastic wafts on the current of the central air system. "You smell that?" I say to Mom over my shoulder. "It smells like action figures and crayons."

"Quiet," Mom says. "She'll hear you."

"I'm just saying, I don't see why we have to go to a kid therapist," I say. "I'm not a kid."

"You're acting like a kid right now."

At the top of the stairs we are the only people in the waiting area because there is no receptionist. Mom instinctively checks her watch to confirm we are on time as we take a seat, then puts her phone on vibrate and drops it into her Kate Spade purse. Mom owns a lot of purses. Kate Spade, Louis Vuitton, Christian Dior. Names that, at once, mean something, and nothing at all. It seems insane to me that anyone could need so many purses, but here we are, getting mental help for me, not her.

The interior temperature of the therapist's office, like all doctors' offices, is a stable seventy degrees, which makes it cold in the winter, and hot in the summer, uncomfortable no matter the season—just like life.

Mom settles in with a copy of *Architectural Digest* and crosses her legs, giving the impression she has been waiting patiently for a while.

I sit with my hands on my knees and study the room. There's a low table in one corner with a basket full of *Highlights* and coloring books, the kind that are supposed to be educational, the kind a kid would never choose on their own. There are dolls and toys spilling out of a trunk that is painted to look like a pirate's treasure chest.

One wall is lined with three plain white doors without names or numbers on them. It reminds me of a game show—we, the contestants, waiting to see which door will reveal a doctor. Mom and I have visited so many therapists over the years that, whichever door reveals one, I am not expecting any surprises.

After a few minutes, about the time Mom starts fidgeting over whether we should knock on one of the doors (it's a new car!), the center door opens and out walks a middle-aged lady with a smile that doesn't reveal any teeth.

She greets Mom first, who is, after all, paying the bill, and then invites us into her office. The doctor directs us to a couch and two chairs and lets us choose where we sit. Mom hesitates, as if it is some kind of test, then chooses the couch.

We have a lot of experience with therapy and Mom is on her guard to carefully portray all signs of normalcy. I know that Mom has taken the seat on the couch assuming I will sit next to her. Then we will appear as a family should, with mother and son wanting, or at least willing, to sit together on the same piece of furniture. Instead of sitting next to Mom on the couch, I take one of the chairs. By choosing the chair and sitting apart from Mom, it gives our new therapist the impression we aren't close, have intimacy issues. I'm probably qualified to be a therapist myself by now after so many sessions.

Instead of taking the other chair, Dr. Lineberger sits on the couch near Mom. It's an unexpected move and I don't know how to interpret it. Despite the Botox, I can tell Mom is surprised, too.

Now that she is sitting across from me, and she has done something unexpected, I take the time to study Dr. Lineberger more closely. She's older than Mom, with highlighted blond hair that disguises her gray hair instead of covering it. She wears a neatly tailored suit that makes her figure ageless. Her face is unlined and serene.

Most people will say that they don't judge others based on their looks. And most people are liars. My dad was a good-looking guy and—not to sound like some kind of perv—my mom is really beautiful. People always used to comment on how striking my parents were as a couple. Most of the time people don't believe Mom is in her late forties, and I'm used to hearing them tell her how young and beautiful she looks. Her response is always a small smile, just enough to show polite thanks, not enough to make it obvious that she agrees with her admirers.

Inevitably, someone who was overwhelmed by my parents' beauty would turn to include me in the conversation and find me lacking by almost every measurable marker. I was living, or at least breathing, evidence that the prom queen and the quarterback do not automatically win the gene-pool lottery when it comes to procreation.

Mom once said to me that getting older is harder on good-looking people than it is on ugly people. Her theory is that because ugly people have always been ugly, getting older doesn't bother them as much as it bothers beautiful people. All that really means is that my mom is kind of a narcissist, though never formally diagnosed.

"So, Dane," Dr. Lineberger says, as though there is nothing weird about her sitting on a relatively small couch with a stranger, "your mother tells me you're a senior in high school. Are you looking forward to graduating?"

"I suppose," I say. The word "graduating," taken literally, implies I am advancing to something else. But there is no else, so the end of high school isn't really something I think about or look forward to.

"He refuses to look at or apply to any colleges," Mom says. She makes it sound as if I torture kittens for recreation rather than just being noncommittal about life beyond high school. "The therapist we saw this past winter adjusted Dane's medication to a higher dosage, but it hasn't made much difference."

"Dane has seen . . ." Dr. Lineberger pauses as she flips back through the file she has balanced on her knees. ". . . a lot of different therapists."

"Well, yes," Mom says. She pauses, as if debating with herself whether to put the blame for that on me or her. Truth, or consequences. "We've had a difficult time finding a therapist who could really meet our needs. That's why we're here. We've heard you're the best." Mom punctuates this last statement with one of her cheerleader smiles. The smile that she uses on bank tellers and servers and store clerks when she's bossing them around.

The smile has no effect on Dr. Lineberger as she returns to my file. "I should say," Dr. Lineberger says, "that I would normally be opposed to using medication for a minor patient who is going through a natural grieving process. In fact, I don't see anything in Dane's history that suggests he should be taking so much medication for anxiety and depression. Fifty milligrams of fluoxetine daily . . . that's a very high dosage."

Though she hasn't asked a question, Dr. Lineberger looks at Mom as if waiting for an answer. As a student, I know this is a tactic often used by teachers, and I always avoid volunteering information unless someone asks a direct question. But Mom, already on the defensive, dives in headfirst.

"Dane has always been extremely sensitive," Mom says. "When he first started going through puberty it was almost unbearable. We could never get him to join any clubs or teams."

"I think I can sympathize with that," Dr. Lineberger says with a conspiratorial smile in my direction. "We're not all joiners."

Mom goes on, itemizing my list of failures. "He moped around the house all through middle school and he barely came out of his room."

To be fair, once I discovered jerking off at age twelve, I wasn't just moping in my room. But mothers don't know anything about that, so I don't have a defense.

Dr. Lineberger takes a thoughtful breath and sits back in her seat then says, "And what about you, Dane? What are your thoughts? How often do you feel you really need medication for acute anxiety attacks?"

"I . . ." I pause, because I don't know the answer. "I'm

not sure I've ever had an acute anxiety attack. But it sounds pretty bad."

"Do you ever experience shortness of breath? Racing heartbeat? Do you feel extreme terror or a sense of impending doom?"

I laugh as she makes it all sound like something dramatic or special. "Sure," I say as I turn to Mom for confirmation that all of these are just normal things, things everyone experiences.

But Mom's expression isn't agreeing with me. Her eyes say again that I'm just confirming all of her low expectations.

"Do you have things that you enjoy, Dane? Things that you look forward to?" Dr. Lineberger asks.

"Are you asking me if I'm happy?" I ask, my voice rising with skepticism.

"Sure," Dr. Lineberger says with a facial shrug. "We can start there. Are you happy?"

"Not since I found out my dad was sick, I guess."

Dr. Lineberger nods approvingly, like she's glad I'm the one to bring it up. "I'm sure it was devastating to lose your father, and I'm sorry for your loss."

"I'm sorry," when acting together, are the two most useless words in the English language when someone is talking about death.

Dr. Lineberger seems to sense that she has said something wrong so she quickly continues, "Obviously that's a major issue, but talking through your grief can help."

"If you say so." I drop my gaze as a rash of hot tears breaks out behind my eyelids.

"What about school?" Dr. Lineberger asks. "Do you like school?"

"Not particularly."

"No subject that interests you?"

"I suppose history is okay. I mean, not the reading part, but the pictures—photographs and paintings and stuff."

"Well, that's something," Dr. Lineberger says. "What about girls? Do you have any romantic interests?"

"Are you asking if I'm gay?" I pause to test the idea, but I'm pretty sure I would know by now if I was gay.

"No," Dr. Lineberger says, but she looks almost hopeful for a second, like within minutes she's discovered the source of my anxiety, and has succeeded where other therapists have failed.

"I like girls. I don't have a girlfriend or anything. I was going to an all-boys school until last year."

"Yes, your mother mentioned that until the end of last year you were attending boarding school. What led to the decision for Dane to attend boarding school?" Dr. Lineberger asks, redirecting the conversation to Mom.

Dr. Lineberger changes the script so suddenly that Mom stops—like a rabbit trying to blend in with her surroundings—and looks at both of us with the intensity of threatened prey.

"Brandywine Academy is one of the best prep schools

on the East Coast," Mom says. "Dane really needed to be pushed, to have structure, and be in an environment where he was required to participate in organized activities."

Mom sounds like a brochure for Brandywine Academy, which is like a factory that takes privileged, mostly white kids and prepares them to be shipped to universities that accept privileged, mostly white kids.

From my perspective, "organized activities" meant the ritualized torture I received in the name of school tradition. At Brandywine I spent most days being judged and abused by guys with names like Skip and Trip and Chip. Which are just made-up nicknames, by the way. They aren't short for anything.

"So, you came home last summer?" Dr. Lineberger asks. "Soon before your father died."

Mom takes a breath in, ready to breathe out one of her rehearsed answers, but Dr. Lineberger gives her a warning look to shut her down.

"I came home at the end of the school year. My dad was already too sick to work then. He died two months later."

"That must have been difficult," Dr. Lineberger says, a clear contender for the Understatement of the Year Award.

"It was," I say, my tone clearly implying, *Of course it was, you moron.*

"Do you ever entertain thoughts of self-harm, Dane?" Dr. Lineberger asks as she shifts her pen into a ready position for noting my answer. "Or imagine doing harm to yourself?"

"No," I say, because that is definitely what you are supposed to say when a healthcare professional asks you that question. Just like you are supposed to say no when they ask if you smoke cigarettes, or drink more than a few alcoholic beverages per week.

"He engages in self-destructive behavior," Mom says quickly, as if eager to prove that I really do want to harm myself. "He drinks, and I can smell the fact that he's using cigarettes and marijuana." She wrinkles her nose, as if she is actually smelling them at that moment. I fight the urge to drop my nose into the neck of my shirt and take a deep whiff.

"Well, let's take this one step at a time," Dr. Lineberger says. "It's not a good idea to start making accusations and putting Dane in a defensive position."

As the interview wears on, it seems that although Mom and Dr. Lineberger are on the same couch, they aren't on the same team. I think about getting up to move to the couch with Dr. Lineberger, relegating Mom to one of the armchairs. That would be funny, and I feel a smile crimping my face at the thought.

"I know that the past year has been very hard on Dane," Mom says, cutting in and preventing anyone from noticing my inappropriate grin.

"Tschyeah," I scoff. "A lot harder on me than on you, I guess."

"That's not fair," Mom snaps.

"What do you mean, Dane?" Dr. Lineberger asks, unfazed by my outburst.

"I mean," I say, as I'm still deciding what I mean, "Within a month of my dad dying, his best friend was her boyfriend."

"Chuck is not my boyfriend," Mom says. "Christ, I am way too old to have a boyfriend. He was Dad's best friend. He's been practically part of our family since before you were born. You make it sound like I went on Tinder and brought home a complete stranger."

"You being on Tinder would be a million times less creepy than you dating Dad's best friend," I say.

"Oh, stop it, Dane," Mom says. "What a ridiculous thing to say. What do you think I should do while you're out partying with your friends? Sit at home and be totally alone? Even when you *are* home I can barely stand to be around you. You're angry all the time. Angry at me. Angry about your dad dying. Angry at . . . everything."

Dr. Lineberger sucks in a breath, the only sound to break the silence that follows. "Dane, why don't you try to articulate—put into words—your thoughts about your mother's feelings."

"I know what 'articulate' means," I say, now directing my annoyance at Dr. Lineberger. Instantly I hate myself for saying that because it makes me sound pathetic.

"Okay," Dr. Lineberger says, her voice soothing, a knowing look in her eyes. *Perhaps you know what "articulate" means,* the look says, *but you can't suppress your anger about being reminded what it means.* Poor impulse control. Her pen scratches against the notebook but her expression doesn't reveal anything. "Then why don't you tell us what you think about your mother's observations—about your anger with her, your father."

"I'm not angry with my dad," I say. "He was sick. He didn't want to leave me. He didn't want to die."

"I don't think you're angry at your dad for dying," Mom says. "I think you're angry that it was him instead of me."

Talk about your awkward silences. I don't immediately disagree with Mom, which makes it painfully obvious that it is at least partly true. It's like when someone gives you one of those hypothetical moral dilemmas, designed to determine whether you are a sociopath: *Your parents are both trapped in a burning building and you can only save one, who do you choose?*

The moral dilemma is always presented as a black-or-white kind of choice but, either way, your answer puts you outside the range of acceptable cultural norms. Maybe your mom is a surgeon, so you decide, *Mom's life has more value because by saving her, I'm saving more lives than just hers alone.*

If I'm being completely honest, it's an impossible choice. My dad was a divorce lawyer who negotiated child support payments and property settlements. My mom is a socialite who focuses most of her energy on power yoga and her ever-expanding purse collection. The real moral dilemma is that the collective human consciousness hasn't benefited from either one of them being alive.

I'm not exempting myself from that. As far as the greater human good is concerned, my life is absolutely worthless. Less than worthless, if that's even a thing.

"I don't wish you were dead," I say. "I wish you weren't sleeping with Dad's best friend."

Mom looks like she wants to slap me but Dr. Lineberger cuts her off before she blows her top.

"Do you feel," Dr. Lineberger says, her words coming so slowly that Mom and I both lean toward her as she speaks, as if we can accelerate the conversation by being closer to her words, "as if your mother has betrayed your father's memory by entering into a new romantic relationship?"

"Seriously?" I ask, and laugh. So far, I'm the only person who has laughed during our session. That can't be good. "That's what I just said."

"Dane!"

"Mm." Dr. Lineberger presses her lips together as she makes a note. Mom and I both wait for her to finish scribbling. After what seems like an eternity, she says, "Trudi, I don't want to just gloss over how you are feeling. Do you really feel that Dane wishes you had died instead of your husband?"

"He would never say it," Mom says. Her hands are in her lap, one hand wrapped around her other fist as she fidgets her thumbs together. "But I know it's how he feels."

"If that's what you want to believe, then fine." My voice is tight with anger but I'm not sure why I'm angry. Shit. I pause, trying to get my voice under control so I won't make her right about my anger issues. I have to push down the hurt, tamp it into my lower gut to keep it from spilling out of me, onto the fan of magazines on the coffee table.

Suddenly, I feel like maybe I understand Suzie Landers and her vomiting issues. Vomiting probably feels good when you spend so much time holding everything inside. "I wish nobody was dead," I say. "Okay? How about that? I wish nobody was dead."

"Dane," Mom says as she leans forward, her arms pressed together from elbow to wrist and her fingers interlaced. Her fingertips bloom red as her knuckles turn white from squeezing her hands together. "I'm sorry this past year has been so hard for you. I really am. But it's been hard on me, too. Whether you believe it or not. Your dad's illness sucked the life out of me. I spent all of my time meeting with doctors and managing his home care and worrying about money because Dad wasn't able to work or manage the finances the way he always had. I'm grateful for Chuck and all that he's done to help us. If my relationship with him bothers you, then I'm sorry, but he's really been there for me when I needed someone."

This speech is delivered for Dr. Lineberger's benefit. I've heard it all before. Mom wants everyone's sympathy and doesn't want to share.

"I get it," I say loudly, projecting my voice to shut down anyone who tries to interrupt. "It was hard on you. But that's all you ever say. You talk about how hard it was to manage the house or how worried you are about money, but you've never once just said you were sad that Dad is gone. You never once said you miss him or miss having him around. All you care about is yourself. You don't give a shit about Dad."

Our conversation degenerates the same way it always does, except now we were paying Dr. Lineberger for the privilege of having the conversation in front of her.

"I think," Dr. Lineberger says calmly, as if there aren't two lunatics in her office, "that it's important to acknowledge that you are both grieving in your own way. And we've got plenty of ground to cover. Right now, I'm going to suggest that we start to wean Dane off the antidepressants by gradually reducing the dosage."

"I'm not sure that's such a good idea," Mom says quickly. From the way she looks at me I know she would say more if I wasn't there.

"I'm going to be there with you every step of the way," Dr. Lineberger says. "I'll meet with each of you individually at least once or twice so you can talk about your feelings without competing with each other. Then we can come back together and see what we can do to start mending some of these hurts. How does that sound to both of you?"

Mom shakes her head and presses her lips together as she sits back into the couch. She doesn't look like she's trying not to cry, more like she wishes she had strangled me at birth with the umbilical cord.

"I can help you to learn how to speak to each other in a way that gives validation for the things both of you are feeling," Dr. Lineberger says. "Really, Trudi, Dane's brain is still developing. Our kids look like adults at this age, but they still have a long way to go when it comes to mental and emotional development. I think we should try reducing

Dane's medications and really give talk therapy a chance to address the issues you face as a family. Maybe in the future we will decide that he really needs medication, but I think it has been provided as a crutch by doctors to avoid the real work that a healthy mental state demands. I'm going to give you some literature about mindfulness meditation and am going to recommend that we meet at least once a week for a start. How does that sound?"

"I'm willing to try," Mom says.

"Whatever," I mumble.

We leave Dr. Lineberger's office in silence, the smell of the action figures now nauseating. When we get to the car Mom stops and, still silent, stands next to the driver's side door without unlocking it.

"What?" I ask finally.

The silence continues, but now it looks like she can't say anything, as if she is trying not to cry.

"I just . . ." She stops and sniffles and presses her finger to the corner of her eye, refusing to allow tears an escape. "I guess I just . . . I've never said it out loud before, what I've been thinking. I really have been feeling like you wished it had been me who died, instead of Dad."

"Don't be crazy, Mom. Please? Of course I don't want you to be dead."

"I just mean if you had to choose. I know you were crazy about him. He was a lot of fun."

"Yeah," I say. "He was. In fact, he would have found this conversation hilarious."

Mom laughs at that. "Let's go home," she says. "We need to get dressed for the party."

"I don't want to go."

"Well, that's too bad, I guess."

Even though I've suffered through a Thanksgiving and Christmas and New Year's, each milestone a reminder that Dad is gone, it still hasn't even been a year since he died. There are other milestones to dread. Dad's birthday, my birthday, the anniversary of Dad's death—all waiting in the not-too-distant future, looming shadows like monsters in the closet.

Tonight, another milestone, the annual party that Dad's law firm, Feint (rhymes with "taint") & Riley, hosts for clients and staff. The annual party started almost twenty years ago as a small happy hour and has grown into a full-blown black-tie dinner at the country club. In reality we are celebrating the fact that Feint & Riley, specialists in family law, have made a shit-ton of money by dismantling families, piece by piece. Even if Feint & Riley make you a winner in litigation against your former loved ones, you're still a loser.

In McLean, divorce is a lucrative business because most people have plenty of assets to fight over. Kids, who are always part of the negotiations, are treated just like any other asset—or liability, depending on your worldview.

Before he died, Dad's best friend and business partner was a guy named Charles Feint, who, for some inexplicable reason, goes by the nickname "Chuck." Chuck and Dad had been friends since law school, though the way they talked made it seem like they spent a lot more time partying than studying law. They were also the best man at each other's weddings and Chuck is my godfather, though my baptism was the last time I was in church before Dad's funeral. I guess my parents thought it was only necessary to involve God in birth and death situations.

Chuck's marriage ended in divorce, but, unfortunately, not before the marriage spawned a bad seed. Eric. Dad was Eric's godfather so Dad had no choice but to act as if he really liked Eric, though liking Eric is almost impossible. I spent a lot of time with Eric when we were kids, when our families did everything together. Eric was one of those kids who makes up the rules to games as he goes, always strictly for personal gain. He fixed the system so that I could never be the winner, even though he's only a few months older than I am.

Most of the time Dad judged people pretty harshly and wasn't afraid to share his thoughts out loud. He would say things like, "Dane, half the shit-stains working for me have law degrees from top colleges, but they wouldn't survive a day in the wild." That was an important qualification for Dad, being able to survive in the wild. I think he was speaking strictly metaphorically because Dad's idea of the wild was something like staying in a hotel that has a lower-than-three-star rating.

Eric has always been a jerk, but these days he's a total mess. He is always high and always in trouble, even if most of the time he's not getting caught for it. He's also rich and good-looking, so he's pretty much untouchable. His full initials are EFF, something his parents should have had the foresight to avoid, and so his Twitter handle is @EFFincool, which pretty much sums up his value to society.

Once, Eric stole a credit card from his ex-girlfriend's dad and charged seven hundred fifty dollars' worth of Uber Eats deliveries before he got caught. I'd like to think I have enough imagination to use a stolen credit card for something other than food delivery. Eric got caught because every time he used the credit card he had the food delivered to the same address—his mom's house. Evidence suggests Eric is either the most epically stupid person on the planet, or the most confident. I believe he is both.

I think Eric only breaks the law because he's bored and entitled, which is a lot worse than stealing because, say, you're actually starving. If Eric wasn't rich, he'd be in juvenile detention, for sure. But he barely even got in trouble for the whole credit card thing. All he had to do was earn back the money by interning in his dad's office for part of the summer, the part he didn't spend at the Outer Banks in North Carolina with his mom. The former Mrs. Chuck Feint got the beach house in the divorce and spends half the summer there with Eric, where both of them drink too much to avoid their feelings.

Tonight, Eric and I end up standing near each other in the crowded ballroom. It's not as if he wants to be around me any more than I want to be around him, but we have both felt out the corner that is the farthest point from the podium where Chuck stands with a microphone to thank everyone for choosing Feint & Riley for all of their family law needs.

Chuck doesn't give Eric or me special mention in the speech, mostly because we don't have any particular accomplishments to celebrate. Eric's not going to college next year either, instead taking a year to party in Europe before he starts college. A "gap year" in McLean is code for a kid who didn't get accepted to his top choices for college. Chuck is paying for Eric to go on his trip to Europe, but I think that's because Chuck really wants to pretend like Eric doesn't exist, not that he has any hopes that exposure to culture will make Eric a better person.

I turn now to look at Eric, to gauge his reaction to his father's speech. He catches my eye as he's pouring whiskey from a flask into his ginger ale and gestures with the flask to offer it to me. I shake my head no, and glance around to see if anyone has noticed his illicit drink.

As I always do in the company of Eric, I feel insignificant and ugly by contrast. Even if he's a complete tool, he meets every qualification for alpha male. He's a few inches taller than I am, his shoulders a few inches broader, and, I'm sure, his dick is a few inches longer.

Chuck takes the time to talk about Dad, to tell a funny story about him from when they were in law school together.

It's a story I have heard many times, about the time Dad made homemade wine, which not only got you drunk, but later made whoever drank it have red pee.

Dad used to tell that story, but he included the part about how at first no one admitted their pee was red, all on their own convinced that they had some incurable sexually transmitted infection. Mom hates the story. She used to get irritated every time Dad told it at a social gathering. "Don't, Craig," she would say with a look that was at once annoyed and pleading, but Dad would just laugh and tell the story anyway.

In Chuck's version of the story, he leaves out the part about the STI scare, and Mom doesn't seem to mind the story now that Chuck is telling it. Then Chuck raises his glass and we all have a toast to Dad and his homemade wine. Which makes my throat tighten and my eyes fill with tears for about the tenth time that evening.

And then . . . the Announcement, the good news we've all been waiting to hear.

Now that Dad is dead, Chuck is going to sell the business they built together. Feint & Riley is about to be swallowed whole by the firm of Cargill, Cargill, Cargill & Cargill—possibly the least creative name ever conceived for a company, and a testament to the narcissism of wealthy people, that it isn't enough to have your name on a company logo only once.

Chuck says how grateful he is for Mom's support of the transition. She still has an interest in the business and owns

Dad's 50 percent share. Mom stands beside Chuck at the podium, smiling like a politician's wife. Chuck thanks her for her support of him and the decisions he has made to run the business on his own through Dad's illness.

Chuck puts a hand on Mom's waist, just above her right hip, and holds her close, so their bodies touch from shoulder to thigh. It isn't a brotherly gesture, or even a friendly one. As far as I'm concerned, they might as well be making out in front of the crowded room.

As insignificant as I am, no one notices as I study the faces of the guests. My cheeks flame with a blush as I search for their judgment. I expect to see heads dip together in whispers, to see shock or even disgust on their faces.

But, as I look around, I realize that no one thinks there is anything strange about Mom and Chuck as a couple. Eric doesn't care. Chuck has been divorced from Eric's mother for almost ten years and has had many girlfriends in that time. The fact that Chuck is now in a relationship with Mom probably seems like an upgrade to him.

What Mom and Chuck are doing is disgusting. But no one else seems to care.

I am alone in my horror.

Looking back now, I can see that Dad's funeral was like a first date for Mom and Chuck. They got dressed up and had their friends around and even had the event catered by the Lebanese Taverna, which is really uncool because that was Dad's favorite restaurant. Why would you have someone's favorite food at their funeral? I feel like that should be a faux pas for the obvious reason that the dead person is the only one who can't enjoy it.

Mom and Chuck being so close seems natural to everyone but me. And the party seems like a celebration to everyone. But me.

For me, this party is just another reminder that Dad is gone and isn't coming back. And then I wish, perhaps for the millionth time, that I could leave and never come back, too.

After Chuck's speech there is food and wine and champagne passed around on trays. If you want liquor you have to pay for it yourself at the bar, which is kind of lame. Mom made all of the arrangements for the party herself. She made such a big deal about how much work it was you would think she had an actual job. Between yoga and massages and facials and shopping, it seems to me the only real job Mom has is taking care of herself.

Mom and Chuck are moving through the crowd, mingling with everyone at the party, while Eric and I hug the edge of the room like we're at a middle-school dance.

Eric offers the flask of whiskey to me again, and even though I want to take some, I say no. I worry about somebody seeing me, though I'm not sure why. Nobody here seems to even be aware of my existence.

"Shit, it's already nine o'clock," Eric says after checking his phone for what seems like the hundredth time in the past thirty minutes. "I want to get out of here."

"So, go," I say.

"I don't want to listen to the bitching Dad will do if I leave too early."

A waiter with a tray stops to offer us some appetizers and Eric takes his time looking over the little bits of food to pick the largest and best for himself.

By the time Eric finishes selecting his food the waiter has grown impatient and moves away without offering the tray to me. I'm hungry and start to raise my hand to take one of the appetizers rejected by Eric, but the waiter turns too quickly, and I am left with no other option but to pretend I had been raising my hand to scratch my neck.

"What are you doing tonight?" Eric asks when the waiter is gone.

"This."

"This party is totally lame," Eric says as he glances around at the crowd. Almost everyone at the party is really old, at least our parents' age or older. They stand in small groups talking quietly. Eric's upper lip twists in disgust as he surveys the room. "It's like a wake but without a dead body to make it just a little bit interesting. No offense."

"Everything that comes out of your mouth is offensive."

"So, what are you doing later? It's Saturday night. You're not going out after this?"

"Why? Is there a party or something?"

It's too late. He's already forgotten about our conversation as he's looking at his phone again. "Shit," Eric says. "This girl will not stop messaging me. I slept with her, like, one time, and now she thinks we're in a relationship or something. I've got to block her."

"Well, if you don't like her, why did you sleep with her?" I've never done so much with a girl that I could define it as "sleeping with her," but if I did, I would be amazed if she messaged me after the fact.

Shortly after I started at McLean High School I overheard Eric bragging in the locker room about having already paid for two abortions. As if it was some kind of competition that he was winning. Just the thought of being put in that position myself is enough to keep me a virgin for the rest of my life. And yet Eric treated it as if it was a joke. I feel sorry for those girls. They probably slept with Eric, probably even did it without using protection, because they were so happy to have the attention of a popular, good-looking guy. And then they found out the hard way that he is an unprincipled dick who only cares about himself.

"She's hot, I guess," Eric says, dismissing the girl and the ability to sleep with any girl he wants as a minor irritation. "But I'm definitely going to block her, because next she'll be messaging me something about how she's worried because we didn't use protection. As if I'm going to infect her with something."

I am not worried about STIs because I haven't had the courage to even suggest the removal of pants on the two occasions when I've made out with a girl. It's just one more thing to worry about. "Statistically speaking," I say, "you're more likely to contract an STI than to graduate from college."

"It creeps me out that you even know shit like that."

"It creeps me out that I have to share a bathroom with someone who will definitely contract an STI."

"Girls are all the same," Eric says with a weary sigh, ignoring my insult. "You know what I mean?"

"No," I say with a mystified shake of my head. And truly, I don't know. There's only one girl I care about, but I've never told her because the prospect that she will laugh in my face if I ever did tell her is too real to even think about it. "I don't go out looking for random hookups."

"Why not?" he asks.

"I'm not looking for a random girl," I say. "I want *the* girl."

"Sure. Okay," Eric says. "That sounds exactly like something a guy who can't get a girl would say."

"You're such an asshole."

"What's wrong with you?" Eric asks. "You're even more depressing to be around than usual."

"This is a party for my dad's law firm. And my dad is dead. You have no idea what that's like, okay? No idea."

"I'm sorry," Eric says, and for a second I think I've managed to make him feel bad. "I stopped listening as soon as you mentioned your feelings again. You're always ear-raping people with your problems. Doesn't your mom pay for someone you can talk to? Here. Hold this," he says as he holds his drink out for me to take as he digs in his pocket for something. Once I'm not holding Eric's drink for him he loses interest in me and interacts with his phone instead.

Mom catches me on my way to the bathroom and insists that I come and meet the Cargills, the family that will own the law firm Dad spent his entire life-energy creating.

Introductions are a blur of names I will never remember, and I am awkward meeting new people. It seems so easy for everyone else. They shake hands and says things like "How do you do" and make polite conversation. People always try to make small talk about sports, as if it's a safe topic because I'm a guy and guys are supposed to care about football and basketball. I don't know anything about sports, other than skateboarding and snowboarding. When I meet new people I try to smile but I can feel that my face is a twisted grimace, like I'm holding in a fart.

Mr. Cargill, the senior partner of Cargill, Cargill, Cargill & Cargill, is younger than I expected him to be. He is probably about Dad's age, if Dad were still alive, and he is fit and tan. Chuck is tan, too—at least his face and arms—from spending time on the golf course, but he isn't physically fit. His pants ride high in the back above his large ass, and low in the front below his gut. He pays a tailor good money, but there's only so much that guy can do.

"It's nice to meet you, Dane," Mr. Cargill says. "My younger daughter is about your age but she couldn't be with us tonight. She mentioned something about a party like this potentially boring her out of her mind." Mr. Cargill smiles as Mom and Chuck laugh, too eagerly, at his joke.

I give him a half-hearted smile for his effort and Mom says, "Dane tried to get out of coming, but I wanted him to see that the people who will be operating his dad's firm are really great people."

Mr. Cargill's smile gets bigger and the creases around his eyes are evidence that he has smiled a lot in his life. "That's nice of you to say," he says, nodding at Mom. "And I'm so sorry about your dad, Dane. My own father died when I was in college so I know how hard it must be on you."

Mom cuts me a knowing side-eye as the mention of Dad raises a familiar lump in my throat. I take a minute to wish that Mom was dating Mr. Cargill instead of Chuck and wonder if Mr. Cargill is married and, if so, if his marriage is in trouble.

I am still caught up in the fantasy of the weekends when Mr. Cargill will take me fishing or hiking, where we will have long talks and he'll get me—really get me—as a person. I can see the father-son weekends like a slideshow of Instagram posts—the two of us smiling while holding up a big fish on a hook, the two of us standing at a scenic overlook along the Appalachian Trail, a close-up selfie of us with Mr. Cargill's arm around my shoulders.

"That's very nice of you to say," Mom says, filling in the hole I have created in the conversation. Everyone is staring at me, waiting for my reaction, but I am too flustered now that I have been caught fantasizing about Mr. Cargill as a substitute father.

I mumble an apology, though I'm not sure what I'm sorry about this time. I say something about needing to go to the bathroom, which makes Mom cringe, but it's so much better than saying what's actually happening in my mind.

Then I am walking away, toward the main corridor where the bathrooms are. I walk past the bathrooms and to the front door and out into the night without looking over my shoulder to see if anyone is coming after me. I have to sit in the car for a few minutes waiting for my breathing to slow down and for my brain to stop its death spiral into chaos.

When Dad got too sick to drive, I took his 1982 diesel Mercedes as my car. The car is old enough to be considered vintage instead of just lame. Dad loved his old Mercedes and swore he would never drive any other car. And, though it wasn't really the way he meant it, his prediction came true.

Now the car is like a time capsule of Dad's life. His sunglasses still rest on the dashboard, patiently awaiting his return. Empty packets of nicotine gum lay crushed in the console. Dad was always trying to quit something—quit smoking, quit drinking, quit eating carbs. Usually it was Mom leading the charge, telling him what he had to quit. Mom hasn't eaten a carb since the nineties.

Though Dad always kept the Mercedes in the garage, these days I usually leave it parked on the street, exposed to the elements. The exterior of the car is dotted with withered mulberries from a nearby tree, along with splatters of bird poop. The bird poop consists mostly of mulberries in another stage of the life cycle. Eventually, all living things—humans, birds, mulberries—turn back into shit one day.

The interior of the car is a light gray, the floor mats dotted with purple-black stains of mulberry juice from the berries that get trapped in the soles of shoes. The stains will never come out, like bad memories stamped into a troubled mind.

My mind is definitely troubled. Sometimes I think I'm the only person in the world who is fully awake. Every day we are fed a constant stream of digital horrors—mass shootings, global warming, the continent of plastic trash in the Pacific, genocides and their refugees, and the premature death of young Black men at the hands of law enforcement. There's barely time to feel the appropriate level of outrage or sadness before you're being asked to be outraged or sad about something else. It's impossible to stay on top of feeling sadness or outrage or outraged sadness for all of the people and situations deserving of it. At a certain point I just gave up and attempted suicide. It wasn't a very good attempt. In addition to being a mediocre student and a non-seeded athlete, I am also a failed suicidist.

If you consider that I could have been born in a refugee camp in Bangladesh, or born into the losing side of a civil war in Syria, or born in a town that doesn't have a Starbucks, my life really isn't so terrible. I live in McLean, Virginia, a suburb of fewer than fifty thousand people but that sustains not one, but two J.Crews. When you think about just how terrible life could be—hunger, disease, racial injustice, non-J.Crew clothing—my existence is pretty golden. But those aren't arguments your mind can formulate when you're in the mood to die.

I take out my phone as I sit in the car before I start the engine and type a text to Dad, to let him know I'm thinking about him. I don't know who has Dad's phone number now. It's just another part of him that Mom threw out after he died, like his clothes and his books. She threw out anything that was taking up space or costing her money. It was so easy for her to just let everything go. I wanted to hold on to Dad's things, and Mom asked me, "What are you going to do when you move out? Just keep boxes and boxes of stuff no one will ever use again?" She told me it was better if I moved on, but where I'm supposed to be moving on to? That part is less certain.

Anyway, I don't know if people can get text messages in the afterlife, or if there is an afterlife, but I still text Dad sometimes.

I miss you. Sometimes I hate you for leaving.

The response comes almost right away.

I know, is all it says.

I feel like everybody has moved on but me. You still exist for me.

That's all that matters.

Even though I don't know who has Dad's phone now, it's an older person, I figure, because they always use punctuation and complete sentences and no emojis, though what emojis a spirit would choose to send from the afterlife is almost too depressing to contemplate. I'm surprised that they haven't blocked me by now, but I'm grateful that they haven't. It's like I can still talk to Dad even though he isn't there. When I do text with him, it's like I can imagine he's just on a business trip somewhere. Not dead. Not really gone. Maybe the person who responds to me does it as a joke, a sick thrill. But I don't think so.

I enjoy the drive home, taking the curves with my foot hovering over the brake. Residential McLean is not laid out in a grid like most towns, but instead has winding roads cut into the hills near the fall line of the Potomac River. The whole river valley is a once-upon-a-time forest, now smothered under a blanket of gourmet grocery stores, coffee shops, and yoga studios. In my neighborhood, houses are set back into deep wooded lots with long driveways. There are few streetlights and little traffic to disrupt the quiet.

As I round the last curve in the road before home, the glare of the headlights catches movement and I quickly mash the brakes and the Mercedes rocks on its suspension as I lurch forward in my seat. A coyote is just emerging from the trees at the side of the road, but it doesn't run away from the approach of headlights. It stops in the middle of the road and swings its head in my direction, surveying the Mercedes as a threat. Coyotes are rare, and secretive, like unicorns, so I figure this has to be the same one that I have seen a few times around the neighborhood since Dad died.

The coyote's head hangs low, which makes it seem wary and aggressive rather than curious, but still, he doesn't run. "Wow," I say in a reverent whisper. The moment demands I say something, even though I am alone in the car. Before this I have caught only fleeting glimpses of the coyote. It looks like a small wolf, with a saddle of dark gray fur on his back, the rest of it a shaggy brown, with a bushy copper tail.

I sit there, completely transfixed, willing to watch the coyote for as long as it will sit still and let me.

Dad would have appreciated the coyote. He respected anything that killed rodents. As I sit in awe, I feel connected to the coyote, more connected than I have felt to anyone or anything for a long time. It's part of the mystic web of the universe—the part of Dad left behind when he died.

If you ask someone what animal best describes them or what animal they would want to be reincarnated as, they always say something like a wolf or a lion, or, if they have limited imagination, something like a house cat.

Nobody ever says the animal they most resemble is something common and unexceptional, like a squirrel.

With seven billion people on the planet . . . it just stands to reason that the majority of us would be reincarnated as squirrels. We can't all be mountain lions.

Because Dad liked to chase impossible dreams, his life's goal was to eliminate the squirrel population in our immediate neighborhood. He would trap the squirrels who came into our yard, then relocate them to Great Falls Park. Had it been socially acceptable in a place like McLean, Dad would have shot the squirrels with the .22-caliber rifle he kept in the garage. I'm not sure why he hated squirrels so much. Like a fear of snakes, it was something programmed so deeply into his DNA I don't think he could have explained it if you asked him.

When I was a kid I always felt bad for the squirrels. Dad would bait them with balls of suet and birdseed. Once they were trapped in the steel box, he'd load them into the Mercedes and drop them at their new home in the park on his way to work, a coat-and-tie-wearing vigilante with the noble mission of squirrel population control.

Since Dad died and the coyote turned up in the neighborhood, I'd been imagining Dad's spirit in the form of a coyote. But maybe he was really a squirrel. Probably if my dad had to imagine a fate worse than death without an afterlife, it would be to come back as a squirrel. It was impossible to overstate how much he hated them.

Mrs. Swope, who lives on our street and has to be at least a hundred years old, always feeds the squirrels. It used to drive Dad crazy to see her outside casting sunflower seeds and peanuts into her yard. Everyone in our neighborhood thinks Mrs. Swope is crazy, and I admire the fact that she doesn't give a shit.

The coyote loses interest in the encounter before I do and finishes crossing the road, disappearing into the trees. Maybe he is headed to Mrs. Swope's to kill some of her precious squirrels.

Since Chuck started staying over at the house, I've parked

on the street instead of in the driveway. It's a small act of defiance. The driveway has enough room to park six cars but it's my way of making myself separate and apart from the house that isn't a home.

Even from the end of the long driveway the house is visible because of the light that spills through the large plate-glass windows. Mom always has lights burning in every room. She hasn't gotten the memo about climate change.

As I climb out of the car I detect the faint smell of cigarette smoke, and I turn in a circle looking for the source of the smell. From just down the street, under the shadows of a giant oak tree, is the swell of a cigarette ember.

"Ophelia?" I call out in a hoarse whisper, trying to project my voice without waking the whole neighborhood. "That you?"

"No," a voice comes out of the black hole in the yard. "It's your mom."

Definitely Ophelia. She's the only girl I know who makes "your mom" jokes.

I walk toward the sound of her voice.

"Hey," I say as I saunter the last few yards to reach her. All five feet and glorious eight inches of her is standing there, watching me, waiting for me to say something interesting. After two years of her living next door, my heart still lurches at the sight of her.

"You got a cigarette?" I ask her. I don't really want a cigarette. What I want is an excuse to talk to Ophelia.

She sighs with impatience, but it is too dark to see her

eyes roll. "No," she says, and then, because she can never just let anything go, adds, "You smoked them all."

Ophelia is beautiful but does her best to keep it on the down-low. She hardly ever wears anything but jeans and T-shirts and usually keeps her black curls in a loose braid that hangs to the middle of her back.

In flat feet she is already close to my height, which is an unspectacular five feet eleven inches, which I always extend to six feet if anyone is asking. Until tenth grade I was shorter than many of the girls my age. An alarming growth spurt over the past year had finally propelled me to a whole new class of masculinity.

If she is wearing shoes with a high heel, like she is now, we are eye-to-eye, which makes me feel even less spectacular than I already do on my best day when I am talking to Ophelia. It isn't enough for her to be smarter than I am, or a better athlete, she has to be as tall as I am, too, which makes me hyperaware of how insignificant I am.

Ophelia lives with just her father, who is a colonel in the army. He's strict, especially by McLean standards, where teenagers go largely unsupervised, drive expensive European cars, and only interact with their parents under the guidance of a prescribing therapist.

I am terrified of Colonel Marcus. Everyone, in fact, is terrified of him.

Ophelia and her father moved into the house next door two years ago. They never provided any explanation for why there was no mother in the house, even though the neighborhood gossips desperately wanted the intel. Especially since Ophelia's father is Black, but Ophelia's skin is much lighter than his, so everyone assumes her mom must be white. I've never asked her about her mom because it seems rude to bring it up, and not just because of the color of her skin.

We go to the same school, but Ophelia and I travel in different social circles. Actually, Ophelia has a social circle, a big one, and I am pretty much a loner. She is strictly focused on her grades and extracurricular activities that look good on college applications, which you would think has more to do with her dad's goals than her own. But I think Ophelia would be a straight-A student even if her dad had nothing to say about it. She's also a varsity athlete, and founder of the school's a cappella group, which would be lame if anyone else did it.

During the fall semester she played Kate in the school's production of *Kiss Me Kate*, and I saw every performance. I sat in the back of the auditorium so I could watch her without anyone watching me, and I watched the audience fall in love with her the same way I did.

My mom thinks that my fixation—her word—on Ophelia is about 50 percent proximity and 50 percent unattainability. This is a prime example of why it's never a good idea for me to tell Mom anything personal. She always finds some way to invalidate my feelings.

As my neighbor, Ophelia is immediate and visible every day, which is what makes her, according to my mom, so desirable. Mom often argues that there are many girls my age who are smart and attractive like Ophelia, and infinitely more attainable.

It doesn't take a genius to see that Mom is projecting her feelings about her own situation onto me, and that she has no appreciation for the idea of a soul mate. When Dad died, Mom latched on to the closest, most convenient person as a new romantic partner. I don't think love matters to her at all.

"Here," Ophelia says as she hands me a cigarette.

"Thanks. I'll get you some next time I'm at work."

"You'll buy them? Or steal them?"

"Steal them, of course."

"Figures," she says.

"I'm joking." I'm not. "I'll buy them when I'm working the register. I can't buy them from Mr. Edgar. He won't sell them to me because I'm underage."

"So stupid," she says. "Twenty-one to buy cigarettes is ridiculous. Back in the good old days people started smoking when they were twelve. Like my grandmother."

"Your grandmother started smoking when she was twelve?"

"Sure," Ophelia says. "She smoked for, like, forty years."

"She die of lung cancer?" I ask.

"Nah. She got hit by a bus."

"Jesus," I say as the mental visual of a grandmother getting hit by a bus jumps into my brain uninvited. "Really?"

"I'm just messing with you," Ophelia says with a chuckle

at my expense and, even in the dark, I can sense her winking at me. Ophelia has the unconscious habit of winking when she drops an ironic comment or says something funny, and I envy her cool. I can't wink without looking ridiculous for trying. "You're such a good mark," she says. "You'll fall for just about anything."

"Your dad know that you're out here?" I ask, only to change the subject from my idiocy.

"No-o," she drags the word out on a frustrated sigh. "I had to wait until he was asleep to sneak out."

"Why don't you just use a vape?" I ask. "Get some that smells like berries or bubble gum and he'll just think it's body spray or something."

"You think I'd wear body spray that smells like bubble gum?" she asks, and she sounds kind of angry about it.

"I don't know. Maybe?"

A girl like Ophelia is so complicated. She looks like a girl—beautiful and curvy, with a long, delicate neck—but she's more complicated than any other girl I've ever known. Holding a door for her is okay, but suggesting that she wear bubblegum-scented body spray is not. It's a lot to figure out.

"I don't use a vape because if I did, I wouldn't have a reason to sneak out." Her tone implies that this answer should be obvious. Her logic doesn't make much sense to me, but she keeps on talking and I have to stop figuring to keep up. "I'm grounded. I can't go anywhere unless I sneak around for two weeks," she says, then blows out a plume of smoke, as if blowing out all of the frustrations that come with being awesome.

"Again?" I ask. "What did you do this time?"

Ophelia is always being grounded for something. As far as I can tell she never does anything really terrible. Except maybe the smoking, but she doesn't even inhale so it kind of defeats the purpose, a fact I would never point out to her. Colonel Marcus would probably send Ophelia to a convent if he could. He's convinced that every teenage boy within a hundred yards poses some kind of threat to Ophelia's virginity.

If she is a virgin. Maybe she isn't. Virginity is a mere technicality in the age of social media. It's up to everyone else to tell us who we are.

"I'm flunking calculus," she says.

"Well, obviously you're setting yourself up to fail by taking calculus. How many people take calculus in high school? You got a light?" I ask as I dig in my pockets for a lighter but come up empty.

"Obviously I have a lighter," she says. "I'm holding a lit cigarette."

"Well, can I use it?"

"My point is, why don't you just say that to begin with? Ask me, 'Ophelia, could I use your lighter, please?' since you know I have one."

"Ophelia, could I use your lighter, please?" I ask obediently. Arguing with Ophelia is a waste of time. I know that she is always going to be smarter, one step ahead. I just accept that and don't fight it.

"You want me to smoke it for you, too?" she asks.

"Such a lame joke," I say as she hands me the lighter.

"It is lame," she agrees. "I have no idea why I just said that. I hate it when people use that line."

"Your dad barely lets you go out. You have plenty of time to do homework. So, why are you flunking math?"

"Maybe it's a cry for attention," she says.

"Yeah," I say in agreement. "If anyone has daddy issues, it's you."

"He's such a drama queen. I'm not actually flunking. I just failed the most recent test. I still have a B average and I can pull it up to an A for the semester if I get extra credit."

"I have no idea what you're talking about right now. It's like, I know all of the words, but together they have no meaning for me."

"Why are you dressed like that?" she asks, nodding at my jacket and tie.

"What's wrong with it?" I ask. "Don't you think it makes me look manly?"

She lets out a snort that can be interpreted as a laugh, or a grunt of disgust.

Maybe she's laughing at what I said because she really thinks I'm not manly. That hurts. But I have long ago given up on the hope that Ophelia would ever fall madly in love with me. Or even just find me physically attractive enough to be considered part of the potential gene pool.

I hear the sound of something rustling in the underbrush and instinctively I look over my shoulder, around the yard. Catching the coyote in the headlights earlier, it was almost as if the coyote was showing itself to me. Somehow, I feel like if I see it again, it will be confirmation that the coyote and I have some kind of spiritual connection.

"What's the matter?" Ophelia asks. "You think somebody's going to sneak up and kill us?"

"We're definitely asking for it," I say, not comfortable with the questions that might follow if I mention the coyote. "Two teenagers, hanging around late at night."

"You're safe," she says. "They never kill virgins."

"Very funny."

"I know," she says as she drops her cigarette and scrapes it under her shoe. "I've got to get back."

"I'll see you around," I say, because I can't think of anything else.

"Not if I see you first." As she walks away she tosses this comment casually over her shoulder. I laugh, but her comment hits me as if it has been shot from a bow. I am wounded.

It's only a few seconds before I can no longer see her in the dark. Almost as soon as she's out of sight I think of some cool things I could have said to keep the conversation going.

FOR IN THIS SLEEP OF DEATH
WHAT DREAMS MAY COME

I started working at Mr. Edgar's grocery store almost as soon as I got home from boarding school. That's what it's called, in fact—Mr. Edgar's Grocery. Mr. Edgar is Korean, but his kids all have American names like my friend Mark, Mr. Edgar's youngest son. I know Mark's Korean name, but Mark says it comes out sounding white when I say it.

Mr. Edgar's name is not really Edgar. He bought the store from an old guy who retired and sold the business before moving to Florida. People who are regulars in the store call him Mr. Edgar because everyone knows he owns the place and why would you own a place called Mr. Edgar's Grocery if your name isn't Edgar? His real name is Kwang Cho, but everyone, including his wife, calls him Mr. Edgar. His wife does it as kind of a joke because she likes to make fun of him every chance she gets. But Mr. Edgar has kind of a corny sense of humor, so I think he likes it.

Mr. Edgar's daughter used to help around the store, but once she started going to the community college and working part-time at the school library, Mr. Edgar hired me. Sometimes he tells me that I am a better employee than any of his kids. They all sit around looking at their phones or complaining about having to work instead of being out with their friends.

Before he died, Dad had been after me to get a job. He wanted me to learn about hard work. My grandfather worked himself to death in a steel mill in Ohio. Dad worked himself to death, too, just destroyed himself from the inside out. At first, I got the job just to make Dad happy, figuring I would quit after he died. But I like the time I spend at the store, and Mr. Edgar is the closest thing I have to a father now.

Mr. Edgar feels as if he can trust me and will leave me to manage the store on my own sometimes. Which makes him just about the only person on the planet who thinks I can be trusted with anything.

His store is on a busy street in north Arlington, with lots of businesses and shops and apartment buildings surrounding it. It's the kind of shop that sells more beer and cigarettes than milk and eggs. The front of the shop is floor-to-ceiling plate glass. The windows are filled with posters and hard plastic display signs announcing that Newport is either alive with pleasure or will make you alive with pleasure, I never can figure which, and an electronic sign that features the daily lottery jackpot amount. The current jackpot is an underwhelming $27 million.

The store features some of the specialty Asian groceries that you can't find at a regular grocery store, like those sheets of dried seaweed or the noodles that go in pho. I have no idea what the hell the seaweed is for, but I can't imagine anyone eating it and actually liking the taste. I tasted it once, when Mark dared me, and it's a brittle, salty mess.

Mr. Edgar's store is on the first floor of a seven-story apartment building. I discovered how to access the roof of the building one day when Mr. Edgar asked me to deliver some groceries to old Mrs. Hathaway who lives on the sixth floor. Ever since then I take my breaks on the roof, sitting on the low wall that overlooks the street, watching the world pass beneath my feet.

When I walk down a street I always look up at the roofline, wondering if I will see someone, like me, who sometimes thinks about jumping off a roof. But most people on the street never bother to look up from their phones, never know they are being watched by anyone.

It's about seven o'clock when I take my break, and the street below is busy with people on their way home from work, or on their way to happy hour at one of the many restaurants and bars in this part of north Arlington. I like to imagine where all of the people are going, to destinations more interesting than anywhere I ever go.

I take out my phone and send a text to Dad, just to let him know I'm thinking about him. Soon after, my phone buzzes with a text and I expect it to be from Dad, but it's not.

Harry.

Yo. Wtf? Im straight as shit up in here

Wtfw? I'm busy

Busy w what?

I think about texting him back to tell him to fuck off. I am busy. Busy contemplating my own death after jumping from the roof. What it will look like on social media the next day. Who will find my body. Whether anyone will give a shit that I am gone.

Seven stories. It isn't much. I might actually survive the fall. My body would be broken and twisted, but I could survive. And I would end up a prisoner, a functioning brain inside a broken body. Like that guy in that movie. I can't remember the title, but the guy had a perfectly functioning brain trapped in a paralyzed body, his only means of communication the blink of his eyes.

And that life would be a thousand times worse. It's not as if they were mixing up margaritas to serve that guy through his IV.

I pat my pocket to confirm I still have the bag of Biodiesel I bought from Eric. The fact that he can get good weed is Eric's only socially redeeming quality. Technically, it is still my weed. Harry hasn't paid me for half of it, but he promised to split the eighth with me.

The Biodiesel is good bud. A body high that just makes you feel like Jell-O, right up until you get the munchies and crash.

I want to get hi mafuck

Harry, persistent and annoying.

I take a deep lungful of air, then an exhale that doesn't release any tension. I look down at the ribbon of sidewalk beneath my feet—cold and unforgiving—inviting me to jump.

I look back at the display of my phone. Another text from Harry that is just a series of poop emojis and then his own creation, a stick figure with an eggplant between its legs.

I imagine how pissed Harry will be if I jump and the bag of Biodiesel is found by the cops when they come for the cleanup. In fact, my friends might miss the weed more than they miss me. Except for Joe. He would miss me.

The news story about my suicide would include mention of the bag of weed in my pocket, the antidepressants floating in my veins.

Dr. Lineberger reduced my dosage of the antidepressants after our first appointment. Mom would probably blame her—say, *See, if Dane had been taking a higher dosage he would still be alive.* Chuck would sue Dr. Lineberger for malpractice and, as a way to manage her grief, Mom would turn my room into a yoga studio.

Maybe the cops wouldn't even know about the antidepressants. They probably don't bother to do an autopsy with such an obvious cause of death.

Or maybe they *would* do an autopsy, and the antidepressants would be their confirmation that I had jumped, not been pushed, to my death.

That part would be kind of interesting—the cops doing an investigation to figure out if it was murder or suicide. Of course, I wouldn't be alive to witness it. It was a cool idea, like that movie about that girl who was murdered and her ghost stuck around watching her family and the cops while they tried to find her killer. Once they solved the murder, her ghost disappeared—headed off to the afterlife or just turned to vapor or something.

In a lot of movies a dead person becomes a ghost because they have unresolved shit with the living. People who are murdered, commit suicide, or are trying to stop a bad guy, they get to stick around long enough to fix things. It's possible the movies are right—about everything. After all, the Bible and other religious texts are just stories made up by people. You might as well believe in movies as your religion. You have about the same chance of being right believing in a movie as you do believing in the Bible.

Still, I'm not sure I like the idea of living as an invisible ghost for eternity. I am already pretty invisible at home and at school and it isn't cool.

I lean out as far as I can without pitching over the edge and test the sensation. My skin tingles with a biological survival instinct, though consciously I am not afraid.

Last year I read an article about a guy who jumped from the roof of his apartment building three days before Christmas. He was a famous writer so it was big news, though I had never heard of him. The article didn't mention how tall the building was, but it was in New York, so probably taller than seven stories.

I still think about that guy. I wonder if he changed his mind the second after he stepped off the roof, what his thoughts were on the way down. The article mentioned a wife and a kid.

Three days before Christmas. That just seemed fucking selfish. That guy didn't just leave his kid—he ruined every Christmas that kid will ever have. Everyone is sad enough at Christmastime anyway. Sad that your family doesn't live up to some TV-sitcom standard of happiness, or sad that you aren't going to get that PlayStation you wanted, or sad that your dad has cancer and won't live to see another holiday. Why make it worse by jumping off a building three days before Christmas? And it seemed like the guy had a pretty good life. A famous writer with a wife and a kid. It's not as if he had been homeless or without anyone to love him.

How miserable are you if you can't even hold out for January to jump? Nobody gives a shit about January.

My dad died on a blazing hot day in the middle of August. Nobody gives a shit about August, either. My dad would never have wanted me to hate every Christmas for the rest of my life because of him. Which is sad, because even though he managed to die during the one month of the year without any national holidays, I'll still hate every holiday without him.

My phone buzzes again with a text and I look at it, expecting to see another message from Harry, and planning to tell him to go to hell. But it's not from Harry. It's from Ophelia.

Are you home? she wants to know.

I go through a range of emotions. Elation that she cares where I am—that's the first. Worry that the only reason she's asking me is because something is wrong. Then disappointment as I assume she is probably only bored and just sending me a message to pass the time.

At work, I tell her.

What time will you be home? The question pops up so quickly that she must have sent her message at the exact same moment I sent my response.

Idk have to make a stop on the way home

Msg me when you get home

K

I want to ask her why but decide it will sound too desperate.

After work I drive to Emily's house to meet Harry, Mark, and Joe. They have been texting me repeatedly for the past hour. Not because they are so eager to be in my company, but because I have the weed.

The party scene at Emily's house is one of the constants of our lives. Emily's mom is a bartender and works late four nights each week. At least a couple of nights per week I know I can find my friends at Emily's, hanging out. Parties usually bore me, and no amount of drugs or alcohol can change that.

Emily is a total bro. She can skate, wears Doc Martens with miniskirts, and always knows about the best music by the most obscure bands before anyone else does. She is the universally ideal woman for all guys between the ages of twelve and twenty-four and is, at the same time, completely oblivious to our adoration. She's the kind of girl who dates legends—like Tony Hawk or Dave Grohl—and someone will eventually write a hit song about her.

I used to have a crush on Emily, until I accepted that I would never be cool enough for her to feel the same about me. My crush on Emily was nothing like my feelings for Ophelia, though I'll never be a good enough student or athlete for Ophelia to want me back. It's a vicious pattern. Society conditions us to want the things we can't have.

As is the case with cool people like Emily, her home life is a complete disaster. Emily's mom is single and I've never heard her mention a dad. Her mom is the kind of mom who lets her daughter and her friends smoke cigarettes out in the open, and who has a complicated dating life with guys who are tough enough that no one would ever call them out for wearing mullets. I suppose girls like Emily grow up to be like Emily's mom, still dating guys who attach their wallets to their pants with a chain, or who fill jobs that allow them to have tattoos on their hands and necks. Maybe this is the peak of existence for Emily, but in high school, she is like royalty.

My friends and I used to go to the same elementary school, back when my dad was still getting his law practice off the ground and we lived in a normal-size house and weren't members of a country club. Though I only saw them for summers and winter breaks while I was still in boarding school, I have known them for most of my life. When I returned from boarding school for good at the end of junior year, our friendship picked up where we had left it.

There is Mark, Mr. Edgar's son, who is funny, though his parents don't really think so. His parents think Mark should get his shit together, be in AP classes, and work on college credit so he can get into medical school like his older brother.

Harry, whose family is originally from Vietnam, is loud and often hyper, and he's got a smile that goes on for miles, but he gets less entertaining the longer you are with him.

Joe is the unofficial leader of our group and the closest thing I have to a best friend, but he's so cool it's hard to know if he feels the same way about me. His family is from the Philippines, which is in Asia but he has a Spanish last name. He's explained the history to me, that his grandfather was actually Spanish, though his family is from the Far East, and he was born here. The result of him being truly global in his outlook means that he is comfortable no matter where he is, and ambles through life in a slouch despite the fact that he is barely five feet four inches tall. His smiles are as rare as unicorns and his humor is quick and succinct, like boxing jabs. He is always watching the world around him, but rarely shows much reaction to it. He's as cool as the underside of a pillow, and oblivious to the fact that his long hair and flannel shirts haven't been in style since the nineties.

Together they are the Extreme Sports Asians. That's

what everybody in their school calls them—like a super-hero group. They are guys who don't believe in boredom. They take risks constantly, and boarding—skate, snow, and surf—defines their existence. I'm not really cool enough to be part of their group, but they accept me, and I'm grateful for their friendship. When I am with them, it is the only place I belong without question or judgment.

It isn't clear as time goes on what still holds us together as friends. We have less in common the closer we get to graduation and starting The Rest of Our Lives. Or, maybe more accurately, just Our Lives. But I suppose it is fair to say that with each passing day I have less in common with all of humanity than I did the day before.

By the time I find my friends, my mood is sour and I don't want to be there. We gather into the drug-user huddle to load the dry weed vape, with Harry taking charge of the process.

"Oh my god, I love this bud," Harry says as he hits the vape, then frowns at it because it isn't pulling the way he wants.

"Yeah," I agree. "It's a good high."

"Happy," Harry says with a nod.

"Funny. Not happy," I correct him. "Things can be funny even if you aren't happy."

"Happy is just a state of mind," says Mark, the eternal optimist. He's like a walking meme.

"Yo, shut the fuck up," Joe says, menacing despite his short stature. "Look at this ma'fuck," he says with a chin thrust at Mark. "Born ugly and stupid and all about look-ing at the bright side of life. Who the fuck are you? Mr. Rogers?"

"Ma-an," Mark says, dragging out the "a" in "man" to a high whine, "I don't even know what you're saying. Look who's talking. You're so short you have to slam-dunk your bus fare."

"Dane needs to be sad," Joe says, Mark's insult rolling off him like rain. "Just let him be sad if that's what he wants. God damn, you're always pushing, pushing, pushing. Just chill, man." Joe, the diminutive philosopher, finishes his monologue and then pats his pockets, locating his cigarettes and lighter. "I'm going out for a smoke."

"Hit the vape," Mark says. "I got nicotine right here. Watermelon flavor."

"Nah, ma'fuck," Joe says. "I'm a smoker. I want a ciga-rette. And I want it to taste like tobacco. If I want to taste watermelon, I'll eat a watermelon."

"It's better to smoke a cigarette," I say. "It gives him an excuse to get away from you fuckers." Joe smiles at that and nudges me in my side with his elbow. "I'll come with you," I say.

"Shit, I'll come," Harry says, "if you got a smoke for me."

"I only have five packs left," Joe says, sounding sad about it.

"Yeah?" Harry asks. "So, then you have plenty."

"I told you," Joe says with the tone of impatience he usu-ally reserves only for Harry. "I'm quitting. I bought one carton. Once they're gone, I'm done."

"Well, if you want to quit, why do you care if you give cigarettes away?" Harry asks. "You just get to quit that much sooner."

"Because I want to get to enjoy every last one of them," Joe says, his voice rising with exasperation. "I made a deal with myself to quit after this last carton. I want to smoke the whole goddamn carton. I'm rationing them for as long as I can."

"Well, if you like smoking so much, then why are you quitting?"

The thing about Harry is that he isn't asking this question to be annoying. But he is. Annoying.

"If you like smoking so much, why don't you buy your own fucking cigarettes?" I ask, delivering it like it's a joke, but it isn't.

Since my arrival at the party it has started to drizzle outside, which has had the positive effect of chasing everyone else inside so we have the yard mostly to ourselves other than one drunk guy staggering around aimlessly. His head is down, as if he's looking for something he dropped, or his head hurts too much to hold it up. I feel sorry for him. I know how he feels.

I hate being drunk. Usually if I'm at a party I'll have one beer, nurse it for the whole night. And I only do that to avoid people asking me why I'm not drinking. Puking because I drank too much once was enough times to convince me I never wanted to do it again. Mostly my friends and I smoke weed. The thing with weed is that you get high, and you feel it right away, and then a few hours later, when the party's over, you come down, eat an entire box of cookies, and pass out. With alcohol, you drink and drink and drink and you feel great, until all of a sudden . . . you don't. You can't walk straight, you can't talk right, and it's as if everyone else in the room is in on a joke that you just can't understand. And the joke is you.

It isn't until you're drunk that you wish you weren't. Then it's hours, literally hours, before you feel anything approaching normal again. It sucks.

Drinking also makes me feel sorry for myself. I can cry when I've been drinking, something I can't do sober. And usually I do end up crying when I drink. I hope the drunk guy doesn't come over to talk to us, or start crying. Or both.

Emily's backyard is surrounded by a chain-link fence and there's evidence that there has been some effort to convert the space into an urban oasis. There's a collection of pots on the patio, but the plants have turned brown and wilted. And there's a bunch of wood planks on concrete blocks that probably looked like a viable hillbilly-chic idea for a bench in a Pinterest post. In practice, the effect is a little sad.

"What you want to get into tonight?" Joe asks.

"I don't know," I say. "There's a party over in McLean. I thought about going but I hate most of the people I go to school with."

"So what?" Harry asks. "Will they have beer?"

"If I tell you something, you have to promise you won't react."

Joe holds up his hand like he's giving me a blessing. "You know me, man, I don't judge. Except for maybe that guy," he says, gesturing at the drunk stumbling guy in the yard. "And Harry and Mark because they're idiots. And people who don't eat gluten."

"Yeah, well, that's all valid," I say. "Ophelia texted me earlier. She asked me what time I'd be home."

"And you came here?" Joe asks. "What the hell were you thinking?"

"I had the weed."

"So? You think if Harry had a girl like Ophelia inviting him to a party, or Mark, you think they'd show up to bring you a bag of weed?"

"Absolutely not," Harry, Mark, and I all say in unison.

"Ri-ight," Joe says. "So, what the hell are you doing here? I think she likes you, dude. She's always giving you a hard time. Makes fun of you. She wouldn't do that if she wasn't into you."

"You think? That's how you tell if a girl likes you?"

"Absolutely. If she makes fun of you, or, you know, she asks you what you're going to eat, or whether you're going to be someplace where she's planning to be, like a dance or something. That's how you know she likes you."

"You think she knows how much you like her?" Harry asks.

"I don't like her," I correct him. "I love her."

"You should tell her how you feel," says Mark, because it would never occur to Mark to be afraid to say what he feels. "In another couple of months she'll be gone. And you'll have to live the rest of your life regretting it if you don't tell her."

"Forget it," Harry says. "That's a terrible idea. Dane, you don't tell a girl you're interested in her unless you're sure she's going to say she likes you back."

"I know that."

"Man, that's dumb," Mark says. "You think the reason why some guys end up with a new girl every weekend is because they sit around waiting for girls to come to them?"

"Guys like that, they know the secret—go average early," Harry says. "That's what I say. You don't wait for the most beautiful girl to fall in love with you. If you do that, you'll be waiting forever."

"How is that supposed to help?" Joe asks, impatient with Harry now. "Dane likes Ophelia. He's not looking for a girl. He's already found one."

"That's what I'm saying," Harry says. "You think a girl like Ophelia, who's good-looking and smart and popular, is sitting around at home wondering when Dane is going to call her? No offense, Dane."

"None taken," I say. "I already figured that part for myself."

Joe sighs. "If you say so, dude. I think she likes you."

"Maybe," I say. "But, what if the reason she makes fun of me is just because she thinks I'm an idiot?" I ask.

"That's also possible," Joe says. "But you should be there, finding out. Not here."

I think about all of the useless advice my friends have given me as I drive home and decide. . . . *Forget it. I'm not texting Ophelia. If she really wants to talk to me, she'll text me again.* Which she hasn't. So, I'm not texting her.

I never message Ophelia because I am sure it will make it too obvious how I feel about her. If she texts me, then I respond, but I never send her a random observational text the way I do with Mark or Harry or Joe. It would seem too desperate for me to text her when there is no real reason for me to do so. If I sent her a text about a school assignment or something lame like that, she would be immediately suspicious. She knows I don't care about school.

I've tried to come up with the most disappointing possible reason Ophelia might want to talk to me, just to prepare myself. This is a strategy I use a lot. I think about the most disappointing possible outcome of a situation or any given day so I can anticipate the grief and be prepared for it. I do this especially if it's something that is supposed to be good—like Christmas. Only this year I didn't have to imagine anything terrible about Christmas before it happened. My dad being dead and Chuck and Eric coming over for Christmas dinner was definitely the most disappointing thing that could have happened. And it did.

Another fifteen minutes go by without a message from

Ophelia. Maybe she's gone to bed. Or maybe she's changed her mind.

I can wait.

Often I am awake for hours after everyone else in the house is asleep. I have worries. The worries keep me awake because they aren't worries that can be solved. I think my brain does this on purpose. It actively seeks things that can't be solved. Perhaps, as my guidance counselor at Brandywine often suggested, it's because I am afraid of failure. And I would ask him if the reason he ended up as a guidance counselor at a school where the students could afford great therapy was because he was afraid of failure himself. Our meetings always ended in a stalemate.

I don't want to give up on Ophelia, so I go downstairs to keep myself from falling asleep watching a show. The house is quiet except for the faint sound of the television from Mom's room. After Dad died, and before Chuck started staying over, Mom kept the television on almost twenty-four seven. She watched a lot of cooking shows, which is weird because she doesn't ever cook.

The kitchen is dark but for the glow of the work light over the stove. There is a separate wine refrigerator under the counter. The wine refrigerator can be set to three separate temperatures, depending on the kind of wine you are chilling. Though we look like doomsday preppers in the wine department, it's a clear guarantee we would be the most useless members of the doomsday team. We can't even survive with single-temperature wine.

I help myself to one of the bottles of white wine. My dad was the only one brave enough to drink red wine around Mom's furniture.

The rear deck is visible from Mom's first floor bedroom, so I can't sit there. I go to sit on the front porch instead. The porch light is on but I switch off the security light that casts a pool as bright as sunshine on the front lawn. I take up a seat on the couch on the front porch, with the bottle of wine and two glasses, just in case.

As I sit on the porch the night sounds rise around me. After a few minutes, one thin, high note rises above the chirp of crickets and the distant hum of traffic. It is a cry of loneliness, pleading with an uncaring and unforgiving world.

It is the first time I have heard the coyote howl, and goosebumps rise on my arms and the back of my neck. Perhaps against reason, I feel as if the coyote is speaking directly to me, as if I'm the only person who can really understand what it's like to be something wild in a place where people only want things tame.

Even though I am watching the darkness intently, watching for any sign of the coyote, I jump with surprise and, horribly, let out a yelp when a human figure steps into the glow cast by the porch light. My heart jackrabbits in my chest and my body tenses before I realize it is just Ophelia, out wandering the neighborhood like an unsettled spirit.

"You scared the crap out of me," I say.

"Good," she says. "I was hoping I would."

"You should have called out to warn me."

"But then I wouldn't get to hear you yell like a scared little boy," she says, the only one amused by her wit.

"Ha, ha. You're very funny. Did you hear the coyote?"

"The what?"

"That howl. It was a coyote crying."

"Oh," Ophelia says as she looks back over her shoulder, as if nervous there might be a coyote standing behind her. "No. I didn't notice it."

"Sit down," I say, patting the seat beside me on the wicker couch. "Maybe he'll do it again."

"How do you know it's a 'he'?" she asks, and I shush her.

Ophelia sits and we are silent, waiting to hear the coyote. After a few minutes I can feel Ophelia's impatience as there is only the sound of crickets and the distant hum of traffic from the Beltway.

Ophelia gestures toward the two glasses on the wicker table and says, "You expecting someone?"

"You," I say. "I thought you might turn up."

"Thanks," she says, sounding surprised as I pour her a small glass of wine. She takes a drink, then wipes her lips with the sleeve of her sweatshirt.

I am envious of the glass, of the sleeve of her sweatshirt, things that can touch her lips so casually. I can't look at her mouth without thinking about kissing it, so I try not to look.

"What are you doing out?" I ask, giving up on the coyote. My desire for Ophelia is so present, it seems incredible to me that she can't sense it.

"Oh," she says with a shrug, "I just felt like going for a walk."

"Why?" I ask. "What's wrong?"

"Why does something have to be wrong for a person to want to go for a walk?" she asks with a frown. Incredible how she does that. She's the one who texted me, the one who snuck up on me while I sat in the relative privacy of my own porch, and the one who is out for a walk in the dark in a neighborhood that actively discourages walking by not providing sidewalks. Yet, somehow, I am the one under indictment for asking the simple question of why she is out walking.

"It's dark," I say, selecting the most obvious of the possible answers.

"So? My grandfather used to say that there is nothing more to fear in the dark than there is in the light."

"Did your grandfather get hit by a bus, too?" I ask. "Possibly at night?"

"He's still alive."

"Well, no offense, but your grandfather sounds like a moron. Of course there's more to fear in the dark. Serial killers mostly work at night. . . . And vampires."

"That's not what he meant. He was talking about monsters under the bed. He was saying not to be afraid of the dark."

"Still," I say, my mood shifting now that we are on this subject, "I've never seen a ghost during the daytime, but if I did, somehow I don't think it would be as frightening."

"What do you mean you've never seen a ghost in the *day-time*? Does that mean you've seen them at night?"

"Not like you're thinking." I turn to look at her and am surprised by the warmth of her gaze. I am always struck by how soft her eyes are. The brain behind her eyes is so sharp and cutting, it is hard to understand how her eyes can be like velvet in their appraisal of me.

She pauses then, as if working up the nerve to say something socially unacceptable. "You talking about your dad?"

"I guess. I mean, it's not as if I see my dad walking around the house." I am saying more than I probably should. The glass of wine takes away my better judgment, leaving only my judgment. "I just feel him. Like he hasn't accepted the fact that he's dead yet and is still hanging around. Do you think that's crazy?"

She purses her lips in thought, then says, "The short answer is no."

I laugh. "And the long answer is yes . . . with a 'but.'"

"*The Simpsons*," she says, and slaps my leg so hard it hurts, but I know she is slapping me as a show of affection so I try not to react. I don't want to discourage her from other shows of affection. "That's a funny episode."

"So, if I say I've seen a ghost, that's a crazy thing to say?" I ask.

"I don't believe in ghosts," she says with the simple confidence of a person who has accepted the absence of a god. "I think once you're dead, that's it. There is nothing else. No eternal life. No heaven or hell."

"Believe me," I say, "I hope there isn't life after death. That would suck."

"Why do you say that?" she asks with genuine curiosity.

"This life isn't so great. I definitely don't want to live another one for all eternity."

"That's why people make up places like heaven, you know?" Ophelia says as she holds her glass in her lap and curls her feet up under her on the couch. "We all want to believe that we're going someplace great after this life is over. I mean, what do you think is worse? Believing in a place like hell and you might go there? Or thinking that when you die there's just . . . nothing."

"Definitely hell," I say without hesitation. "I want there to be nothing. Life is already hell."

I don't say that in the privacy of my own mind I have often hoped there is no afterlife, that the people we love can't watch our actions from the advantage of a spirit world. There are many things I have done in the past six months that I hope my father could never see. Even as I did them, I hoped he wasn't watching over me like a guardian angel, shaking his head in disappointment or disgust. I can't even pick my nose anymore without thinking about my dad watching me like some kind of Jedi Force spirit.

"Don't say that," Ophelia says, startling me out of recollections of the things in my life that are secret, from other people, if not from myself. "That makes me sad to hear you say that."

"Why would you care?" I ask. The question comes out sounding angry.

"Of course I care," Ophelia says as she presses one hand to her chest. "I mean, we're friends. Sort of."

"How do you figure?" I ask. "We've never hung out. Not really."

"Is everyone you hang out with your friend? I hang out with lots of people who aren't my friends. Not real friends."

"Maybe not," I say, thinking lately I don't feel like my friends and I have much in common, like they don't struggle with the same thoughts that I have about the uncertainty of everything. "How would you define a real friend?" I ask.

"I care about you," she says, "what happens to you. That's friendship."

"If you say so. I've always gotten the impression that I got on your nerves."

"Oh, totally," she says. "You're getting on my nerves right now."

I laugh. I can't help it. Ophelia purses her lips in an effort to keep from laughing at her own joke.

"See?" I ask, my voice rising with feigned exasperation.

"Just because you get on my nerves doesn't mean I don't like you. That you're not my friend."

"Thanks. A lot. I feel really fucking special now."

"Do you remember last Christmas?" Ophelia asks, with her whiplash-inducing ability to change the subject. "The Dabsons had that holiday party and invited everyone in the neighborhood to drop in?"

"Vaguely."

"It was a couple of days before Christmas and they had

that giant fake tree in the living room. I mean, a white Christmas tree? As if McLean isn't white enough already. Anyway, Mrs. Dabson was talking about her golden child, Jordan, applying to schools and she made some comment about how lucky my dad is because it's going to be so easy for me to get into a good college and get a scholarship. And she didn't mean because I'm such a good student or a great field hockey player."

"She meant because you're brown," I say.

"Exactly," Ophelia says.

"Mrs. Dabson is a lunatic. I wouldn't worry about anything she says."

"You were there," Ophelia says as she nudges my shoulder. "You don't remember?"

"If it involved our neighbors I probably blocked the whole thing from my memory. It's possible I was really high." I do remember the conversation, but I hadn't given it any thought at all since it happened. I'm used to being the person who says whatever is socially unacceptable. I'm enjoying the fact that I did something memorable enough that Ophelia would take any notice, so I let her finish telling me the story.

"You were standing right there." Ophelia's voice rises with exasperation. "And after Mrs. Dabson made that comment there was an awkward silence and then you said, 'I guess it's too bad Jordan isn't brown, too. They'll have to actually judge his applications based on his grades.'"

"Well, it's true, right?" I ask. "She was being a racist asshole."

"Yeah, but I couldn't believe it when you said that," Ophelia says. "It was the first time I realized you weren't a total creep."

"That's . . . flattering."

"In fact," Ophelia says, "it made me realize you were pretty cool."

"I'm waiting for the 'but.'"

"There is no 'but.'"

We are both quiet for a minute and I wonder what she's thinking. The human mind is the last great frontier.

"So, why did you text me earlier?" I ask.

"I just wanted to talk to you," she says with a shrug. "Is that okay?"

"Sure. But why?"

She places her glass on the table and shifts in her seat to put her hands under her thighs, drops her head to one side so she's looking right at me, then opens her eyes so wide it looks like it must hurt. "I don't know. Maybe it's because I have a big crush on you."

I laugh at that. "Very funny."

After taking another sip she says, "Why would you assume I'm being funny?"

"I never thought about you being into any guy, I guess," I say, carefully dodging her question. This is another lie. I worry about Ophelia being with other guys all the time. No guy is really good enough for her, present company included.

"What did you think?" she asks, misunderstanding what I said. "That I'm into girls?"

"Well, you do play field hockey." In order to cover my reaction to her joke about having a crush on me, I have to create a diversion, say something so insulting it will distract her from my horrific pain and make her forget it.

"Oh," Ophelia says, her forehead wrinkling as I meet and exceed every low expectation she has for me. "So if a woman plays a sport, that makes her a lesbian?"

"Nah," I say. "Just field hockey . . . and softball."

She appraises me silently, one eyebrow arched in judgment as she waits for me to finish making a fool out of myself.

"Maybe boxing, too . . ."

"I take back what I said about you being cool," she says.

My plan, which has been working beautifully since the start of senior year, is to always be just enough of a dick that Ophelia will never catch on to the fact that I am in love with her. If she finds out . . . well, I'm not sure what will happen, but for sure I will be rejected, and, by extension, humiliated. And because she is my neighbor, my rejection and humiliation will be an ongoing, daily ritual.

She takes a deep breath and lets out a sigh before saying, "But not gymnastics because that's girlie. They wear leotards and makeup and have glitter in their hair."

"I guess so," I say. "I wouldn't think of a girl who does gymnastics as being a lesbian, no."

"And not beach volleyball," Ophelia says helpfully, though she isn't really trying to be helpful at all, "because those outfits are sexy."

I know that she is ridiculing me—not just telling me that I am an idiot, but proving it, too. "Okay, I get it," I say. "Now I'm the asshole."

"You said it, not me."

"You definitely said it."

Finally, I have said something to make her smile. I mean . . . finally. I have known Ophelia for two years, and before this moment I couldn't swear under oath that she had teeth. And, really, she is only laughing about the fact that I am an idiot, so it isn't exactly the kind of smile I have hoped for, but I'll take it. That smile makes me feel good. It makes me feel better than good. It makes me want to do a bunch of other shit that will make her smile.

"So," I say, "you're not into girls, but you don't have a boyfriend. Why not?"

"Why don't you have a girlfriend?" she shoots back.

"I asked you first."

"I don't have a boyfriend because I can't be in a romantic relationship," Ophelia says, as if shocked by the suggestion. "My parents have never provided me with a positive example of a romantic relationship."

"Nobody's parents have ever provided them with a positive example of a romantic relationship. That's what television is for."

"Seriously, my mom is the most unsuccessful married

person to ever live. She's had two husbands, three live-in boyfriends, and one guy who dated her just because he needed a kidney donor and thought she might be a match."

"Did she do it?" I ask. "Did your mom give the guy her extra kidney?"

"It's not really an 'extra' kidney, is it?" Ophelia asks. "Not if you're still using it. My point is, the people who have raised me are emotional cripples. I'm the last person who should be in a romantic relationship."

"I've tried to kill myself," I blurt suddenly. "I'm not sure what's worse. The fact that I tried to kill myself, or that I failed at it."

"That's kind of funny," Ophelia says, flipping her head to look at me in a way that makes her hair jerk out of her face and lay obediently over one shoulder.

"Not really," I say with a grimace.

"I mean, not funny that you tried to kill yourself. That's tragic. But the way you think about it—failing at suicide is the ultimate failure."

"This is your therapy session, not mine," I say as I resettle in my seat and remind myself not to get too comfortable. "So, you think just because your parents got divorced, and that your mom is bad with . . . interpersonal relationships, you just give up on love?"

"What I'm saying is that I have no point of reference. I don't know what a successful romantic relationship looks like. So, any relationship I enter will probably end badly."

"Everything ends," I say. "Usually badly."

"You know what I think? I've always thought that if I ever do have a boyfriend he would have to agree ahead of time on a date that we end our relationship. That way there's no anxiety about when it will happen. We both know it's coming. That way we're prepared. And if we still like each other, still like spending time together, then it will still end. But it won't be bad. It will just . . . be."

"That's a terrible idea," I say.

"Why is it a terrible idea? Killing yourself—that's a terrible idea. But just deciding to be happy and enjoy each other for a while? That's not terrible."

"So"—I decide to go along with her crazy for a minute—"you just pick some arbitrary date?"

"Well, I figure the first couple of months, that's the best time of any relationship. You're still getting to know the person and you want to spend all of your time with them. So, say two or three months. You pick the date ahead of time and then you just walk away." As she says this she waves her hand out and away from her body, like she's throwing a Frisbee. "Then it's not like anybody is getting dumped."

"Or dying," I say.

"Right. It's just . . ." She pauses and shrugs. ". . . over."

"Maybe you're right," I say. "Maybe if you knew the outcome ahead of time, then being in a relationship would be okay."

"So, you don't have a girlfriend? Have you ever had one?"

"I don't think so. No. There was one girl, I used to have a

huge crush on her. But I only saw her when I was home in the summer and she always had a boyfriend."

"Does she go to our school? Do I know her?"

"No. You wouldn't know her."

"Well, what's your excuse now?"

"I don't have a girlfriend because there's nobody who wants to be my girlfriend. I always manage to say the wrong thing."

"Yeah, but you do that on purpose," Ophelia says, and it surprises me.

"Only to you," I say. "I only say the wrong things on purpose to you."

"Why?"

"I like to give you good reason not to like me upfront. That way I never have to wonder why you don't."

"Don't what?" she asks.

"Don't like me."

"I just told you that I don't think you're a total creep."

"Well, I guess that's pretty good."

And then, the worst possible thing happens. A car pulls into the driveway and I recognize Eric's certified, pre-owned Audi.

"Crap," I say as I sink down into my seat, trying to become invisible.

"What?" Ophelia asks.

I only sigh in response as Eric is already almost to the front step.

"Hey," he says with a surprised smile. "Ophelia, what are you doing here?"

"Just hanging out. What about you?"

"My mom would lose her shit if I was coming home this late. I stay here because my dad and Trudi go to bed early."

"Sounds reasonable," Ophelia says.

I wish she would stop talking to him so he will go inside and leave us alone. As much as I hate interacting with Eric, I hate the idea of him interacting with Ophelia more. She's beautiful and smart, but she's also kind of a nerd, so I doubt Eric has paid much attention to her before now.

"What are you up to, Dane?" Eric asks as he jerks his chin in the direction of the bottle of wine, half empty, on the table in front of us.

"Nothing," I say.

Ophelia and Eric both wait as if I might say more, but I don't.

Eric picks up the wine from the table and drinks straight from the bottle, not even bothering to ask if one of us wants more before he puts his cooties all over it. Typical Eric. The largest piece of cake is always his.

"Dane never mentioned you guys were friends," Eric says to Ophelia.

"That's because you and I don't talk," I say.

"Sure, we do," Eric says. "You're just always depressed about something so you never want to hang out."

"Dane and I aren't really friends," Ophelia says. "I just use him for sex."

Eric laughs at that, and it makes me hate him a little more than I already do. Ophelia is joking, of course, but the fact that they both think wanting to have sex with me is a joke makes me feel lonelier than ever.

"Good luck in that department," Eric says. "Have him tell you about STI statistics. He knows a lot about that. Right, Dane?"

Ophelia says nothing, just takes a sip from her wineglass. I couldn't swear it, because of the dark, but Ophelia's cheeks look flushed, like she might be blushing, and I wonder if she's embarrassed because she really likes Eric, is attracted to him.

"Well," Eric says as he lifts himself off the porch rail to his full height, "I guess I'll leave you guys to do . . . whatever you were going to do before I got here. See you around."

"Good night," Ophelia says as Eric opens the screen door and slips inside.

I say nothing, just wait for the sound of the interior door shutting before I relax by degrees.

"Fucking asshole," I mutter under my breath.

"Why do you dislike him so much?" Ophelia has a habit of asking questions that are uncomfortable or hard to answer and then watching, rather than listening, for a response. Her dad, the Colonel, is the same way, and it always makes me wonder if his work for the military includes Black Ops interrogations.

"Why don't you dislike him more?" I shoot back.

She shrugs one shoulder. "He's always been pretty cool to me."

"Of course he has," I say, and it sounds like an accusation. "Because you haven't slept with him. Guys like Eric are only nice to you because they want to sleep with you."

"Really?" she asks, unmoved by the anger in my tone. "You think that's the only reason a guy would be nice to me?"

"You know what I mean," I say, but Ophelia isn't ready to let it go. I know from experience she will latch on to my idiotic remark like a pit bull and shake it to death.

"You're not nice to me. Does that mean you don't want to sleep with me?" she asks.

"When have I ever been not nice to you?"

"Um . . ." She pauses as if she's really considering my question, then says, "I don't know. Maybe right now."

"This isn't mean," I say. "This is just honest. You're naive to think that if a guy like Eric is being nice to you it's because he's a nice guy, doesn't have some ulterior motive."

"An ulterior motive?"

"Like sex."

"Oh, come on. Why do I have to be the victim?"

"Let's just forget it," I say, thinking that Eric already did his best to ruin the end to a pretty awesome night. I've had Ophelia all to myself for a half hour.

"Talking to you is exhausting sometimes," she says.

"You should try being in here," I say as I tap the side of my head. "I'm exhausted all the time."

"You don't give anybody a chance to be anywhere near inside there," she says, pointing at my head.

She waits in silence and I'm not sure what she wants me to say. I'm confused now, and angry after seeing Eric—him treating my house, my life, as if everything is open for him to take.

"I should go," Ophelia says, and, for sure now, I get the sense she's waiting for me to stop her, to say something meaningful.

"Good night, Ophelia. I'll watch to make sure you get home okay."

Dr. Lineberger greets us and gestures for me to enter her office. Mom stays behind in the waiting area.

The days are growing warmer but Dr. Lineberger hasn't reset her thermostat. Seventy degrees. Warm enough that in the puddle of sun that spills through her office window, I feel as if I could sleep.

"It's good to see you, Dane," Dr. Lineberger says as she does her routine of waiting for me to choose a seat before her.

This time I take the couch so I can stretch out a bit, and she takes one of the chairs.

"How are you?" she asks as she settles in across from me.

"I'm okay."

"I thought our last meeting was really productive," she says. "Maybe we didn't solve anything, but you and your mom were both honest about your feelings."

"I guess."

She nods but watches me and waits to see if I'm going to

say any more before she says, "So, let's talk about your father. You miss him, of course. But your mother has said she thinks your response to losing your father has been extreme, that you can't manage the grief and you aren't getting any better as time passes. What do you think about that?"

"I don't know. What's an acceptable amount of sadness after your dad dies?" I am hoping there is a real answer to this question. I am not just asking to be a smartass.

"I wish I had an answer for that question," Dr. Lineberger says, which maybe is the right thing to say. "I guess what we want to figure out is whether there is an underlying depression that is compounding your grief, making it unbearable. Grieving is one thing, harming yourself is quite another. Your mother told me that you have had a suicidal episode in the past."

"My mom told you about that?" I ask. It surprises me that she has told Dr. Lineberger about the time I tried to overdose. It was a misguided effort. Prescription pills almost never work if you really want to kill yourself. Street heroin, or a combination of pills and alcohol, that's a lot more reliable. Just ask Amy Winehouse, or a hundred other celebrities.

"I didn't try to kill myself after my dad died," I say, feeling like this is an important point. "It was before I even knew he was sick. I just really didn't want to go back to school. I hated it there."

"You must have really hated it a lot, if being dead was preferable to being away at school."

It's kind of a funny thing to say, but I don't think she is trying to be funny.

"Honestly . . . ," I say, then pause to decide how honest my next words will be. "I'm not sure what I was hoping for when I did it. And I did end up going back to school. I told my parents I wanted to go back. I took all of those pills just so they wouldn't send me back, would be too worried to let me go. But then when the time came, I didn't want to stay home. As much as I hated it there, staying home seemed worse. And now"—I shrug, a gesture that is woefully insufficient to express my uncertainty—"I don't know what I want. I don't feel much about it now. I'm just kind of . . . numb. Awake. Asleep. It's all the same to me."

Dr. Lineberger is, for once, not writing in her notebook as I talk. She seems riveted by my story.

"So, this sadness," she asks, "it was there before your father died? Before you even knew he was sick?"

"Yeah. I guess. I'm not sure 'sadness' is the right word. Hopelessness, maybe. What's the point in trying, if tomorrow you wake up and there are just new problems to solve, new mountains to climb?"

"What kinds of problems, Dane? Can you give me a specific example?"

"I don't know. Problems like a school assignment I don't want to do, or problems like climate change. One is manageable but pointless; the other is too big to fix. It just seemed easier to shut down."

"So, just to use your climate change example, what if

you did focus in school, went to college and got a job in developing clean energy alternatives, and contributed some small part to a global solution? Why do you think you can't be part of the solution?"

"You don't know me very well, but if you think I'm going to be part of the solution to any of the world's problems, then the situation is even more bleak than I already thought it was."

Dr. Lineberger cracks a small smile at that but says, "I'm just suggesting that, maybe, having a goal, and working toward it, is more productive than just giving up and hiding under the covers."

"I guess."

"Everyone feels the way that you do, Dane. When we stop and take the time to worry, it can seem overwhelming. Our goal here, together, is to look at ways you can feel like that there are things you want to accomplish, achievements that can make you feel good. A good goal right now would be learning to manage your grief about your father. We've got a reality to deal with. And it's preventing you from moving forward with a life for yourself."

"I guess it's hard to get over my dad being gone, because he's not really gone. He's still . . . hanging around."

"You mean his memory? Things that remind you of your father?"

"That too, I guess. But no, I mean, like, he's still there." I hadn't planned on telling Dr. Lineberger any of this but now that we're talking about it, I figure . . . what the hell?

"Elaborate, please," Dr. Lineberger says, and tugs at the hem of her skirt as she settles in to get comfortable. "That is, tell me what you mean."

I know what "elaborate" means, but this time I resist the urge to tell her so.

"I mean he's still here. His spirit, or whatever."

"Are we talking about ghosts?" Dr. Lineberger asks.

"If that's what you want to call it," I say, hoping to seem agreeable.

"You've seen your father's ghost?" If she thinks I'm crazy, I don't think she's supposed to let on about it, but I can hear it in her voice anyway.

"Not exactly. See, there's this coyote that lives in the neighborhood. He turned up right after my dad died. I guess I kind of feel like this coyote . . . it's my dad. Only reincarnated. He hangs around the neighborhood. Like he's keeping an eye on the house. On me. Do you think that's crazy?"

"'Crazy' isn't a word I would use. It isn't a clinical diagnosis. If you are having hallucinations, actually seeing your father's ghost, that might be one thing. But just sensing that his spirit lives on in this . . . coyote? Perhaps you are just holding on to his memory in a way that feels comforting. You can imagine he's still there, even if he's gone."

"I suppose," I say, noncommittal as to whether I agree with her assessment.

"Have you talked about this with your mother?" she asks.

I laugh. "No way. She would definitely think I was crazy.

I mean, she already does. That's why I'm here. Talking to you."

"I think you're here because your mother cares about you, Dane. She wants you to get better."

"Well," I say, "we have different opinions on that."

THUS BAD BEGINS, AND WORSE REMAINS BEHIND

Mom wants us to spend more quality time together. She tells me this as I'm lying in bed trying to get ten more minutes of sleep before I have to be up for work. I'll agree to anything just to get her to stop talking. I think she is aware of this and that is why she makes suggestions like "dinner together as a family," whatever that means, when I am still half asleep.

Just like Mom was always trying to get Dad to quit things, she's always trying to make people do things that she decides are best for them. I don't think she has started in on Chuck yet, getting him to quit eating prime rib or to stop drinking so much scotch. Maybe once she starts in on him about that stuff he'll lose interest in her like he did with his ex-wife.

"Are you working today?" Mom asks.

"Mph." I'm only barely awake, so my response is noncommittal.

"Until what time?"

"What?" Now I'm mostly awake, but I still have no idea what she's talking about.

"What time do you finish work today?"

"The store closes at six."

"So, you're off at six o'clock?"

"I *just* said that. For the love of God, Mom, please. What time is it?"

"It's ten o'clock, Dane. For goodness' sake. Most of the world has been awake for hours."

"I'm off at six. Okay? And only old people have been up for hours. Now shut the door so I can go back to sleep."

"I'm going to make reservations at the club for seven. Don't be late."

"You could just send me a text to tell me this."

"This is exactly what I'm talking about. We live in the same house and we text instead of talking."

"Shut the door, Mom."

She sighs as she leaves and shuts the door—hard. My last therapist said he thought Mom was passive-aggressive. He wasn't a very good therapist, but he sure had Mom figured out.

When I arrive at the country club at seven fifteen to meet Chuck and Mom for dinner, I notice Eric's Audi in the parking lot. The dread that I am already feeling becomes a rock in my stomach and I think about leaving.

They are already seated at a table in the dining room when I arrive. There are three phones on the table, but Mom must have told everybody not to look at theirs. Mom is old enough that she still wears a watch, the real kind that only tells the time, and she looks at hers the second she sees me walking toward them. Classic passive-aggressive.

"Glad you could make it," she says, passively. Then she smiles, aggressively.

"We'll see if you change your mind about that," I say as I take the empty seat and unfold my napkin.

"We've already ordered," Chuck says, but not in a mean way. His smile is apologetic and I almost feel bad for hating him so much.

"There's Dave Ingram," Mom says. Mom places the tips of three fingers on Chuck's wrist and nods at the middle of the room. Her voice is low and conspiratorial. I'm thankful that Dave Ingram has distracted her from torturing me. Probably because there's something tragic about Dave Ingram, and she's always interested in anyone who suffers more than she does.

Chuck doesn't have a lot of neck agility, so he has to half turn in his chair in order to see where Mom has indicated. Mom rolls her eyes slightly at this because Chuck is being so obvious.

"He had to have six inches of his colon removed," Mom leans forward to say to all of us, "it was so full of polyps."

"Oh my God," I say, fighting back the bile in my throat. "Why do you know that?"

"His wife, Miriam, is in my Bikram yoga class," Mom says, still directing a side eye at Dave Ingram and his family.

"Six inches is a lot," Chuck says.

"Not actually," Eric says with a laugh.

Chuck and Mom don't seem to hear Eric, but even if they do, they don't get his joke. Which is typical. Middle-aged people spend more time thinking about their colons than they do about dicks.

"Maybe it was six centimeters," Chuck offers helpfully.

Mom grimaces with doubt at Chuck's ignorance about the human digestive tract. "I don't know. Six centimeters doesn't sound like much. I'm not even sure how long six centimeters is. . . ."

"Dane, you can show her what six centimeters looks like." Eric is grinning at me over the top of his glass as he lifts it to drink. "Am I right?"

I ignore him and pretend as if I'm listening earnestly to Mom and Chuck, as if the length of Dave Ingram's colon is something I've wanted to know my whole life.

"Well, either way," Mom says, gesturing with her hand so that we all can't help but admire her acrylic nail tips, glowing white under the crystal chandelier, "they had to cut out a big part of his colon. And Miriam didn't say it, but I know he eats a lot of red meat and he won't drink any of those juice blends like the ones I make for you."

"That's victim-shaming," I say.

Now they're all staring at me, either with a question or, in Eric's case, confusion. I'm not really sure what victim-shaming is, or why it's bad, but I've heard Ophelia express outrage about it during some of our conversations. Mom sometimes talks about Dad's cancer like it was an inevitable result of his lifestyle. It makes me nuts. Kids get cancer all

the time and it's not like a six-year-old is out smoking cigarettes or drinking martinis.

"What?" I ask as they all keep staring at me silently. "It
is. It's victim-shaming to say that Dave Ingram lost his colon because he made bad choices about the food he ate." I
shrug as I take the opportunity to look across the room at
Dave and his family, who all look pretty happy at their table.
They look like a family should. I can just imagine what
Thanksgiving or Christmas is like at the Ingram household.
Everybody is so fucking grateful that Dave just lost part of
his colon, not his whole life to cancer. Losing six centimeters
or six inches of his colon was probably an eye-opener, and
everyone in the family was woke to the fact that they could
lose Dave at any time. And now, here they are, reveling in
their togetherness as a family. It's almost beautiful to watch.

"Eric was just telling us about the plans for the senior trip
to the Shenandoah," Mom says, disrupting my enjoyment
of the Ingram family's annual Christmas tradition with all of
them in their ugly sweaters, posing for photos in front of a
big stone fireplace, opening presents around a massive tree,
a real one, not the fake kind my mom puts up every year
because she doesn't like pine needles in the carpet.

"You're going to need new hiking boots," she says, pointing one of her perfect nails at me.

"I'm not going on the senior trip," I say, deciding this as
I say it.

"Why not?" Eric asks. "It's going to be . . ."

He talks for what seems like a really . . . really long time.

God, I'd give anything to see the world through Eric's eyes. He's got everything all figured out—just waiting for graduation to launch him into his gap year and being an adult useless turd, instead of a pre-adult useless turd. Why does he spend time on homework or participating in extra-curricular activities? He honestly believes that all that shit really matters.

"I'm not going," I say, slowly, "because the senior class trip is gay. I mean, not gay like it's insulting to homosexuals, but . . . you know." I'm editing as I speak, thinking about Ophelia's accusing glare if I use the word "gay" to mean anything negative. "Like, I think it's going to be lame."

"Jesus, Dane," Mom says, her teeth gnashing at the *s*'s in "Jesus" as she reaches for her wineglass.

We all ignore Mom's outburst, each for our own reasons. Chuck wants to pretend as if everything is fine, it's all cool. I hate her tactics, but I can never formulate an effective response to them—which, by the way, is how passive-aggressiveness works.

"Jeez, Dane," Eric says, choosing the politically correct way of taking Jesus's name in vain. "I feel like your hostility is unfair. The student association has invested a lot of time in these activities." His mouth is curled into a predatory smile but I'm the only one who notices it. He doesn't give a crap about the student association. He's just hoping to get loaded, and probably get some girl drunk so he can take advantage of the situation. And now he's doing his best to make me look like a whiny baby in front of Chuck and Mom.

"I get that, Eric," I say, "and I appreciate you. Group activities just aren't my thing."

"The oysters are here," Chuck says with obvious relief and too much delight as a platter is set down in the middle of the table before us. It's a large metal tray, piled high with ice, a dozen oysters lying open on the half shell in front of us. There's a pause as everyone else at the table picks up their phones to snap a picture of the oysters. Like the proverbial tree falling in the woods, it's hard to say you actually enjoyed something unless you convince your social media followers that you did.

The oysters are large, the size of a human ear, and in the same shape. They glisten under the candlelight and, as the light flickers, the oysters seem to be shivering, or breathing. I put my hands on the sides of my chair and the weight of my legs on the backs of my hands. I do this whenever I feel like I might fly into a million pieces.

I read somewhere that when you order oysters on the half shell, the oysters are actually delivered to the table still alive. The oyster only dies when you bite into it, or when your stomach acid starts to digest it. I don't know if that's true or not, but it sounds true. And, anyway, who really gets to decide the difference between life and death, numbness and pain? For all we know, oysters have an elaborate belief system that correctly explains the meaning of life and the universe.

Chuck and Eric dig into the oysters, slurping the quivering little bodies right off the rough shells. They are greedy and sloppy about it—their mouths wet with oyster juice. There are dainty forks for removing the oysters from the shells, and these they use to spoon little heaps of cocktail sauce onto the oyster. They add lemon juice or a dab of horseradish, anything to conceal the actual taste of the oyster. The condiments are added like a solemn ritual, as if the oyster's entire existence has only been in preparation for this moment, a Viking send-off for a mollusk.

All I can think about is the pain the oysters must be experiencing, and Chuck's indifference to it. Maybe the whole situation, Mom dating Chuck, forgetting Dad—maybe that's all her. Maybe Chuck is an innocent victim. But now that I'm watching him, the Oyster Killer, relishing the taste of each little death in his mouth, it's killing more than just the oysters.

The oysters' shells are still drenched in seawater and the smell emanating from them is metallic. The cocktail sauce makes the oysters look as if they are swimming in pools of their own blood.

Of course, I can't really hear the oysters screaming in agony. Oysters don't have mouths, or even central nervous systems, as far as I know. But watching Chuck and Eric eat the oysters is filling me with anxiety. I can hear their jaws working against grit and slime amid the intermittent screams of the oysters.

And, oh God, another thought occurs to me, that for people who come back for life after death, being an oyster is probably a lot worse than coming back as a squirrel. Maybe coming back as an oyster is the reincarnation equivalent of hell. Or not. Life for an oyster is probably pretty simple, like being a monk. Maybe there is some joy and peace in that simplicity.

But I doubt it. Especially if the end result is to be eaten alive by a guy like Eric.

I don't know why I can't ever stop thinking things like this. Why my mind has to go tripping down rabbit holes that are uncomfortably tight, dank, and dirty.

I'm still sitting on my hands, doing an okay job of pretending like everything is cool with me, when Chuck makes a noise from the strain of trying to dislodge an oyster from its comfortable home. The guttural sound coming from his throat dislodges my cool, right as his knife dislodges the oyster.

I stand quickly, tipping my chair over as I do, and take a step back from the table. My legs become tangled in the legs of the overturned chair and I fall to one side, wrenching my calf painfully against the steel chair frame.

A waiter rushes over to help me but I'm already on my feet. Chuck, Mom, and Eric are all staring at me. Mom and Chuck both stand to help me, but not Eric, who isn't even trying to hide his amusement.

"Dane, what's the matter?" Mom asks, her voice screechy, adding even more drama to the situation.

"The oysters are still alive," I say, trying to explain myself while at the same time realizing that I can't. There's a painful throb in my shin from my conflict with the chair and I want to touch my leg, to look at my injury, but people in the dining room are staring and I'm afraid that by drawing attention to my injury I'll shine a spotlight on my humiliation.

Mom and Chuck exchange a knowing look.

"It's okay," Chuck says to the waiter who has just finished righting my chair. "Thanks. Everything's okay."

"It's not okay," I say. I can feel the sweat of Chuck's palm through the fabric of my sleeve and I shake his hand away in disgust.

"Dane, you're making a scene," Mom says, and she's right. I am making a scene. The Ingram family is staring at us. Just a few minutes ago we were discussing Dave Ingram's colon, and now the Ingrams are discussing my frontal lobe and poor impulse control.

Chuck holds my chair for me and signals for the waiter to come and take the oysters away. The salty smell that reminds me of blood still lingers even after the oysters are gone.

"Wow," Eric says as Chuck takes his seat again. "Was that crazy, or is it just me?"

"Just don't worry about it," Chuck says. He glances at me and gives me a tight-lipped smile. Part of me wants to thank him, but I can't bring myself to do it. It's like I've been sworn to a code—a Chuck-and-Mom-hating code—and my pride won't let me back down.

Somehow I make it through the rest of dinner. Mom and Chuck are doing their best to keep the conversation going. We've exhausted any discussion of Dave Ingram's colon, and school and end-of-year activities are not safe topics, so they seem at a loss to find something to talk about. When Mom does speak to me, her voice is a soft coo, like she's speaking to an injured dog.

As Chuck is signing for the check I'm already halfway to the door. For once Mom doesn't try to stop me or to talk to me about anything. I make it all the way to the car before the tears come. Once I'm inside the Mercedes, the display of my phone is a blur as I type out a message to Dad.

This sucks this sucks this sucks. I don't know how to stop feeling this way. When is it going to stop?

Radio silence.

I throw my phone so hard against the dash that it ricochets off the windshield and ends up in the passenger seat. Another cracked screen. Mom has only recently stopped bitching about the last one.

Just then I see Mom and Chuck walking toward me and I hurry to start the car and back out before they have a chance to wave me down or try to stop me.

The ride home is dangerous because I can't really see through the tears. I think that maybe I'll run off the road or end up in an accident because I can't see. When the cops come they'll think I'm drunk but I'll say, *No, officer, I'm just under the influence of sadness.* That thought makes me laugh and now I am crazier than ever while my face is puffy and sopping wet, and I'm laughing through my snot.

On Sunday I leave the sanctuary of my room by climbing through the window onto the low-pitched roof over the front porch. It's only about a ten-foot drop to the soft pine mulch of the flower bed below. I've snuck out of the house this way so many times that there is a smooth place at the edge of the roof where the shingles have broken under the weight of my hands.

I hurry to fire up the Mercedes and pull away from the house quickly. After I leave the pristine streets of McLean, I ride on waves of potholes through north Arlington, to the neighborhood where the Extreme Sports Asians live. The neighborhood is not a bad one, but the houses are all of modest size, and close together, with midsize Japanese- and Korean-made sedans in every driveway—most of them gray. As if the very existence of everyone in the neighborhood is gray so they drive cars of the same color.

I pull up in front of Joe's, a two-story brick house where he lives with his mother and father, two brothers, his grandmother, and his great-aunt. His great-aunt makes me uncomfortable. Her smile is more crazy than happy and she always makes me feel as if she knows things about me that even I don't want to know. Her mind is still in the Philippines, where she lost it, before the family came to America. She lived through a war, Joe told me once, but it isn't a war in our memories or in our textbooks. Joe was born here, in Arlington, and his family has been here since his mom was young, but you wouldn't know it by going inside their house or eating dinner with them. The house always smells like the exotic spices his grandmother uses for cooking.

Joe is riding his skateboard slowly down the front walk,

then flipping the deck between his feet so that it spins once and lands on the wheels again. He hops in the car with his deck resting between his knees, and we drive to the trailhead at the end of a dead-end residential street to wait for Mark and Harry.

The Wall is a legendary skate site, hidden deep within a wooded area that borders Great Falls Park. We call it "the Wall" because the guy who originally introduced the Extreme Sports Asians to the site called it that. Maybe the name had started as a reference to the Pink Floyd album. Nobody still using the name has any memory of where it came from, but it's been handed down over the years.

The Wall is an old bent that once supported a bridge span, with a brick arch that now supports nothing but the sky. The bridge was demolished long ago to make way for a massive overpass, but the old bridge support remains and is a perfect bank for executing tricks.

The guy who introduced my friends to the Wall when they were in ninth grade has since graduated from high school and disappeared into adult life. And now the Wall is like a lost city, or a pharaoh's tomb, shrouded in legend.

The site was first discovered and modified by skaters in the early eighties, their names and graduation years etched into the crumbling bricks, their spirits haunting the cool quiet under the arch. Over the years, new generations of skaters have dragged metal plates, concrete blocks, and hundreds of other pieces stolen from construction sites or salvaged from dumpsters. Most of the wooded area that is outside the protection of the actual park is a dumping ground for beer cans, rubber tires, and any other trash you can imagine, but the area around the Wall is pristine, like a skater conservation area.

It's crazy to imagine that the original skaters, those guys who first discovered the site and struggled under the weight of those abandoned construction materials, are now old enough to be our parents. But we don't think about them that way. They are preserved in our minds like the Lost Boys, living out eternity as skate rats with uneven haircuts, listening to *Louder Than Bombs* and *40 Oz. To Freedom*, and putting new layers of stickers on their decks.

I park the Mercedes on the dead-end street and roll down the windows before I cut the engine. There is a six-pack of beer in the trunk, which I grab and put on the console between us as we sit in the car waiting for Harry and Mark.

The beer is warmer than I expect it to be—hot, in fact, from being in the trunk of the car. Joe doesn't take one of the cans for himself, so I offer him a drink from mine. He sips only enough to wet his throat and makes a disgusted face as he passes the can back to me.

"You get cancer from drinking out of these," he says. "The lining of the can. It's some kind of plastic that gives you cancer. You're just going to get cancer sooner by leaving it in the trunk to get hot like that."

"Where did you hear that?" I ask idly, wishing for a cigarette but knowing I can't ask Joe for one. He's down to the last few packs of his carton. He enjoys each of the cigarettes so much so that you would think he is quitting heroin. I can't ask him for a cigarette. But I want to.

"I don't know," he says. "I guess I read it somewhere."

"Well, how do you know it's true?" I ask.

"I just know. I told you, I read it somewhere."

"Everything gives you cancer, if you use enough of it," I say, dismissing the threat. Cancer at some unknown future date doesn't sound so terrible when you are ambivalent about living. Cancer takes choice off the table. Besides, people our age just accept cancer as an anxiety-inducing inevitability, like climate change or a dying ocean. "Ophelia told me her grandma smoked for, like, forty years."

"She die from lung cancer?" Joe asks, and his question makes me smile.

"Nah. She got hit by a bus."

"Shit," Joe says, not catching the joke. It is funny, that. Ophelia is really fucking funny. She gives you the story and, you think, the punch line. But then there it is. The bus. Waiting in the wings. I miss Ophelia right then and wonder where she is and what she's doing.

We're both silent for a few minutes, which is one of the nice things about having Joe as a friend. He doesn't fill every silence with words.

"Hey, Joe," I say as a thought occurs to me. "You've been only smoking . . . what? Like three, four cigarettes a day, huh?"

"Yeah. 'Bout that."

"So, you know, three, four cigarettes a day, that isn't so

bad. I mean, you could smoke that many cigarettes a day for the rest of your life and never get sick from it. Right? You'd be more likely to get cancer from drinking beer out of a can." I hold up the can from which I am drinking in a mock toast to our inevitable deaths from cancer.

"You know what that sounds like?" he asks. "That sounds like something an addict would say. An addict can make any justification, as long as he gets to keep doing the drug he wants to do."

"I'm just saying, if you can get by just smoking a few cigarettes a day, why not just keep doing that? You like smoking. So why do you want to give it up so bad?"

"That ain't the point, bro," Joe says as he feels around in his pocket for one of his rationed cigarettes. Just talking about smoking is making him want to smoke. "I want to give it up because I don't want to be a slave to cigarettes. If I don't have to have them, that would be one thing. Like having a beer. I have one because I want one, not because I have to have one. Smoking is an addiction. It has power over me."

"I don't see it like that," I say. "When I have a beer or a bong hit or something, it makes me feel better. It makes me calm or makes me not give a shit about everything happening in my life. Sometimes I need that."

"Which makes you a slave to it," Joe says with an emphatic nod. "Right? You feel better with it, can't get by without it. Same thing, ma'fuck."

"I suppose," I say. I feel like there is more I can say to prove my argument, but I lose interest in the subject as I settle back into the driver's seat, my head resting where my shoulders should be. "Hey, Joe, do you believe in ghosts?"

"Of course, dude. I'm Asian."

"Yeah? Is that a thing? All Asians believe in ghosts?"

He thinks about it for a few seconds, squinting through the cigarette smoke that coils around his head. "Yeah, probably. My grandmother sees ghosts all the time. Usually she sees my grandfather."

"He died and then came back to haunt her?"

"It's not like that. You know, it's like if a bird sits on the windowsill all day, hanging around the house, she'll say it's my granddad coming to check on us. Or she'll misplace something and then later she'll find it and say my granddad helped her find it. Like, subconsciously she knew where to look because he was telling her where it was."

"You think she's crazy?" I ask.

He takes a minute to think about my question. He goes through the smoker's ritual of tapping his cigarette on the top edge of the window, blowing on the ember to clear it of gray ash. If Joe doesn't think his grandmother is crazy for calling a bird on her windowsill his dead grandfather, then maybe me thinking my dad has been reincarnated as a coyote isn't so nuts. Maybe if my family were Asian I would just be considered normal.

"No," Joe says finally. "I don't think she's crazy. I think

she misses him. When I was a kid I thought it was weird. But now, I just think she's lonely."

"I get that," I say.

When Harry and Mark arrive on their boards we enter the trail together as a pack. Now, we are the Lost Boys, in a place where time has no meaning. A place where you will never grow up, and never grow old.

It is a short hike to the Wall. Harry scats the opening lines of the Pink Floyd song as we wind our way along the trail. I never liked that song much. It makes me think of the older guys we run into down at the park sometimes, the ones who did too many drugs in high school and now live in limbo between the teenager and adult worlds.

The Wall isn't just a place where teenagers go to party. It's a place where you can escape a shitty parent, or forget that you suck at school, or pretend like you are already grown and there's no one to tell you what to do.

Though we are surrounded by deep woods, there is always the reminder that people, and too many of them, are close by—the sound of planes overhead, and the distant hum of traffic on the clogged arteries that circle the city.

The trees and undergrowth are not the pristine specimens found in the Shenandoah National Forest, only an hour's drive west, a place where my friends and I go for hiking and camping trips or for snowboarding in the winter. The trees in this park are weary, and they struggle against the indignities inflicted upon them by humans. Their roots rise up against the immovable foundation of the old bridge and twist like coiled snakes above the eroded surface.

The stream that flows just below the bent is about thirty feet wide and shallow. The water appears still; the only evidence of movement are the bits of trash that bob along the surface until they come to rest against piles of brush or rocks. The stream swells after a rain and leaves trash stranded as a marker of high water.

"Hey, Joe," Harry calls out as Joe and I climb to the top of the bent above the makeshift half-pipe. "You need a boost to get up there?" Harry stands below, grinning up at us, like he has been dying to use that line for a while.

"Man, shut up," Joe says. Joe has a pretty low threshold for tolerance of other people. The fact that he still hangs with Harry is a testament to how far back they go.

I ignore my friends and their taunts of each other and scrabble my way up the steep incline to reach the top of the bank.

When you practice tricks on a skateboard, you have to accept that there will be lots of failure. The majority of those failures aren't even close to fatal. And even though I am an experienced skater, meaning I have my share of scars and mended bones, I never expect to get hurt. I suppose you could say that if a person gets on a skateboard and performs tricks that are potentially fatal, then that makes them reckless, or stupid. But the thing is—life itself is guaranteed to be fatal.

That's the way skaters think. Real skaters, anyway. If you

aren't living, really living, by taking risks, then you might as well be dead already. When I'm skating with my friends, it's the only time when I feel like taking a risk is worth something.

Get busy living, or get busy dying. That's a line from a movie, though which one I can't remember. And those words have stuck with me. Most people walking around are just living to die. But skaters . . . we're dying to live. Each day of the predictable mediocrity of school or work is another life sentence. If that's all there is . . . well, then that's not enough.

Joe and I take turns skating the length of the concrete cap of the bent and hopping the double-sided ramp perched in the middle. We practice the move over and over again. Each time my feet leave the board and I fly into the air, the edge of the bent rises up to fill my entire world. In reality there are probably only about two or three feet between my feet and the top of the structure during the hops, but it feels like a mile of air separates me from a solid surface.

The prospect of falling makes my scalp tingle and my finger pads sweat. In normal people that would be called fear. The biological indications of fear still work, even if I don't feel afraid.

The human brain is wired to feel instinctive fear of heights, snakes, deep water—fear that comes in super handy at times. Even people who are too depressed to live feel instinctive fear.

From our vantage point on top of the bent we can see

through the trees to the winding path we walked from our cars. The trees have not finished forming their dense summer canopy, which makes it easy to see the scar of red clay earth.

"Who the hell is that?" We all notice the movement of people on the path at the same time, but it's Harry who speaks first.

"Probably a bunch of amateurs," Joe says, dismissing them.

"Crap," I say when I recognize one of the interlopers. "That's Eric."

"Did you tell him you were coming here?" Joe wants to know.

"Why would I do that?" I ask, directing my impatience for Eric at Joe.

Eric and his friends arrive like a grenade detonating. "What up, losers?" Eric calls out to us, though we have done our best to pretend as if we didn't notice their arrival until then.

Joe's irritated sigh is audible, but his expression doesn't even flicker.

Eric and his friends have a cooler full of beers and they settle down near the edge of the water.

"Dude," Eric says with a grin in my direction, "what was up with your little freak-out at dinner?" He turns to his friends to get them in on the joke on my behalf. "We went to the club and had raw oysters and this dude starts freaking out. Yo, he was like, 'The oysters! They're still alive!'" Eric's voice rises to a falsetto as he mimics me.

"Shut up," I say, resorting to a childish comeback.

"The oysters!" Eric cries again, as he knows now that he's hit me in the soft underbelly and goes in for the kill. "You are truly nuts, Dane. Were you scared of them? Or you felt sorry for them?"

"I feel sorry for anything that goes near your mouth, you prick." That's a little better than my first comeback, but not by much.

Eric's friends are looking at me with guarded interest, while my friends pointedly ignore Eric and avoid looking at me.

"What happened to your hair?" Joe asks Eric, and I'm grateful to have him on my side.

"I got the tips frosted," Eric says, forgetting to finish me off as he brushes his hand over his head. "The whole soccer team got theirs done."

"Yeah? Did you go to the same salon where your mom goes?" Joe asks.

"Man, shut up."

Eric and his friends have ruined my day of skating, the way he ruins everything that is good in life. There is no way to ignore them as they fill the available air with their stupid jokes. They speak almost constantly, using volume to dominate the space with their toxic masculinity. I can tell they are high because they keep laughing at the dumbest things. They have to laugh at their own jokes because nothing they say is funny enough to make the rest of us laugh.

Joe and I keep taking turns hopping over the ramp; with

each jump we get higher and land closer to the edge of the bent. It is a test to see how high we can jump while still leaving enough room to land and stop our boards before we hit the edge.

Eric watches us for a few minutes, but not being the center of attention bores him. I can feel his need for the spotlight to be on him as he says, "There's a party tonight at that girl Shana's house."

"I heard it was at your mom's house," Joe said.

"Very funny, Flip," Eric says. I broil at Eric's use of the racial slur but Joe doesn't even flinch. I have heard Joe use the word "Flip" to describe himself before, and I have heard Mark and Harry call him a Flip when they are teasing him, but I figure it is like the N-word and only other Asians are allowed to say it. In fact, my friends have a lot of culturally derogatory shit they say about each other, but in a way I will never understand, and I can't participate.

Eric's friends are dropping comments about the girl Shana, about how she will sleep with anyone. Winking and nudging each other about her low standards. I feel bad for Shana, and a little guilty that I'm glad they have turned their attention to picking on her instead of me.

"You guys probably don't go to parties where they have actual girls, anyway," Eric says.

"Nope," Joe says. "Just your mom."

"Stop talking shit about my mom," Eric says as he takes a few menacing steps forward.

"Stop calling me a Flip," Joe says. Joe never raises his

voice, never even changes his expression, but Eric backs down and doesn't use the word "Flip" again.

The corner of Joe's mouth lifts in an almost imperceptible smile. Eric tried to take him on for a few rounds, but Joe got the KO on decision.

After his exchange with Joe, Eric directs his comments to his buddies but they are still talking about girls. Guys our age spend a lot of time thinking about girls. Maybe not real girls, like the girls we know at school, but the girls who are just objects on a screen or a page.

I am not really listening, trying to force their voices into the background and pretend like they aren't there. But then Eric and his friends are talking about Ophelia and I am straining to overhear.

"Hey, Dane," Eric calls out to me. "What's the story with Ophelia? You hitting that?"

"I don't know what you mean," I say, trying to keep my voice level, indifferent.

"Of course you don't," Eric says, and turns to his friends, seeking their approval. They all laugh obediently, and I can feel heat climbing my face.

"I never really noticed before, but she's pretty hot," Eric says, and I'm not sure if he's doing it on purpose to get under my skin. But he is. Under my skin.

"She's not your type," I say. "She doesn't have an idiot IQ."

"Yeah, well, she doesn't need to be a great conversationalist," Eric says. Cue laughter at his stupid joke from his friends. "Do you have her number?"

"I don't really talk to her much. I just see her around sometimes."

"No worries," Eric says. "I can get it."

I'm agitated now, thinking about Eric making the moves on Ophelia. Nobody seems to notice. It always amazes me that the shitstorm inside my mind is never visible to anyone on the outside.

The last jump I make over the ramp that day is the jump I make to put Eric in his place. It is my best. I catch air and hang there for so long that I have time to see the sun glinting off the stream as it slithers over the rocks; have time to notice the angle of the sun as it cuts through the immature leaves that have sprouted on the bigger trees; and have time to clearly read Joe's lips from the other end of the bent as he says, "Oh, shit."

Part of my body lands on the safety of the concrete, but most of my weight is beyond the edge. I land on my shoulder against the concrete and feel it scrape my arm before I tumble over the side. My muscles strain, as if they might be able to perform some miraculous feat of strength and save me from falling. But my arms find only air, and I land facedown on the packed earth below. My skateboard clatters beside me, and the *clunk* as it hits the ground next to me is like a mallet ringing a gong. And the gong is my head.

The impact of my chest against the ground knocks the wind from me and I spend an agonizing minute making that horrible whooping sound as I try to suck air into my starved lungs. The minute is probably more agonizing for Mark and

Harry as they stand over me, helpless to do anything until I can fill my lungs.

I sense Joe scrambling down after me, but then my consciousness slams shut like a closet door and I, trapped on the inside, become a prisoner of blackness.

The next thing I am truly aware of after my fall is that I am in the back seat of the Mercedes, my head in Joe's lap. Mark is driving and I feel gratitude that at least they have sense enough not to let Harry drive.

"Shit," I say as I screw my eyes shut against the pain in my head. I let go with a string of curses after that as I first put my hands to my face to rub away the ache in my head and then think better of it when the skin I touch is raw and sensitive. It feels as if a massive hand slapped me from my forehead to my knees, and I think how strange it is that while most of my body hurts, my lower legs feel perfectly fine. I want to scrunch my entire being into my lower legs, the only part of me where there is no hurt. Joe shushes me and holds my shoulder as I squirm, as if I can really retract myself into my calves and ankles.

"Holy shit, man," Harry says. "That was fucking epic."

"Shut up, Harry," Mark and Joe say in unison. But for once, I don't mind Harry's commentary. It distracts me from the pain, which I am now able to sort into categories as a way of keeping my mind occupied.

The worst pain is the pain in my head, an ache that comes

in waves, each more excruciating than the last. Wherever we are going, I hope it is toward some kind of pain medication.

"Anything broken?" Joe asks.

"My head," I say through clenched teeth. "My head is broken."

"We're here," Mark says. "What do I do? Park?"

"Just pull up to the entrance and drop us off," Joe says.

"It says that way is just for ambulances," Mark argues.

"We are an ambulance," Joe says.

"You're taking me to a hospital?" I ask in alarm.

"Dude," Joe says, "you need it."

The efficiency with which Mark, Harry, and Joe get me into the emergency room makes me realize that in the event of doomsday, they probably aren't the best teammates.

I sit slumped in a chair, holding my head in my hands, with Mark and Harry sitting uselessly on either side of me, while Joe goes to the reception desk to talk to someone.

The waiting room is much noisier than I would have expected. There is a television hanging from a stand in the corner, and a dozen or more people are waiting. None of them look sick. Maybe I don't look sick, either.

I study my body as if I'm not inside of it. My left sleeve is torn and has a streak of blood on it. My chest burns when my shirt rubs against it and I am afraid to lift my shirt to look at it, mostly because anytime I move, the pain in my head comes rushing back full force.

The pain in my head is bad, but now there is something

so much worse. Smells of the hospital start to fill my head, and soon after, the images come. When my eyes are shut, a slideshow plays on the back of my eyelids. Dad, in life, his body shaking with laughter. His laugh was always over the top, his whole body in on the joke. I loved his laugh. In one recurring dream his hands reach out to me, so big they fill my entire world, as he helps me down from the monkey bars at the playground by our old house. There are gaps in the slideshow, the years that Dad was working so much we hardly ever saw him. He was always gone before I got up in the morning and often got home only in time to say good night when I was on my way to bed. The last images in the slideshow are of Dad after I returned home from boarding school. Dad is thin and frail and his skin is yellowed and dull. By the end it is hard to believe he is the same person who raised me. He is so changed physically, it's impossible to believe he is the same person inside.

Joe returns with a woman wearing hospital scrubs. She has an iPad resting on her hip and a stethoscope around her neck. "Are you Dane?" she asks me. It is a very innocent question and probably she is nice, but all of a sudden my heart is racing and I can't catch my breath and there is a weight, like a lead blanket, on my chest and arms. My mind goes into a spiral of fear and panic and I have this terrible feeling that something bad is about to happen and I am powerless to stop it and it is going to happen. Right. Now.

"No," I say.

"He hit his head," Joe offers as explanation. "But he's definitely Dane."

The woman's forehead wrinkles in confusion and she asks, "Do you not know who you are?"

"I'm Dane," I say.

"Uh-huh," she says. "Dane, do you know what today's date is?"

"It's Sunday."

"Okay. How about the date? Do you know what year it is?"

"Seventeen," I say, hoping that this is the right answer and that now everyone will see I am perfectly fine.

"He's seventeen years old," Joe says, his voice hushed as he looks into the face of the woman to judge her reaction.

It feels like being drunk, like everyone is in on a secret but me. And then the most alarming thing of all happens. I start to cry. They all stop to watch me. Even Harry, by some miracle, is quiet as they all watch me sob. Tears run down my face and puddle at the corners of my mouth. I lick the puddles and the water is just the right amount of salty—like snot—and tastes good.

"I want my dad," I say, my voice a strangled sob.

At the same time Joe and Mark both put a hand on my back.

"His dad's dead," Mark says, and there is a question in his voice, and the question is whether everyone else is in agreement that the current situation is crazy.

Though Joe isn't a big guy, he never takes any shit from anybody. His tone of voice is changed as he speaks to the woman now. "You gonna stand out here asking him questions he can't answer all night? Or take him back to see a doctor?"

"We'll need to call his mother to get his insurance information," the nurse says, unmoved by the ice between Joe and her.

"I'll take care of it," Joe says.

Mark calls his dad to let him know where he is and Joe calls my mom. They both show up at the hospital. Mr. Edgar takes the Extreme Sports Asians home and Mom stays with me. She sits by me in the emergency room while we wait for the doctors to tell us something.

I haven't said much since my failure to identify the date, afraid that anything I say will be evidence of permanent brain damage. *If I can just get some sleep,* I keep thinking, *I'll be fine.* But they are intent on keeping me awake. Every time my eyes slide shut, someone starts saying my name in that insistent way, like the sound of your mom's voice in the morning when she's waking you for school. So annoying, and no way to sleep through it.

When I finally do say something, it comes across as weird. I have been quiet for so long, my mind tripping through a half-awake, half-dead place.

"It smells like Dad dying," I say, which, to be fair,

doesn't make a lot of sense to anyone who can't read my thoughts.

"You're not going to die," Mom says quietly as she squeezes my hand.

"No. The hospital. The smell reminds me of Dad being sick." There. That made more sense.

She's quiet for a few minutes then says, "I hated it, you know? The fact that the house had those hospital smells in it while he was dying. After he died I kept lighting scented candles, trying to get rid of the smell. But it was like cigarette smoke. No way to get rid of it unless we gutted the place."

"Maybe we should have been smoking in the house," I say, and I'm trying so hard to speak clearly but I think it might still be a mumble. "Cover the smell of death with the smell of dying."

She laughs so I think she understands me, then fluffs my bangs away from my forehead with her fingers. "You're so much like him," she says. "Maybe that's why you make me crazy."

"Mmph." I am drifting off to sleep again but trying to play like I am still in the conversation.

"I could use a cigarette right now," Mom says with a sigh. "Why weren't you wearing a helmet? You go out skating God knows where and don't even wear a helmet? Not smart, Dane."

"Nope," I say. "Not wearing a helmet. I'm not eight."

"That's something an eight-year-old would say."

It occurs to me that my mom is incapable of just saying she's worried and upset. Her response to crisis is irritation and sarcasm. The same reaction she had to Dad dying. It's something to think about, but my head hurts too much and my thoughts slip through my grasp and disappear into the void.

After what seems like an eternity, the doctor comes in to tell us what we already know, that nothing is broken but that I have bruising, including a bruised brain. I am to rest but Mom is supposed to wake me frequently, and if I start to vomit or seem disoriented I am to be brought back immediately. Disorientation is a pretty normal state for me so I'm not sure how Mom will know if I need medical help before it's too late.

On the ride home I keep my eyes shut against the brightness of the sun and the next thing I know Mom is shaking me awake in the driveway. She offers me something to eat but Mom's idea of food usually involves something revolting and healthy like quinoa, so I just shake my head and trudge up to my room. Normally I would be starved after no lunch or dinner, but there is bile at the back of my throat and my stomach is too knotted to feel hunger.

I am dimly aware when Mom comes to check on me, when she brings me ginger ale or tells me I should really take a shower and change out of my dirty clothes.

When I wake again I am unsure if it is the same day or

I've slept through to the next. I'm so hungry I figure I must have slept through the night.

There are voices coming from the kitchen as I walk downstairs and I'm surprised to find Mom and Chuck sitting together at the kitchen island. They stop talking as soon as I enter the room and they both look guilty, so I figure they've been talking about me.

"Morning, son," Chuck says.

I hate it when he calls me that. I'm not his son.

"Why are you here?" I ask.

"Dane!" Mom says, shocked at my rudeness.

"What?" I ask. "I mean, it's a workday, right? Wait, what day is it?"

"It's okay, Trudi," Chuck says, and puts a hand on her arm. To me he says, "This is why we decided to sell the firm, Dane. Your mom and I wanted more days that we could just take off and forget about work."

"You guys are pretty good at forgetting things," I say, which is a lame response, but I can see from their reaction that it's had the desired effect.

"I was just getting ready to wake you. I made an appointment for us to see Dr. Lineberger today since you're home from school anyway," Mom says, going for casual and failing miserably. I know what she's thinking about. The scene I made at the club with the oysters, the things I said at the hospital.

"Why don't you guys go see her together?" I ask. "Maybe she can help you deal with your guilt."

"That's enough, Dane," Mom says. She shakes her head in disgust and says to Chuck, "You see? I'm trying. I'm the only one."

Mom storms out of the room and all we hear is her bedroom door slamming. Chuck looks really uncomfortable. More uncomfortable than I feel when I'm in his company, which is a lot.

"You know, Dane," Chuck says as he removes his reading glasses, "your mom loves you very much. She was terrified when your friend called from the hospital."

My anger with Mom and Chuck is instinct now, so ingrained that I barely have any control over it.

"I don't need you to tell me how my mom feels about anything."

He twirls the reading glasses between his chubby fingers as he bites the inside of his lip in thought. "Well, I just wish you could take it easy on her. All she wants is for you to be happy."

"Does she?" I ask.

"Yes. You make it difficult for her, and for yourself, by moping around the house and always giving her a hard time."

"Well, I'm sorry if my feelings are inconvenient for everyone."

"I understand you're upset about your dad," Chuck says. "We were all sad to lose Craig. We miss him. But life keeps going, you know?"

"Not for Dad."

"Well . . . right," Chuck says, "but I mean for those of us who are still alive. We're all still alive and we have to keep going. Your dad would want you to be happy."

God, he is so annoying.

"If Mom wants me to be happy," I say, "then she shouldn't be sleeping with my dead father's best friend, pretending like Dad never existed, letting you move in here and throw your weight around as if this is your house."

My open challenge doesn't cause even a ripple.

"Your mom is human, Dane." If this is his defense against his complete disregard for the bro code, it makes me want to vomit. Vomit on his starched white golf clothes and the polished granite countertops.

"Please stop talking," I say. "I'll be out of your life soon enough."

Chuck's eyes drop to the countertop, right where I had just imagined the splash of my stomach contents, and sighs dejectedly.

I go outside to escape Chuck and the screaming in my ears and take out my phone to text Dad. He's the only one who ever understood where I was coming from.

I don't know what to say to people to make them understand how I feel—what I feel.

I keep my phone in my hand, waiting, needing the lifeline of a text from Dad. I'm not disappointed.

I'm sure that's a lonely way to be, he says.

He's right. That is the feeling. Loneliness. More than sad. Sad and misunderstood at the same time.

I say stupid things all the time because I just want everyone to know what it feels like to feel horrible. How it feels when people don't listen. Don't understand.

I understand.

"So, Dane," Dr. Lineberger says, "I've spoken to both you and your mom about what you went through individually, about your father and what he went through, but I'd like for us to discuss it together."

She pauses, waiting for me to respond. The silence roars in my ears as they both wait, Mom watching me, and Dr. Lineberger politely looking at her notes instead of staring at me.

"Okay," I say finally.

"Why don't you tell me your perspective on things. I mean, tell me from your point of view."

I know what "perspective" means.

"I came home from school at the end of my junior year, expecting to find things normal, I guess. But my dad was . . . pretty sick by then. It was obvious as soon as I saw him. He was skinny, for one thing, and he was wearing a hat in June, to cover the fact that he had lost most of his hair."

"And you hadn't seen your dad since . . . when?" Dr. Lineberger asks, though her pen never stops scratching in her notebook.

"Uh . . . January, I guess. Right before I went back to

school. My mom got me into some exchange-student thing. I went to France for spring break and stayed with a family there. She wants me to learn how to speak French."

"It's an international language," Mom says, cutting in.

"So is English," I say with a side-eye at Mom. "Besides, I took four semesters of French at Brandywine and, to be honest, you're not really getting your money's worth."

"Okay," Dr. Lineberger says. "Let's stay focused on when you arrived home at the end of the school year."

"I still can't speak French," I say, wanting it to go on the record in her notebook.

But Dr. Lineberger just smiles and doesn't make any notes about it.

"Uh, so . . ." I pause as I try to think back and remember last summer. "I guess Dad had given up. You know, when people talk about cancer they talk about people going into battle against it. But it's more like a siege. The cancer attacks and has better weapons and more soldiers. That's not really a battle."

Mom practically dives for the box of tissues that sits on the coffee table. "We tried everything," Mom says into her tissue. "Radiation and chemo and medical marijuana and special green tea I ordered online from Japan. We really tried." Mom takes a deep breath and dabs carefully under her eyes to keep her mascara from running.

"It's okay, Trudi," Dr. Lineberger says. "We talked about this and it's okay for you to cry. Dane probably needs to see it."

My own eyes fill with tears and there is a hard lump in my throat as I tell the rest of the story. I didn't remember a whole lot about Dad or the things he said or the time we spent together that summer. The process of dying was like a full-time job for all of us.

While Dad lay dying, my parents' bedroom became a public space, with a rotation of hospice nurses who came to give Dad his medications and try to keep him comfortable. Mom and I were still living, but we did everything on autopilot. We became cold, our bodily functions slowing down, as if we were dying, too. The hospice nurses brought their own warmth with them and did not bleed it into our spaces. Everything in our house was cold.

The nurses had witnessed the death of so many people they were able to predict, almost down to the minute, when Dad would die. In the days leading up to his death, they would say things like, "It won't be long now." And then, finally, on Dad's last night, after listening to his breathing, the oldest of the nurses said, "I think he'll be gone late tonight or in the early morning." Then she left us, with the pall of her omen and the smell of her lavender-scented lotion hanging in the room.

And she had been right. Dad died the next morning.

We watched him most of the night, waiting for each breath to be his last. There was nothing violent about Dad's death. Just a shuddering breath, and then nothing. Here one minute, gone the next. And there was nothing profound about the last moments of his life. His final intelligible words were, "It smells in here. Let the dog out."

He was right. The room where he died did smell something awful. But, he was wrong about the dog. We didn't have one. I had always wanted a dog, but Mom thinks dogs are dirty and a nuisance, which is pretty much Mom's attitude toward having a kid, too.

Dad died lying on his side, curled up like a child. The nurse waited only a few minutes out of respect for Mom and me, then confirmed he was actually gone. She turned him onto his back, stretching his legs to their full length, and crossed his hands over his chest under the sheet. His legs were impossibly thin. The cancer had eaten everything between his skin and bones but for the corded muscle and ligaments. He lay on his back, peaceful and serene, and, as far as we know, he's been in that position ever since.

When I finish speaking everyone is quiet for a few minutes. Mom sniffles and dabs with her tissues and I sit in the armchair, like a witness on the stand.

"Now, Trudi," Dr. Lineberger says after she has given us a chance to get our shit together. "Talk to us about your decision to keep Craig's illness a secret from Dane."

"It wasn't my decision," Mom says quickly. "Craig wanted to keep it a secret. He thought, if he got better, then we would have worried Dane for no reason. And, if he didn't . . . well, I guess he just didn't want Dane to worry. He thought it would be too much with . . . everything else Dane had been through."

"How does that make you feel, Dane?" Dr. Lineberger says, a line straight out of every movie with a psychiatrist.

"How does it make me feel?" I ask, but rhetorically. "It makes me feel like shit."

"In what way?" Dr. Lineberger presses.

"In every way," I say, my voice rising to a whine because I'm too impotent to be a shouter.

"Uh-huh," Dr. Lineberger says as she continues to scrawl merrily along the page of her notebook. The scratching—the constant scratching—of the pen against the page grates on my nerves.

"Can you stop that?" I ask. "Please. I mean, if you have something to say about how I feel, how about you just say it, instead of writing about it in your little book there?"

Dr. Lineberger stops and carefully places her pen on the open notebook. "I'm sorry. It helps me, later, when I review notes of our sessions, so I can think about our conversations when I am not actively listening."

"Yeah, well, it makes me uncomfortable."

"Okay," Dr. Lineberger says, flashing me a sunny smile. "Go on."

"I wanted to tell you," Mom says, as if she wants special points recorded in Dr. Lineberger's book.

"You should have," I say.

"I know. But your dad insisted and, you know," she says with a shrug, "he was the one who was dying."

I hate her for that little shrug. It's as if she is shrugging off all responsibility for the way I feel.

"You know," Mom says, "your dad could be very difficult

to live with. I mean, he was funny, what most people would call charming. And he was so direct. He liked to shock people by being so direct." She stops and smiles at some memory that Dr. Lineberger and I can't see. "But he was a difficult man to live with. . . . I don't know." Mom looks out the window, working up the courage to say more. "I sometimes think that if he hadn't died, maybe we wouldn't have stayed married. Maybe we'd be sitting here talking about our divorce instead."

I lean forward and put my head in my hands. "Just stop."

"Why?" Mom asks. I can sense her turning her gaze back to me, away from the window.

"It's none of my business. The way things were between you and Dad."

"But it's your business if I date Chuck? It's your business if I don't seem sad enough about Dad being gone?"

"Stop," I say.

"Yes," Dr. Lineberger says. "I think we've covered enough ground for today."

And, just like that, the timer on our feelings runs out. It's time to stop feeling again for this week.

When we arrive home Mom is halfway across the porch before she realizes I am not right behind her. I am hanging back, near the car. I'm mad at her for the things she said at our appointment with Dr. Lineberger, but I don't know what to say. It feels like being trapped in the closed loop of eternity. Every way I turn I end up at the same dead end. Anger and disappointment. I'm tired of being trapped in it, a rat in a maze.

"What's wrong?" Mom asks.

"Nothing. I just don't feel like going inside right now." The house is her turf. I want the option to leave.

"You're not going anywhere, Dane. You have a concussion."

"I know," I say, irritated by my own impotence. "I'm not going anywhere. I just want a few minutes outside. By myself," I add firmly.

"Fine," she says, and turns to go inside without me.

The street is quiet. All normal people are at school or work.

I walk to the end of the driveway and down the street, just far enough to be out of Mom's sight from the house, when I see the golden heap in the shallow ditch beside the road. At a glance, the mottled pile looks like dried leaves, but once my brain adjusts to what it is seeing, I know it is the coyote.

His fur, which had been lustrous and beautiful in life, is matted and dull. The heavy morning dew of spring has clumped his hair into wet peaks.

The coyote is lying with its front paws crossed, his chin resting on its forelegs, with a streak of rusty dried blood across its haunches. Because of the thick fur I can't see where the coyote's flesh is torn, and I don't want to.

From his position I can reconstruct the final minutes of

his life. He must have been struck by a car, then dragged himself into the sanctuary of the ditch. Just seeing the coyote lying there dead, or knowing that he had faced a violent death, isn't what bothers me. It is the knowledge of his lonely, painful struggle to the side of the road, the world black and uncaring around him. He worked impossibly hard, first to get himself out of the road and out of danger, then trying to make himself comfortable, and dying in the process. Those last moments or, God forbid, hours of his life must have been torture. To be sad, lonely, or scared, to suffer cruelty and neglect, without a living soul to care about you.

Left here at the side of the road so close to the house, I know who is responsible for the coyote's death. It had to be Chuck. He always takes the curve just before the driveway too fast, as if to prove that he is some kind of expert driver just because he drives a Mercedes SL-class.

Chuck probably got back late from the club, after a few too many bourbons, and caught the coyote crossing the otherwise quiet street. Chuck wouldn't have stopped, wouldn't have gone to check if the coyote was dead or alive, wouldn't have cared enough to put the coyote out of its misery.

Though I had seen the coyote a half dozen times and heard its cries at night, I had never gotten closer than twenty yards from it. Now that the coyote is dead, I still feel nervous about getting too close, but I want to know the feel of its fur.

I crouch and scoot forward in crab fashion, watching

intently for any signs of movement. Maybe the coyote is just injured and sleeping. When I am only two feet away, I make myself still, even hold my breath, as I watch the heap of golden hair for the subtle rise and fall of respiration.

Nothing.

I reach out my hand and hold it over the coyote and hesitate, my fingers moving as if over an imaginary piano keyboard. The fur is not perfectly soft like a coat or rug. It is damp, and gritty with dirt, the shaggy outer coat knotted like rope in some places.

The flesh underneath the fur is cold and hard. Colder and harder than marble, or concrete. The coldest thing I have ever touched.

"What the hell are you doing? Checking for a pulse?"

I'm so startled by the voice that I topple back from my crouch, away from the coyote, as if he has moved suddenly.

Above me stands Colonel Marcus. He's out of uniform, wearing sweatpants and a T-shirt and spotless running shoes. Even in casual clothes his appearance is neat and tidy as always, as if he's prepared for an inspection by the Joint Chiefs. His hair is no more than a few millimeters long and his hairline is neatly shaved.

"N—no," I stammer. "I mean . . . I guess. I thought he might just be injured."

"Hmph." Colonel Marcus bends at the waist and puts his hands on his knees as he peers at the coyote. "What are you doing home?" he asks, his eyes narrowing to accusatory slits.

"Skating accident," I say, and tap my head. "I hit my head."

"Oh. Well, you seem all right."

"I have a concussion," I say, wondering, as I do, if I sound too defensive. "The doctor said I should stay home and rest."

"Well, get a shovel and a trash bag," he says, issuing a direct order. "I'll help you get it into a bag. It'll stink up the neighborhood if we don't move it."

I hurry to comply and return with a metal spade and a leaf bag from the garage. Colonel Marcus holds the bag, the top rolled down so he can hold it open wide at the mouth. As he supervises, I gently nose the spade under the side of the coyote. The body seems to cling to the wet leaves and muck beneath it, and I can't get the spade more than an inch or so beneath the body. I can feel Colonel Marcus's impatience as he watches me prod the coyote tentatively.

"You can't hurt it," he says. "It's already dead."

"I know, I just—" I break off what I am saying to catch my breath. It's exhausting to maneuver the shovel, the dead weight of the coyote much heavier than I imagined it would be. As I try to slide the shovel under more of the coyote's weight, I worry I will put the point of the spade through the skin, cause further injury or damage.

"Here," Colonel Marcus says, losing patience and holding out the bag for me to take. He takes the shovel roughly from my hands and, with brute force, slides the blade under the coyote with one thrust. The shovel head scrapes against the ground, but my brain hears the crunch of bones and the tear of flesh.

Colonel Marcus's indifference to the grim horror reminds me of a movie I have seen. The movie was two hours of unrelenting bloody battle in the streets of some foreign city. In the movie, Army Rangers collected the disembodied limbs and mangled torsos of their fellow soldiers with a sense of duty and responsibility to leave no man or, apparently, no part of a man, behind. I wonder if Colonel Marcus has been hardened to the realities of death as a soldier. I think about asking him, and then think better of it.

I hold out the bag, my arms extended to keep the horror as far from me as possible. Colonel Marcus curses as he tries to angle the stiff body of the coyote into a straight—or at least manageable—line. The coyote fur laps over the edge of the bag and the lifeless body seems to fight the confines of the plastic.

"Pull the bag around it," Colonel Marcus says, his voice tight with exertion.

We struggle for another minute before the coyote is finally covered in its burial shroud. Then he takes the bag from me and spins it to twist it closed.

"I suppose if the bag is closed it's okay to put it in the trash," he says. "Pickup is tomorrow."

"The trash?" I ask, my voice cracking with alarm. "I—I don't think we should just throw him away."

He stops, one eyebrow raised with a question. "What do

you think we should do? Have it stuffed and put it on the mantle?"

Ophelia definitely gets her sense of humor from her dad. But Ophelia's wit is like a paring knife. Her dad's, like a machete.

While I am thinking this, Colonel Marcus is standing there, holding the dead coyote in the black leaf bag, wondering why the fuck I am such a weirdo that I don't want him to throw away a piece of roadkill.

"I think I'm going to bury him," I say.

"Come again?" he says.

"The coyote," I say. "I think I'm going to bury him. I don't . . . I don't want him to just get thrown out with the trash."

"Son, are you on something?" he asks.

"No," I say with a shake of my head. "No, sir. I just—I guess I kind of think of him like a pet."

"A pet?"

"He's been living in our yard," I say. "It's hard to explain."

"Yeah," Colonel Marcus says with a nod. "I guess it is."

"Anyway, I'll . . . uh . . . I'll take him." I step in and gingerly put my hand around the twisted part of the bag. Colonel Marcus has been holding the bag with only one hand, but when he releases it I'm not prepared to take the weight. The bag falls to the ground between us and I have to use both hands to lift it. I don't want the coyote's body to touch me, even through the bag, so when I lift it, I am holding it out away from my legs, the bag swinging like a pendulum.

My shoulders ache from the strain within seconds and I am unsure how to end the conversation gracefully with the dead coyote between us.

"You got it?" he asks, and he seems to be asking me more than just whether I am able to lift the bag on my own.

"Yeah, yeah, I've got it."

"Because I'm heading out to watch Ophelia's field hockey game, but if you need help . . ."

"No, I'm fine. Really. Thanks for your help," I say. I can feel Colonel Marcus's eyes following me back up the driveway to the house as I struggle with the weight of the bag.

I place the coyote bag just inside the garage and start to wipe my sweaty palms on the legs of my pants, then think better of it. I enter the house through the garage door.

When I return to the kitchen Mom and Chuck are sitting at the counter drinking coffee. They are both looking at their phones, but Mom puts hers down when I come into the kitchen.

"What are you doing?" Mom asks me. "You should be resting."

"I have some stuff I need to do first," I say.

"Like what?" Mom asks, but not in a suspicious way, more like she is actually pleased I have something to do.

"You know that coyote that's been living in the yard?"

"No-o, no. Coyote?" Mom turns a quizzical eye toward Chuck but he is deep into his phone. Either the conversation isn't registering for him, or the phone is a prop he's using to hide his guilt. It's impossible to tell which. I have used the phone-scrolling technique to hide interest and emotion many times before and am at once frustrated and relieved to see how effectively it masks people and their innermost thoughts.

"There's a coyote," I say slowly, my gaze still on Chuck. "Or, I guess I should say, there *was* a coyote." Now Chuck does look up. He's wearing his reading glasses and when he raises his head his eyes are startlingly huge, out of all proportion with the rest of his face. The effect makes Chuck look shocked by what I am saying, but then he removes the glasses and his eyes are normal again—a watery blue and set a little too close together.

"The coyote, he's been living around here. I've seen him coming from our backyard a few times. The first time I saw him was right after Dad died." I pause and wait for them to catch up. They exchange a look, but it isn't a look that says they are mystified by the coincidence of Dad's death and the coyote's sudden appearance.

"And what about the coyote, Dane?" Mom asks, her tone cautious now, like she is wary of any discussion about Dad in front of Chuck, as if I might accuse her again of being unfaithful to Dad's memory.

"He's dead," I say, and Mom winces at the word. "The coyote. I just found him on the side of the road."

"Oh," says Mom, glancing again in Chuck's direction. "Well, that's very sad."

"I put him in the garage, but I need to bury him," I say. "It can't wait or he'll . . . ." I stop. I had started to say that the body would start to stink, but now that Dad is a corpse, too, I don't like to think about what eventually happens to living things once they are dead.

"Dane," Mom says, suddenly sure of herself now that she has been given something to make her worry, "that thing is a wild animal. You shouldn't be handling it. What if it's got fleas and you catch something? What if it has rabies?"

"It's in a plastic bag, Mom. I'm not going to catch anything from it."

"I think you can only get rabies if you are bitten by an animal," Chuck says.

"You think?" Mom asks. "You want to take a chance on rabies if you aren't sure?"

"God, Mom, no one is going to get rabies from a dead coyote in a bag," I say.

"Dane, why on earth would you bring a piece of roadkill into the garage? We should just call Animal Control and let them pick it up from the side of the road."

"I can explain," I say, but when I start to talk, I realize maybe I can't explain. "The coyote, he's got a den or something near here. I used to see him around late at night. And I guess I got the idea . . ."

"What?" Mom asks, her eyes wide as she looks at me, like it is the first time she has ever seen me, and she isn't sure what I am.

"I got the idea that he was . . . like . . . Dad. Reincarnated."

Now Mom and Chuck don't look at each other. They are very consciously making the effort to not look at each other for fear of what they might see in each other's expression. There is no logical place to take the conversation now. It reminds me of that movie with the woman who gets sent to a mental hospital and you think she's not crazy because you're seeing the whole thing from her perspective and then—surprise twist—turns out she really is crazy and she's been tricking the audience the whole time.

"I realize that sounds crazy," I add, just to give them the impression that we are all on the same team. *See? I'm sane, just like you guys. I just don't express it as well.*

Mom's reaction surprises me as she says, "Dane, I'm not sure I understand what's going on here. You're worrying me." She reaches across the counter to cover my hand with hers but then remembers the dead coyote I have been touching and thinks better of it.

But even though she's afraid I'll give her rabies, suddenly she is transformed into the protective mother I haven't seen since I was a little kid, when bigger kids would pick on me on the playground. Dad would tell her I needed to learn to settle things on my own, learn to survive in the wild, but Mom would go charging in, making threats and scolding the kids who were being mean to me. Even if it is only for this moment, that mom is back.

"Anyway, I just wanted to give it a proper burial. I thought . . . ," I say, my gaze fixed on Chuck's face as I speak slowly, "maybe Chuck could help me."

Mom's eyes soften with pity and her head tips to one

side. Now we are both looking at Chuck, Mom with a silent appeal for him to treat me gently, while I study his reaction.

"I'm sure Chuck would be happy to help you," Mom says when it becomes clear Chuck isn't going to say anything.

"Great," I say, pretending as if Chuck has been the one to agree willingly.

"I have a tee time scheduled," Chuck says, at once hopeful and terrified.

"I'm sure it won't take long," Mom says, her eyes pleading with him.

Chuck stares at Mom for a few seconds while I act as if nothing is unusual. Mom's pleading look is unrelenting. Finally, Chuck has no choice but to say, "Okay. Okay, yeah. I'll help you after I get dressed and we eat something. I want to eat before . . . well . . . before."

"Forget it," I say, my words acid on my tongue. "I know you don't want to. Neither one of you gives a shit about anything."

"Dane," Mom says, but not like a warning, just with alarm.

"What?" I ask, my voice rising. "'Dane' what? I said, just forget it. Forget everything. Just leave me alone." I'm afraid my voice falters on this last part as I hurry for the safety of my room, where I can lose it in private.

After slamming my bedroom door I pick up my phone and sit on the end of the bed, rocking and holding my stomach, which hurts like hell. I stare at my phone, not knowing what I'm looking at or for, and then I text Dad. It's a text that rambles and doesn't make any sense.

Just be calm, a text from Dad, *Be calm. Take a deep breath. It's going to be okay.*

But a message, coming from Dad right now, when he's gone for a second time? It freaks me out.

I want to text Ophelia or Joe, anybody who can help me to feel normal right now. But the normal world is in school or getting ready for a field hockey game and isn't going to respond. I throw my phone in frustration and lie down on my bed, curling into a ball and holding my stomach as the ache becomes unbearable.

When I wake, the house is quiet. My face is puffy and damp, like I have been crying in my sleep. It hurts to open my eyes. The lids have to be peeled apart, glued together by sleep that scratches against my corneas.

I go to the bathroom at the end of the hallway and splash water onto my face. I don't know what time it is.

Downstairs, the house feels empty, but I know Mom is there. I can feel her, hearing me through the walls. Mom emerges from her room and tries to smile, but fails.

"How are you feeling?" she asks, and seems worried about what my answer will be.

"Where's Chuck?" I ask, ignoring her question.

"Oh, he's . . ." She waves her hand. "He went golfing. He thought maybe we needed some time, just the two of us."

"How long have I been asleep?" I ask, expecting her to say a month, or a year.

"Just a couple of hours."

"I'm going to bury the coyote," I say.

"Dane." Mom speaks to stop me as I am headed for the garage. "Maybe you should just leave it for today. I don't want you getting upset."

"I've already been upset for a while, Mom. I want . . . I need it to be settled."

"O-okay. It's not in the garage. I had Chuck move it."

"Where is he?" I ask.

"Dane, please, can we just talk about how you are feeling? Dr. Lineberger said . . ."

"Mom, I'm fine. I just need to bury him. Where is he?"

She sighs and gives up. "It's on the side of the house. Chuck said he was going to move the bag to the side of the garage."

I walk out the garage door and feel her eyes following me, but she doesn't say anything to stop me.

The coyote's funeral will be only the second I have attended in my life. The first, of course, was Dad's.

Dad's funeral had been in a cathedral because Dad's family was Irish Catholic, but as far as I knew, he hadn't set foot in a church since I was baptized. I don't know what he believed, because we never talked about it. Other than using expressions like "God damn it" and "Jesus H. Christ," Dad didn't have much use for God or any of his holy helpers.

Maybe he believed in God and an afterlife and heaven and hell, but even if there was a heaven, Dad would probably never make it there. In addition to blaspheming God's name, he used words like "fatty" and "retard." Compelling evidence of his moral turpitude.

Dad's funeral had been almost like any other social event—it was catered and there was a bar and people got dressed up and a lot of them seemed happy to see each other. The church service was more like a business conference since most of the people knew Dad because of work or through the club. Though there were some people with tears in their eyes, I was the only person who cried. A few people got up to say nice things about Dad, but nobody said they missed him so much it might kill them.

Chuck delivered the eulogy, which was full of jokes and golf references that I didn't understand but that made the crowd rumble with chuckles of appreciation. I felt completely alone at Dad's funeral, just like I did at any social event—always on the outside, even when I was right in the middle of everything.

As I sat in the church listening to people talk about Dad, I could imagine him sitting beside me, delivering wry commentary about everyone there. Dad believed in unvarnished truths because he was never hurt by them.

I find the coyote in its death shroud on the side of the house, next to a pile of cinder blocks that are left over from the installation of the shed. The idea of the coyote being inside a plastic bag makes me uncomfortable, like it will suffocate him, though rationally I know the coyote is beyond caring, or breathing.

I think about burying the coyote, but then I imagine the coyote under the weight of the dirt and rocks, imagine him panicked and smothering. I step back and turn away from the coyote's corpse, willing myself to think of the coyote as just an object, nothing that can feel.

When I was a kid, I remember thinking that even in-animate objects had feelings. I was always careful to make sure that my stuffed animals and toys were comfortable, not just dumped into a toy box. If Mom decided that I wasn't playing with a toy, she would take it from my room, saying it was time to get rid of it. That always made me cry and I would promise, swear, that I would start playing with the toy again, just so that it didn't get hurt feelings.

The toys would eventually go into a box. Mom would help me pack them carefully, making sure that they were comfortable and safe, and she would tell me that the toys would just go into storage in the attic to save for later. The toys wouldn't be unhappy, she told me, they would just go to have a rest until I had a child and then my own kid could play with them. That all sounded very reasonable to me at the time.

Burying the coyote would feel wrong, the way it felt wrong to drive Dad to the cemetery and just leave him there. It still feels wrong, knowing Dad is in a box in the ground, a box from which he can never escape.

I'm not going to let that happen a second time.

There's a pile of wood in the corner of the yard, not far from the garage along the property line. We don't have a wood-burning fireplace, so the wood isn't useful. It's just a pile of branches deposited by the guys Mom pays to mow the lawn.

I carefully place the coyote bag on top of the pile of wood, then go the garage to find the can of lighter fluid and the long-handled lighter Dad used for the grill. Mom wanted him to use a gas grill because of the mess the charcoal created, but Dad always insisted it wasn't really grilling if you used propane. After I douse the pile with lighter fluid, I hold the lighter at arm's length to set the pile ablaze.

The lighter fluid burns quickly and releases an oily black smoke. It takes longer than I would expect for the flames to take hold, but once they do, the fire quickly spreads among the dead leaves that are still attached to the branches and sticks in the pile.

I stand only a few feet from the fire and watch for a few minutes, but then there is the smell of burning plastic and hair and I have to step back.

A shimmering red outline of the coyote is visible in the flames now and I don't want to look anymore. I have to turn away. My heart aches and I have to tell myself over and over that the coyote can't feel it anymore. *He can't feel. He can't feel. Dad can't feel. Only I can feel.* And that part seems really unfair.

The flames are lower now that the lighter fluid has

burned away and I hear the weight of the coyote sink into the burned leaves that collapse into ash beneath it. It is not a raging fire anymore, just a smoldering heap, the coyote's shape, I am grateful, indistinguishable from the rest of the pile.

I walk inside, the last of Dad disappearing into the swirl of smoke from the funeral pyre behind me. I'm careful to take off my shoes before I enter the sliding glass door on the deck and start upstairs, thinking I'll take a shower, maybe make a sandwich. Despite my nap earlier, I am tired and my hunger has returned.

In my room I strip out of my clothes. My shirt smells powerfully of smoke even though I barely got close to the fire. I am tangled in my sweatshirt for a moment as I struggle to pull the hood over my head. The removal of my sweatshirt leaves me spent and exhausted and all I can do is lie down on the bed until my head stops spinning.

The smell of smoke is still strong in the room. I take deep breaths, hoping that the smell will start to dissipate now that my sweatshirt is off and lying in a crumpled heap on the floor. But the smell seems to get stronger and stronger.

I'm just so tired. So very, very tired.

When I hear Mom from the first floor her voice is a high screech, so I can't understand what she's saying. My head protests as I sit up and swing my legs over the edge of the bed. As I open my bedroom door I hear Mom clearly now, and her screams take on meaning.

"Oh my God, oh my God! Dane, are you in the house? Dane! Where are you!?"

I'm not sure what I had been expecting. "Involuntary admission to a mental health facility" sounds bad. You imagine there would be shouting and/or restraints, or some kind of tranquilizer involved. In reality, Mom just fills out a few forms and, because we have awesome insurance, I am no longer her problem.

I tried to explain to Mom, to Chuck, to the firefighters, to anyone who would listen, that I hadn't been trying to burn down the house. The fireman said it only took fifty gallons of water to put out the fire, barely more than a bathtub full. He said that we were lucky.

He meant that we were lucky the fire hadn't spread to the garage or the deck. He meant that we were lucky we hadn't lost our house, or our lives.

But Mom hardly feels lucky to have a son who is an arsonist who builds funeral pyres in the backyard. She doesn't feel lucky that neighbors came out to watch as three fire trucks, an ambulance, and several cop cars blocked all traffic on our street while the fire was extinguished. She doesn't feel lucky to have a son who is a lunatic.

And now I'm confined to a facility with rooms that are a lot like the cheap hotels you see in movies when the bad guys are trying to lie low.

I have a twin bed with a plastic cover on the mattress

and a matching nightstand and dresser with no pulls on the drawers and nothing inside them. I also have a bathroom that is just a toilet and sink but the toilet has no lid, or even a seat, really. It's just a smooth stainless-steel bowl with a wide lip on it. This makes me wonder about what type of self-harm I could do, or if anyone has ever successfully committed suicide, with a toilet seat. But I can't Google it because they have taken away my phone. There isn't anything electronic in my room except for overhead lights in the bedroom and bathroom, and these are recessed into the ceiling with covers on them that can't be removed without a tool.

I am issued a pair of rubber slides with a Velcro closure over the toes and an outfit that is like hospital scrubs but in a pattern that designates me as crazy rather than employed by the hospital.

My room is so quiet that the only sound is a persistent hum from the lights and the occasional sound of a toilet flushing from the rooms on either side of me. It is morning, and as I lie in bed after a mostly sleepless night, I stare at the ceiling and mull over the events that have landed me in the hospital, replaying all of it in my head like a movie. At first glance, I suppose my reaction to the coyote's death could be interpreted as over the top. It wasn't the same as Dad dying, even if in my mind, the coyote *was* Dad.

I probe the inside of my head with questions, like poking your tongue at a sore in your mouth to test if the sore is growing or changing. Yes, I am sad about losing my dad; yes, I am angry at my mother and Chuck. But none of that makes me crazy. I am an inconvenience to the people who are trying to pretend as if everything is great. No dysfunction—nothing to see here. We are all normal, well-adjusted, happy people. In fact, the more I think about it, the crazier they all seem. I am the only one who is sane.

So, why am I here, and they are out there?

The other people in this facility are all my age or younger, but they seem to have real problems. There are drug addicts, and anorexics, and cutters. I suppose, in their eyes, the real difference is that I am not only a danger to myself, I'm a danger to other people. Which isn't really fair. After all, the whole thing with burning the coyote is just a projection of my grief.

In the afternoon we meet as a group for a check-in. We're supposed to tell everyone what color we are feeling. We don't have to talk about why we're feeling that color, or even what the color means if we don't want to. We just have to say a color.

I am surprised to find out that the group is coed. I guess I was expecting guys to be separated from girls, like in prison. But when I walk into group that first day there are eight people, and five of them are girls. I recognize one of them—Suzie Landers, the bulimic girl Dr. Lineberger is supposed to have cured. The counselor is a young guy named Ted. He's old enough to be out of college, I guess, but he dresses like his mom still picks out his clothes. His shoes are brown leather loafers with tassels. I keep my focus on the tassels, which quiver anytime Ted gets animated as he talks. I don't speak at all during that first session and Ted doesn't ask me to. I am the only person who doesn't volunteer a story.

Ted calls on Suzie to start the group session and you can tell she's experienced. She doesn't even seem to care that there are other people listening to her. Suzie chooses the color orange. Then she talks about how when she used to binge eat she would always eat a bag of Cheetos first. That way, when she was vomiting all the food up later, she would know when she got to the bottom because her vomit would turn orange. She sounds as if she misses Cheetos a lot.

I'm looking around the room, sneaking glances at the reactions of other people as Suzie talks. I'm wondering, does all of this sound bonkers to everyone else? Because it sounds fucking nuts to me. And if I'm in here with these people, then that means Dr. Lineberger, my mom, they must think I'm as out of touch with reality as Suzie is with her color-coded vomit. And that's not good.

During group I don't have to tell my story, but I do have to say my color. I have a hard time choosing what color to say. It's all I'm thinking about as they go around the room. While people are talking about all the terrible things they've done to themselves and to other people and all of their failures and hurt feelings and drug use, I'm just sitting there trying to think which color I should say. Gray seems too obvious, like I haven't put any effort into my color. But purple or even green seems ridiculous. In fact, any color in the rainbow seems ridiculous, other than maybe blue. And then you're right back to being too obvious. Blue. Gray.

Depressed. But what the hell else is there? Aubergine? It must be nice to feel so comfortable with talking about your feelings that you can say any color that comes to mind.

My mind is so consumed with the color-choice struggle that I am panicked and my palms sweaty when the circle gets around to me.

In the end I go with orange, just like Suzie. Ted asks me why I said orange and my answer, which I think is pretty good on the fly, is "Because orange is slightly less angry than red."

Ted nods approvingly and lets me off the hook as he moves on to the next person. I spend the rest of the session looking at my hands in my lap, but when I look up I catch Suzie watching me. She doesn't even try to conceal the fact that she's watching me.

Suzie is so small. She's petite anyway, but with her bulimia she's so thin that she can curl her entire body into the pocket of her chair. And she looks tired. And weak. And pale. And veiny. And it makes me think of Ophelia because Ophelia is the exact opposite of all those things.

Really, anything makes me think of Ophelia.

After group we get to eat lunch. The food is laid out on a folding plastic table in the same room where we had group. There are sandwiches and chips and a salad.

I end up at the table next to Suzie, who is holding a plate and looking at the food with an expression of regret.

"No Cheetos," I say, then realize that's probably a terrible thing to say.

But she smiles and doesn't seem offended. "Is that the

real reason you chose orange as your color, too?" Suzie asks. "Because you love Cheetos so much?"

"Who doesn't love Cheetos?"

"My mom doesn't love Cheetos," Suzie says, and I figure she's not really talking about Cheetos anymore.

"I chose orange because I couldn't think of any other color," I say. "I had to copy you."

Suzie smiles at that. "You want to sit together to eat? We could go outside."

"We can go outside?"

"Sure," Suzie says, shrugging one really delicate shoulder. Her collarbone is so thin and sticks so far out from her neck that I think it could break if I barely poked it with my finger. "It's miles to the nearest bus stop. They know we're all too fucking pathetic to walk that far."

She's joking. I think.

We walk out through a side door that opens onto a court-yard enclosed on three sides. The view through the open side of the courtyard is of a large field with woods beyond. I imagine making a break for it. Like that scene with that girl running from the Nazis in that movie.

It's only a twenty-minute drive to my house from here so I figure we can't be too far from civilization. But I have no money. No phone. After a day without my phone, I don't reach for it instinctively every few minutes and I wonder what I'm missing in the world. We could have been invaded for all I know.

Suzie sits down at a round concrete table with benches

that are also concrete and shaped like two half-moons. I take the bench opposite her and dig into my food. I'm not eager to eat but the food is a good distraction from the fact that I don't know what to say.

"So," Suzie says, "what are you in for?" The corner of her mouth lifts up into a quirky smile.

"Um," I say. That's it. My entire answer. Where to begin? "My mom and my therapist think I'm a danger to myself. And others, I suppose," I say, thinking about the fire. "And I see ghosts."

"Really? Like that kid in that movie?"

"No. God. Not like that. I think my dad was reincarnated as a coyote. And my mom's boyfriend hit the coyote with his car so the coyote is dead now, too."

"Oh," she says as she pushes her food around her plate. Truly, there isn't much else you could say while still being polite. And Suzie seems like a pretty nice person. It occurs to me that she hasn't actually taken a bite of her food yet.

"What about you?" I ask, as if I haven't noticed that she's the size of a fifth grader.

"I have a bad relationship with food."

"Yeah. The Cheetos. You mentioned. You actually like throwing up?"

"Nobody likes throwing up," she says, but not in a mean way, like it's a stupid question. "It's how I keep from gaining weight."

"You think that would be a bad idea?" I ask, unsure if that's a rude question.

"Let's talk about your problems. I'm sick of talking about mine. Ghosts are more interesting than an eating disorder."

"Or, we could just talk about something else," I say.

"Okay."

I wait, hoping she will go first. With girls you usually don't have to wait long for them to fill any silence, and Suzie doesn't disappoint me.

"You have a girlfriend?" she asks.

"No."

"I don't have a boyfriend," she says, and I'm worried that she'll say we're perfect for each other. *You're crazy, I'm crazy. It's a good fit.*

My plate is near empty. "You going to eat that?" I ask her.

"Probably not. Why? You want it?"

Even though the food isn't great, now that I have started eating, I realize how hungry I am. I didn't eat at all yesterday. And I wonder how Suzie goes without food on purpose. "Sure. I'm starving. I didn't eat yesterday. Won't you get in trouble for not eating?" I ask as I take her plate and start to eat her food.

She sighs. "I have a weigh-in once a week. My mom always comes. It's like she enjoys watching me suffer."

"I feel that way too sometimes. About my mom, I mean."

"I won't be here much longer. I haven't been gaining, so they'll send me back to a residential place that specializes in eating disorders. The last one I went to, a girl actually died while I was there."

"Shit. No kidding?" I ask, thinking what I'm not supposed

to think, that people who starve themselves are legit crazy—there are much easier ways to leave.

"Well, she died at the hospital. But they had to call an ambulance from the group house."

"She actually starved herself to death?"

"Heart failure. It's pretty common. She had been sick for a long time."

"You think that could happen to you?"

"Maybe," she says with a shrug, like dying is nothing compared to being fat, or even normal size. "Look," she says with a nod toward something behind me. "The squirrels. They come when they see me because they know I'll toss most of my food. They're trained."

It's a surreal moment, her bringing up squirrels like that. I figured I was the only one who thought about squirrels.

"If you died and were reincarnated, what animal would you come back as?" I ask.

"God, I don't know, a dolphin, maybe. I like the water. The idea of being free."

"If you like being free so much, why don't you get better so you don't have to keep staying in places like this?"

"Yeah, I guess," she says, noncommittal. "What about you?"

"Honestly," I say, "I'd probably be a squirrel."

Mom comes to visit me on the second day of my incarceration. We're going to sit down with Dr. Lineberger to talk after my two nights in the hospital, though I don't really think of it as a hospital because I'm not sick. I think of it more as a minimum-security prison.

We meet in one of the generic offices at the residential facility. It's smaller than Dr. Lineberger's regular office and there is just a desk and two straight-backed wooden chairs where Mom and I sit.

When she arrives, Mom kisses me and hugs me and I let her. I know she's worried because after the coyote and the fire she doesn't just think I'm disturbed, she knows it.

There are things she has to say, and I can tell from her expression that she has been trying to come up with the best way to say them.

Dr. Lineberger starts with an easy question. "How are you, Dane?"

"I'm fine." Most of the time when people ask you that question, they really just want you to say that you're fine so they can go about their day. Today, I will not get off that easily. "I feel . . . better."

"Why don't you start by telling me about the coyote."

"I told you about him. A while ago. I really wanted to think about him as my dad. He had become like a . . . symbol. And I guess, once the coyote was gone, too, I just . . . ," I start to say "snapped" but want to avoid any words that imply some kind of psychotic break. Instead I say, ". . . got upset."

"Your mother mentioned that you were cremating the coyote. That you started the fire as a sort of funeral."

"Okay," I say, knowing I have to be careful, "it does sound

a little nuts, but I swear I didn't mean for anything bad to happen."

"Were you still thinking of the coyote as your father then?" Dr. Lineberger asks. "Was it like a second funeral for your father?"

"No. I know it wasn't really my dad. I just didn't like the idea of burying him. The coyote, I mean. Maybe my dad, too. I don't know. Somehow it seemed wrong."

Dr. Lineberger waits for me to say more. I'm not sure what else there is to say, so I say the same thing again. "I never really believed the coyote was my dad. It was just something, maybe the idea, that I liked. That he was still there. I don't know."

"Well, it's good that you can talk about it, I guess," Dr. Lineberger says, maybe not with as much enthusiasm as I would have hoped. "I'm glad you feel open to experiencing and sharing your feelings."

"I'm still sad about my dad. But I wish I wasn't stuck in this place. I wish I could go out into the world and finally be on my own. Move on to something else."

Dr. Lineberger turns to Mom then and asks her how she's feeling about everything.

"Scared," Mom says after taking a long minute to think about it. "I'm scared because I feel like I don't know my own son. And I should know him better than anyone. And, I guess, a bit angry. With myself, I mean. I feel like I've failed as a mother."

"You didn't fail, Mom," I say. "This isn't about you. The

way I feel about Dad being gone . . ." I stop, knowing what I think but not feeling okay with saying it out loud. But I know I have to be honest or they are never going to let me leave this place. "We don't share that. Okay? The way I feel about Dad being gone isn't the way you feel. And that makes me feel lonely. Alone. Sometimes I wish I had a brother or a sister because at least I would have one other person around who knows exactly how I feel."

"Do you think it would be helpful to be part of a group?" Dr. Lineberger asks, sounding hopeful.

"Like group therapy? Like we have here?" I ask skeptically. "No. The problems these people have, they aren't my problems. It doesn't make it any easier just knowing there are people more messed up than I am."

"I meant like a group in which the other members are kids who have experienced the same thing. The loss of a parent. If your grief makes you feel lonely, maybe you need to be around other people who have had the same experience."

"Maybe," I say, but only because I want to sound as if I am open to Dr. Lineberger's idea. It wouldn't be the same. Other people who have lost a parent aren't people who have lost *my* dad.

"We don't have to decide anything right now," Dr. Lineberger says. "But maybe you will consider it. There are programs we can access."

"Maybe," I say again, and again, it means no, but I'll wait to fight that battle later.

After our meeting, Dr. Lineberger says I'm ready to come home. Everyone seems tentatively able to accept that, despite how crazy my actions seemed, I wasn't really trying to cause harm to myself or anyone else. But now I am going to be expected to go to therapy twice per week. And Mom has started talking about medication again.

I'm reminded of a movie I saw about these people who live in a facility, like this one, and they are on a steady stream of medication that keeps them catatonic. The medications made it impossible for them to physically react, or even talk. But probably they are like that guy in that other movie, who was paralyzed and could only blink his eyes to communicate. And what he really wanted to communicate was a primal scream at the horror of being a prisoner trapped in his own mind.

As soon as I get home I ask Mom to let me go hang out with my friends. She agrees, with conditions. I'm supposed to text her every thirty minutes and share my location with her on my phone.

When I get out to the Mercedes, it doesn't start, and my heart sinks with disappointment. I head back inside the house, wondering what address I can use to get an Uber to the Wall. Mom and Chuck look up with surprise when I enter the house through the garage door.

"The Mercedes won't start," I tell them.

"That car costs more in maintenance than it would to just buy a new car," Mom says.

I open my mouth to speak but Chuck cuts me off before I can say anything.

"It's okay," Chuck says, and puts a hand on her arm. "I'll call the garage and have it towed in. It's probably just a bad battery or something."

I'm grateful to Chuck for sticking up, if not for me, at least for the Mercedes.

I text Joe and he arrives about thirty minutes later in his dad's Toyota Corolla, which rolled off an assembly line sometime in the early part of the twenty-first century.

"Dude," he says as he leans over to look at me through the half-open passenger-side window. "I've been texting you for days."

"It's a long story," I say as I climb into the car.

"Okay."

"You got a cigarette?" I ask him as I pull the shoulder belt over my chest.

"Seriously? I've only got two packs left."

"I don't care, man. I need it more than you do. Hand it over."

Joe takes a moment, struggling with his inner addict before he concedes, and says, "We can share one."

There's nothing worse than sharing a cigarette, but I'm in no position to argue.

As soon as I start telling my story, explaining what happened and where I have been, Joe forgets to care about the cigarette. He responds with a low whistle, the only indication that he is listening intently to me, when I tell him about everything that happened before the coyote's funeral. And he only interrupts me when I tell him about Suzie Landers and her Cheeto-orange vomit indicator.

"Man, that's messed up. You think Cheetos taste the same on the way up as they do on the way down?"

"I don't know. I've heard that only works with bananas."

"What the fu-uck?"

"Yeah, my dad told me that."

"How does . . . did . . . he know that?"

"I have no idea. Anyway, as far as the world knows, I'm just recovering from a skating accident. At least I think there's no way my mom would tell anyone the truth. It's too embarrassing for her. It's just . . . you know, in combination with my little freak-out at the club, and maybe that one time I tried to commit suicide . . . it gave my mom and the therapist the impression that I'm totally gone, mentally."

"Well, you know," Joe says, warming up to what he's got to say, "your mom called me. She asked me about what you've been into lately, like she was feeling me out to see if we're into meth or something."

"That's all she said to you?"

"She asked me if I knew anything about a coyote. The whole conversation was kind of crazy."

"I'm not crazy," I say, feeling like I can say this truthfully now.

"Uh-huh," Joe says. He rubs the length of his index finger along the line of his lower lip as he thoughtfully watches the traffic light where we're stopped.

"What?"

"I didn't say nothing, bro."

"But you thought it. You think I'm crazy."

"There's lots of people crazier than you are."

"Is that supposed to make me feel better?"

"I think it's supposed to make me feel better," Joe says after considering the question for a minute. "So, where are we going now?"

"The Wall. I want to skate."

"You just got a concussion, like, four days ago."

"I don't care. I want to go."

"Maybe you are crazy."

That night, as I'm plugging in my phone I hear a noise outside on the roof, just outside my window. It's a noise too substantial to be a twig falling from a nearby tree or the scuffle of squirrel feet. In my mind the noise is big enough to be a monster, or a garden-variety serial killer.

I have left my room via my window a thousand times to sneak out late at night, or just to leave without having the hassle of interacting with my mom. Before this moment it had never occurred to me that some psycho could use the easy access of the porch roof to break into my room.

When I finally work up the courage to peer out the window, Ophelia is crouched only a few feet away and I scream. Holy shit.

I open the window to stick my head out.

"What the hell?" I say. "How did you get up here?"

"I climbed the tree," she says, as if it's a totally normal thing for her to be sneaking into my room. "Isn't that how you do it?"

"I usually only sneak out. I just walk in the front door when I come back."

"Well, are you going to let me in?"

"I guess so."

I don't even have time to worry about whether I have dirty underwear on the floor or some other cripplingly embarrassing evidence of my humanity.

Ophelia clambers in through the open window and makes a lot of noise rattling the blinds and stomping.

There's a knock at my bedroom door followed by Mom's voice, saying my name with a note of concern.

"What?" I ask.

"I thought I heard a scream," Mom says.

"Probably the TV," I say. Ophelia nods, her eyebrows raised and lower lip pooched out, clearly impressed with how easily the lie has come.

"You sure you're okay?" Mom asks.

"I'm fine," I say, my voice raised so she can hear me through the door.

"For goodness' sake, Dane," Mom says, "open the door."

I hold up my finger to my lips, indicating Ophelia should remain quiet. She twists her fingers, turning an imaginary key at her lips, as I walk over and open the bedroom door, just enough to stick my head out.

"What?" I ask her.

"Don't *what* me, Dane. I feel like I have every right to be concerned."

"Fair enough," I say, hoping that if I'm agreeable she'll drop it and leave me alone. "It's been a long week, Mom."

"I just wanted to make sure you were okay."

"I am. I'm fine. Okay?"

"I'm going to go to bed. You should try to get some sleep, too."

"Okay."

"I love you, Dane."

"Thanks." All I can think is that if this is going to end in a rare hug, how am I going to angle my body so Mom can't see Ophelia? I don't think Mom would be all that upset. She would probably be grateful I am doing something as normal as sneaking a girl into my room. But it would have been a lot better if Ophelia had come to the door like a normal girl.

Mom leans in to give me the hug but I hug her with just one arm and pat her gently on the back. "Good night, Mom," I say, hoping it will get her out of there.

"Good night," she says, and she's smiling.

"That was really sweet," Ophelia says after Mom is gone.

"I guess."

"Where have you been? Why haven't you been in school?"

"Oh, I was in the hospital," I say. "Skating accident."

"Really?" Ophelia's eyes widen with surprise. As proof, I pull up my shirt to reveal the purple bruise on my chest that has faded to a gruesome blend of greens and blues.

"Ouch," she says, and, without any warning, puts out her

hand to touch the bruise. Her fingertips are cool and only rest on my chest for a second, but they brand my skin. I am looking at her hand as she touches my chest but when our eyes meet again, her cheeks are flushed pink. I can feel heat in my own face and know my cheeks are redder than hers.

"I had a concussion. My head got the worst of it," I say, my voice breaking like I'm still in middle school.

"Oh," she says. "I guess that's good. If it was just your head it wasn't too serious, then." Her expression is almost apologetic. "Sorry. You set up the pitch. I had to swing."

"No worries. I'd have been disappointed if you didn't."

This is a bald-faced lie. I was enjoying her sympathy, the closest thing I have gotten to real affection in a long time. Her joke hurts me. More than it should.

"There were firetrucks in front of your house the other day when my dad and I got home from my field hockey game. What happened?"

"Oh, that," I say, dismissing it casually. "Chuck was burning some brush and it got out of hand."

"I messaged you to see if everything was okay. You never messaged me back."

"I'm sorry. I didn't have my phone while I was in the hospital." This isn't a lie. I was in a hospital and didn't have my phone. Ophelia waits for me to say more, but I'm not volunteering anything.

"So, this is your room," Ophelia says as she bounces into a seat at the end of my bed. "I've always wondered. Man, you get your own television. My dad won't even get cable. If I asked for a TV in my room he'd tell me to go to hell."

"I hardly ever watch it," I lie. I'm not sure why I feel compelled to lie about how much time I spend watching. Somehow, I just sense that it would make me seem boring and uninteresting to Ophelia. "You want to watch a movie or something?" I ask. The television could give us both something to look at other than my obvious infatuation.

I sit on the desk chair because she is sitting on the bed and I don't want to make her uncomfortable.

"What are you doing?" she asks.

"Just . . . sitting."

"Why don't you sit over here?"

"I didn't want you to think I was trying to put the moves on you or something. Just because you're in my room, you know?"

"I'm pretty sure if you had any moves, you would have used them on me by now," she says, and if I didn't know any better, I would say she sounds kind of disappointed I don't have any moves.

We end up sitting side by side at the end of the bed, me rigid with anxiety and Ophelia with one leg tucked under her, the other bouncing idly against the end of the mattress.

I surf the channels for a while until I finally give up, and land on a reality show about some guy who has multiple wives. The guy already has three wives and he's brought out this new woman he's dating to introduce her to the other three wives, see if it would be a good fit.

"We're going to watch this entire show," says Ophelia. "That's how they suck you in. We'll sit through thirty minutes of commercials just in case we get to find out about their sex lives."

"They're not going to talk about it," I say with confidence, though not enough confidence to use the word "sex" in front of Ophelia.

"But it's the only thing we want to know. How can they not mention it?"

"How do you think they met?" I ask. "They're Mormon so it's not like he's picking them up in a bar or something."

"Tinder," Ophelia says without hesitation.

"No way. I don't think they're allowed to use Tinder."

"How can a religion that started two hundred years ago have Tinder restrictions? Have you ever used Tinder?"

"I go on it sometimes out of curiosity. I wouldn't say that I use it."

In truth I have never swiped right on a girl because I am too afraid that if I did, I would never get a match. And then I would have confirmation that every girl on Tinder and, by extension, the world, has taken a pass on me.

"What about you?" I ask.

"No way," she says. As she's speaking she stands and circles to the head of the bed, then flops down to recline on my pillows. "My dad says that dating apps are how serial killers look for victims."

It's too awkward for me to turn all the way around in my seat to talk to her so I get up and go to sit against the headboard with her. I grab a pillow and put it on my lap, a way to hide myself, to be safe in her presence.

"That sounds like something your dad would say," I say. "I suppose you don't really need a dating app."

"Why? Because I'm not a serial killer?" she asks, her brow wrinkling in confusion. "How do you know I'm not?"

"I guess I don't. Are you going to sneak in here some night and kill me in my sleep?"

"No," she says, and then smiles. "If I kill you, you'll definitely be awake for it."

There doesn't seem to be anything to say to that, so we go back to watching the show in silence for a while. Ophelia is the one to break the silence. She usually has a lot more to say than I do.

"Why did you say I don't need a dating app?" she asks.

Because the answer is obvious, I speak without thinking. "Because pretty girls attract all kinds of unwanted attention. You don't need a dating app for guys to make your life uncomfortable."

"You think I'm pretty?" she asks.

"I know you're pretty. Though sometimes I forget because you're mean to me."

"Mean to you?" Her voice rises as her eyes widen with surprise. "I'm not mean."

"I didn't say you were mean, just mean to me sometimes," I correct her. "Don't worry. I get it. A pretty girl like you, if you're too nice, guys get the wrong idea. You have to keep everybody at a distance."

"You're the first person to ever tell me I was pretty," she says. "Well, other than my dad or my grandma or somebody. But they're supposed to say that. It's not like I would believe it coming from them."

"Give me a break. You can look in a mirror. You can see that you're pretty."

"Is that so?" she asks. "So, when you look in the mirror, do you see a hottie?"

I laugh and put up a hand to cover my face. "You're making fun of me now."

"I should go," Ophelia says with a sigh.

"You don't have to."

"No," she says. "I do. My dad wakes up in the middle of the night sometimes."

"I'll walk you," I say.

We walk downstairs and Ophelia is being careful not to make any sound to avoid alerting Mom, though I'm not worried about it. At the edge of the driveway we stop, lingering, like neither one of us really wants our time together to end. I start looking around the yard, like I always do, hoping to see the coyote, and then I remember that he's gone and isn't coming back.

She says good night then and I say, "I'd walk you home, but I only have on socks."

"I'm fine on my own," she says.

And I think, *Yeah, she really is fine on her own. She doesn't need me.* And that makes me sadder than ever.

I take out my phone and text Dad while I'm waiting

to see if a scream pierces the night during Ophelia's walk home.

I'm in love with this girl, I type to Dad.

I put the phone back in the pocket of my hoodie, waiting another minute to make sure she's made it home.

My phone buzzes with a reply from Dad. *Tell me about her.*

I would have told my dad all about Ophelia. I could talk to him like that. He always said I could come to him to talk about anything—man to man. So, I take the time now to tell him all about her, probably the longest text I've ever sent anyone.

THERE IS NOTHING EITHER GOOD OR BAD, BUT THINKING MAKES IT SO

In boarding school skipping class was an impossibility, but it's easy to ditch class in a regular public high school. So easy that it surprises me anyone goes to class at all. But whenever I show up for school, there they all are.

The whole concept of excused versus unexcused absences is completely flawed anyway. I'm seventeen, for Christ's sake. In many cultures that would render me fully human. I could own cattle or fight in wars. At the very least I'm capable of determining when I need a break from school, which is almost universally considered a failed system anyway.

I have always looked forward to English class, though not because I like reading, or even particularly my English teacher, Ms. Guinn. I'm in AP English, which is kind of a joke and I'm not really sure why I'm here. I look forward to it because it's the only class I share with Ophelia. Not only that, but I have a seat at the back of the room, with a perfectly unobstructed view of her where she sits two seats over and one seat up from me.

When I arrive at English that day Ophelia is already in her seat and Ms. Guinn is talking. I figure our relationship, if you can call it that, has moved to a different level since she snuck into my room the night before, but now that I am in Ophelia's presence around other people, I'm unsure what to do with my expression or my eyes, so I don't look at her as I make my way to my seat.

Ophelia always comes prepared and has something to contribute to class discussions. I like it when she speaks up in class so that I can watch her without it seeming weird.

I am lost as the class discusses *The Great Gatsby*. I haven't done the assigned reading. Usually I just learn enough about a book by reading a summary online and from the class discussions to pass the tests. When the reading was first assigned I had opened the book, but just kept reading the same page over and over. The words didn't really come together in a way that made sense to me.

During class discussion I watch Ophelia's lips moving as she speaks, her head tilting thoughtfully to one side as she listens to other people's comments, and the crease at the corner of her perfectly almond-shaped eyes. Her black curls seem to have life of their own, quivering with emotion, or tumbling across her shoulders when she turns her head.

When the bell rings, releasing us to our next class, I am still watching her. I watch as she puts her books in her backpack and leans over the flat of her desk to say something to the girl who sits in front of her. I watch as she bends over to pick up the hair tie that has fallen from her desk. Her hair falls to one side in a current of dark waves, the fluorescent bulbs above sparking blue fire in her curls.

"Dane," Ophelia says, like she's already said my name more than once to get my attention.

I realize I have been looking at her hair, staring at it, obsessing about it, and I quickly check in with my facial expression to see if I've been revealing my innermost thoughts.

"What?" I ask, then say, "Sorry," because it is my instinct to apologize for who I am and what I think.

"I was just asking if you're feeling better."

"Yeah," I say, eager to conceal my embarrassment about being caught watching her. "Yeah, I'm fine."

As we are walking out of the classroom Ophelia falls into step beside me and is just turning to say something else to me when Ms. Guinn stops me by calling out my name above the din.

"Dane," Ms. Guinn says again, though I am trying to ignore her.

Seriously?

Ophelia stops and gives me a questioning look. I shrug in response to her silent question. "What did you do?" Ophelia asks.

"I don't know," I say, which is an honest answer. I have a feeling whatever Ms. Guinn is going to say to me, I don't want anyone to overhear.

"Catch you later," Ophelia says, and, I can't tell for sure, but maybe she is disappointed to be leaving me behind.

Ms. Guinn gestures for me to approach her desk and I go to stand before her.

Everything about Ms. Guinn is medium. She isn't fat and she isn't thin. She isn't tall and she isn't short. Her hair has started to show streaks of light gray but her natural hair color is a mousy shade of khaki so it's as if she has had gray hair for her entire adult life. She doesn't have a defining feature. Today she looks tired.

"We've missed you this week."

"I seriously doubt that, but it's nice of you to say."

"Is everything okay with you?" Ms. Guinn asks. The question surprises me. Teachers don't usually go out of their way to ask how a student is doing. Other than how we did on a test or an assignment, I don't think they are obligated to care. At Brandywine Academy the teachers didn't show concern for the personal feelings of students, either. After all, we could afford better therapists than they could.

"Yeah. Sure. I just had a concussion from a skating accident." The more I repeat this explanation, the truer it sounds. It is true that I had a brain injury, just maybe as much from grief and sadness as a skating accident.

"You know, I'm still waiting on your overdue report about the American author of your choice. I really want you to turn it in, even if it's so late now that you can't really get any credit for it."

"Yeah, that's the thing," I say, trying not to come off smart-mouthed, just honest. "There's no real incentive for me to turn it in if I won't get any credit for it."

"Well, like I said before, I think you should complete it and turn it in, if only to build your self-confidence academically."

"You were serious about that?" I ask, blinking a few times in surprise. "I'm sorry. I thought it was a joke."

"Do you think your education is a joke?" She's so earnest. It seems impossible that she isn't shining me on.

"Is that question strictly rhetorical?"

She ignores my response and plows ahead with her agenda. "I was looking at the list of colleges our seniors will be attending. I noticed that you had 'undecided' next to your name."

She hasn't actually asked a question. I wait.

"So, you haven't committed to going anywhere?" she presses.

"I didn't apply anywhere."

Her forehead creases above the bridge of her nose. "May I ask why not?"

"Sure," I say with an affable shrug, and wait again.

After a few seconds, realizing that I am going to make this conversation as awkward as possible, she tilts her head and her eyes become warning. "Why," she says, and waits for a dramatic pause, "did you not apply to any colleges?"

"I didn't really see the point. I don't like school much. My dad went to college for seven years and he had a job he hated and that stressed him out. All he did was work. And then he died before he ever got to retire and enjoy anything."

Most people would stop now, express some sympathy

about my dad. Or their eyes would cloud up with pity, and they'd let it go. But not Ms. Guinn. She ignores the subject of my dad and says, "I know that high school can be pretty boring for an intelligent person like yourself. But once you get beyond all this, school can be quite interesting."

"You think I'm intelligent?" I ask. "What gave you that idea?"

She smiles, as if she thinks that maybe now I am the one shining her on. But I can't remember anyone telling me they thought I was smart before.

"Yes, Dane. I think you're intelligent. Maybe you don't work as hard as you could, but you're perfectly capable."

"Well," I say, thinking as I do that my logic won't come across as reasonable once I say it out loud, "I guess I figure school doesn't really matter. What's the point?"

It occurs to me that what I have said is somewhat insulting to Ms. Guinn. After all, she has spent her entire adult life teaching people like me. People who don't care about books that some expert, probably some expert who has been dead for a while, decided were great works of literature.

She seems puzzled, maybe unsure how to argue against my line of reasoning. It is an awkward position for her, having to defend why a student should care about the books that are required reading for graduation. Suddenly I am curious about what argument she is going to offer.

"I know that right now," she says slowly, considering her words, "it seems like none of this is important. But if you want to eventually have an interesting job, to have some reason to look forward to getting up in the morning, the course you set for yourself now really does matter."

"I just don't see myself going to college."

"So, what's your plan?" Ms. Guinn asks. "Sit around playing video games for the next sixty years?"

"Sixty years?" I repeat loudly, with some alarm. I try to imagine living another sixty years. Fail. Then say, "I guess I never really thought about it." Because I haven't. I have never pictured life beyond right now. I think of myself like that character in that movie where the guy ages backward and his childhood is the end of his life instead of the beginning. It's an interesting idea, but kind of a stupid movie.

"You know," Ms. Guinn says, her voice gentle now, "sometimes, when people are depressed, it can make it hard to find a reason to get out of bed in the morning." Her cheeks redden slightly, as if she has said too much, and I wonder idly if her coffee mug is filled with something other than coffee.

"Are you telling me that because you're depressed?" I ask. "Or because you think I am?"

The corner of her mouth turns up with a smile at my question and she says, "Maybe both. It is sometimes depressing to teach high school English. My audience isn't exactly going crazy for me like I'm Kanye West or something."

"I would maybe steer clear of pop-culture references when you're talking to students," I say. "Especially Kanye West."

"Oh?" she asks. "Is he not famous anymore?"

"He's still famous," I say, "just more of a punch line than a metaphor."

"I see," she says, and I get the impression, definitely now, that she is poking fun at me, at the world, with everything she says. "Anyway, I'm just saying I can relate. Being a high school English teacher is a pretty thankless job."

"Well," I say, "I wouldn't get too down about it. You get summers off, right? Not a bad gig."

She laughs now, as if I have said something intentionally funny. "Dane, I'm not really concerned about my own happiness at the moment. I was thinking that you might be struggling yourself. Struggling to find a good reason to get out of bed in the mornings."

"Why would you care about that?" I ask, genuinely mystified.

"I'm not an English teacher just because I love literature, you know?" she says as her forehead wrinkles with the question. For a second she reminds me of my mom, the way her eyebrows will disappear behind her bangs when she asks me questions like that, questions for which I am supposed to know the answers, but never do.

"Oh?" I say, reverting to the kind of response that makes you seem present in a conversation, while letting the other person lead until you can catch up.

"I had a pretty shitty high school experience," she says.

The way she uses "shitty" isn't the way most adults do when they use foul language around teenagers, as if they are trying to sound like they're "hip to our jive." She says it as if she has a pretty good grasp of swearing vocabulary. Like she would be more comfortable if she could swear all the time. I have never noticed it before, but Ms. Guinn is actually kind of . . . cool. And now I am really listening to her, interested in what she has to say. "I spent ten years teaching in an inner-city school," she says as her shoulders go slack and she sighs, as if some huge weight has been placed on her. Then she turns to pull open one of her desk drawers, using the distraction to minimize our connection as she continues with her story. "It got to be too much. Being around those kids—smart kids, decent kids—who were just victims of the hand they had been dealt. It made me feel helpless. I was powerless. I wasn't doing a goddamn thing to improve their lives." She punctuates her use of another swear by slamming the drawer shut, giving up on busying herself with something to distract from her emotions. "So, I took a position here. Figuring it would be like a vacation. Everyone at this school has plenty of money. Nobody's hungry or living in a house without heat or running water. But I was wrong. The kids here are in just as much pain as they are anyplace else."

She seems embarrassed now and is looking around the room, looking at everything but my face, too uncomfortable to look me in the eye.

I feel the need to comfort her somehow, give her a boost. She's sad, and angry with herself, two feelings with which I can intimately relate. I reach out to put a hand on her shoulder—just a brief touch, because it isn't socially acceptable for teachers and students to really care about each other, and say, "You want a Klonopin? I have some on me."

Her laugh is sudden and explosive, and then she shakes her head. "No. No, I'm okay."

"Well," I say as students for her next class are filing in, "I've got to get to my next class." I am edging toward the door, unsure how to end the conversation.

"Sure. But Dane, listen," she says, turning suddenly serious. "You can't experience joy if you don't also experience anguish. Don't give up on joy. Okay? Don't give up on joy, and I won't, either."

Her eyes and voice are pleading and I don't know how to respond so I just say "Okay" and give her a weak smile.

"Do you need a tardy pass? You'll be late for your next class."

"That's okay," I say with a reassuring smile. "I think I've already failed it for the quarter anyway."

Her eye-roll in response is more playful than annoyed and she waves me out the door.

As I walk to my next class I think about Ms. Guinn and her sadness. She seemed so genuine in her disappointment about not having more of a positive impact on the students she teaches. It makes me sad for her, so much so that I try to shake away the feeling before it can settle in too deeply.

For a moment I wonder if my conversation with her will become an important memory, like those moments in childhood that for some reason stick in your brain, like a briar clinging to your pant leg. It seems to me that you don't really get to choose which moments get lodged in your memory. No way to tell your mind which memories you want to become stuck there.

Part of me hopes that it is a memory I will carry with me. It's just a moment in time that will disappear with all of the rest when I die. Like memories of my dad from my childhood, which only exist as long as my brain does.

Business is slow at Mr. Edgar's after the early-evening rush of a Friday. I am just killing time until my shift ends at nine. I dust the shelves, and the cans of things like water chestnuts or chickpeas—things that will sit on the shelves for years. They will probably only get used if there is ever a zombie apocalypse and the store gets looted.

Mr. Edgar comes up from his office while I am cleaning the glass doors of the beer coolers. "Employee of the month!" Mr. Edgar shouts.

This is our own inside joke because, technically, I am Mr. Edgar's only employee. Sometimes his wife works the register and occasionally Mark will work a shift. But I am the only employee who isn't related to him by blood or marriage.

I do my best to give him a smile. The joke is so old and he uses it all the time. "When do I get my plaque?" I ask him. "I noticed over at the Burger King they put a photo of the employee of the month right up by the register where everyone can see it. Why don't we have that here?"

Mr. Edgar waves his hand at me, as if to say, *Just wait.* "Stay with me for another nineteen years, Dane. I will buy you a gold watch."

"Can't wait," I say.

It's so much work to maintain an appearance of nice and normal for other people. I go back to my glass cleaning, thinking about Mr. Edgar and his recycled jokes.

I like the time that I spend in Mr. Edgar's store. When I arrive at work I always feel like a weight has been lifted from my chest. As if, somehow, I'm safer within the familiar routines of my job and the predictable nature of Mr. Edgar.

It's dark out now, my shift almost over, when the bell on the front door announces the arrival of a customer. The bell is just another constant of my shift and I ignore it. Mr. Edgar is working the register and I'm restocking the drink coolers.

The new customer walks into the rear aisle where I am working and stops a foot away from me, as if waiting for me to get out of her way. I am unloading a hand truck full of boxes, so it is obviously going to be a while. But instead of saying "excuse me" or something, the person just stands there, impatiently patient, waiting for me to acknowledge my faux pas of working for a living.

It's only because I feel the weight of her impatience on me that I turn to look at the person standing behind me. And when I do, it almost takes my breath away.

Ophelia.

She is wearing a short skirt with a wraparound sweater

that creates a deep vee at the neck. Her shoes are high-heeled and extend the line of her legs to almost impossible lengths.

"Hey," I say when I realize I have been staring at her without saying anything for longer than is socially acceptable for a non-special-needs person. "You surprised me."

"I know. What are you doing tonight?"

"Working."

She sighs. A sigh that is so long and so dramatic, it's as if our conversation is the most disappointing thing that has ever happened to her. More disappointing even than her parents, or her first time having sex.

"I mean," she says slowly, "what are you doing after this?"

"Oh. Nothing, really. I was going to meet up with some friends."

"There's a party at Andrea Marcinkevicius's house. You know her?" Ophelia asks.

"Not really."

Everybody at McLean High School knows Andrea Marcinkevicius. Her last name is a complete disaster, but the end of it is pronounced like "itches," so that's what most people call her. Her friends use "Itches" as a term of endearment, while others use it as a witty reference to STIs, with varying degrees of hilarity. Most of us know Andrea in the same way that people know the Kardashians, which is to say I know what she looks like and who she has dated, but I don't really *know* her.

Andrea is, perhaps, the most popular girl in school—maybe

more feared than adored. Her parents are legendary for leaving her home alone while they travel for a week at a time.

"I'm not friends with her or anything," Ophelia says as her face scrunches into an adorable frown.

"If you don't like her, why are you going to her party?" I ask.

"I mean, it's not like I dislike her. It's just that she's . . . overconfident, I guess."

"Yeah." I nod in agreement. "Confident people are the worst."

"Anyway," she says, raising her voice to keep me from saying more, "it will be a good party. You should come."

"Maybe. I'm supposed to meet up with my boys. They don't go to McLean. They won't know anyone at the party."

"It doesn't matter if they know anyone," Ophelia says. "The place is going to be mobbed with people."

"I thought your dad had you on house arrest. How are you going to a party?"

"My dad has a thing tonight for work and he didn't want me to stay home alone. I told him I was going to a friend's house to hang out."

"He doesn't want you to stay home alone because he's afraid that you'll get murdered? Or that you'll have a guy over?"

"Oh, please," she says with a roll of her eyes. "I'm sure he'd rather I get murdered than have consensual sex with a guy my age."

I laugh because it's funny, but I feel my cheeks get hot at her mention of sex. Just watching the word on her lips is enough to give me a half hard-on.

"I told him I was hanging out at a friend's house. I just texted him to tell him I'm going over there to eat popcorn and watch a movie." As she says this she holds up the lighted display of her phone and wags it in the air. "I'm not entirely convinced my dad doesn't have some kind of tracking app on my phone, so I had to give him Andrea's address and say I was going over there."

"Your dad is preparing you for a life of crime."

"I'm texting you the address," Ophelia says, ignoring my comment.

"Who are you going with?" I ask.

"I'm going with Eric. He's the one who invited me."

"Eric?" I ask, incredulous. Dear God.

"Yeah, what's wrong with Eric? You practically live with the guy."

"What's wrong with Eric? Are you seriously asking that question? He lip-synced a One Direction song at the winter talent show." If I'm being honest, what's really wrong with Eric is that he's a better student, a better athlete, and an all-around more qualified boyfriend for Ophelia than I am. Except for the fact that he's evil.

It's my belief that any girl who has been with Eric would testify to regretting it.

I never thought of Ophelia as a girl who would fall for that trap, but I had seen plenty of smart girls become the victims of a guy like Eric. And I never could figure out why.

The fact that girls never fall for me is the most compelling evidence I can point to that I am one of the good guys.

I can't explain any of this to Ophelia. One, I'm not comfortable talking about sex with her. Or suggesting that she might have sex with Eric, just in case it gives her ideas. And two, if I try to tell her how evil Eric is, it will just make me sound like I'm jealous and pathetic—in other words, a little too close to the truth.

"So, what?" Ophelia asks. "So he has bad taste in music. It's not a federal offense."

"Yes. It is. It's really offensive."

"What are you getting so hot about? I'm just going to a party with him. He asked me and he offered to drive."

"Just because he offered you don't have to accept. He's evil."

"You're being dramatic. What do you have against Eric?"

"Ophelia, seriously. The guy is bad news. He goes out with a different girl almost every weekend. He's a . . ." "Predator" seems like a strong word. But it fits Eric and his MO. "Creep." Not strong enough. I wish that I had the courage to tell her the truth. Throw down my rag and bottle of cleaner and take her in my arms. Tell her Eric could never deserve her, and neither could I, but I want to try to be worthy. It's one of the impossible goals I've talked about with Dr. Lineberger—to be worthy of Ophelia. Or even just ask her to a movie or something.

"He's a . . . ? What?" she asks.

"You know what?" I say, frustrated now because there's no way to win with her. "Forget I said anything. If a guy like Eric is what you want, then I hope that's what you get."

"I never said I wanted Eric. I just said he's giving me a ride to a party. What are you getting so mad about?"

"I'm not mad."

"You are mad," she says, and sounds like she's enjoying herself. "If I didn't know any better, I'd say you were jealous."

"Well, you'd be wrong. It doesn't matter to me what you do. I'm just telling you that Eric's bad news. And if you think he's a good guy, well . . . then I just lost all respect for you."

"Oh yeah? Is that your thing? Respecting women?" Before I even have a chance to respond she waves her hand, dismissing any answer I might give. "So, I'll see you there?"

"Maybe."

She just shakes her head as she leaves me then and goes back to the front of the store, to the display of impulse items on a rack near the register. I move to the end of the aisle so I can watch her without being seen, behind an end cap of Cheetos and Doritos and flavored popcorn. While she studies the processed meats and nut mixes, I have time to study her the way I want.

She trails her fingers along the Slim Jims and packages of beef jerky as she seems to debate between teriyaki beef jerky and the supersize Slim Jims. The mental image of her lips closing delicately on a Slim Jim sends a shiver of excitement through my core, but then she dismisses the meat altogether and plucks up a bag of wasabi-flavored trail mix instead. In the world of snack food, I am a Slim Jim, and Ophelia is wasabi-flavored trail mix.

Ophelia texts me the address for Andrea's party but I don't respond to her message. And I have no intention of going. Instead I meet up with my friends and we take our skateboards down to the park near the pavilion. I'll hang out with my friends and drink a few beers and skate and think about a girl instead of being with one and it will be like a thousand other Friday nights.

It's dark but there's a couple of streetlights around the pavilion, just bright enough to kill your night vision if you try to go outside the puddle of light. My phone buzzes in my pocket with a text but I ignore it. It buzzes again with another text a couple of minutes later. Finally I take out my phone and the display is full of notifications, all of them meaningless. Except for one. Just Ophelia's name, in clear black letters outlined in its gray box, is enough to make my heart skip in my chest. Then I notice that there are seven messages from her in my inbox.

I've never sent more than two texts in a row to anyone without a response. At least not sober, I haven't. It just isn't done.

Where are you? 10:52 PM
Are you coming? 11:07 PM

I really need you to answer me 11:13 PM

I can't believe I'm such an idiot 11:15 PM

Why aren't you answering me?!?!?! 11:20 PM

Dane I really need you to come get me 11:30 PM

Please come 11:31 PM

If she's drunk, she must be an amazing typist.

I hold up my phone to show the guys.

"She's drunk," Joe says without hesitation.

"Maybe," I say. "You think I should answer her?"

"I guess," Joe says, "unless you think it's too late and she's already dead."

"Very funny," I say as I read the messages again. "She's not much of a drinker. She might be in trouble."

"Then let's posse up and go get her," Mark says.

Andrea's house is mobbed with people when my friends and I arrive. We split up to explore the house and look for Ophelia. Harry and Mark are obviously enjoying this as an adventure and not taking the whole situation very seriously.

I don't find her anywhere on the first floor. I don't see Eric, either, and I'm ready to assume that they have already left. I decide to take one more pass through the house to be sure.

On my second pass through the house I am distracted by the rising noise of a dozen people chanting outside. I step out though the sliding glass door onto the deck in time to see Harry do a keg stand. I'm irritated, though not really surprised, by Harry's antics, but then I notice Eric among the crowd on the deck. He is with a girl, but it's a girl way too small to be Ophelia. Eric's arm is draped heavily over her shoulders, but she doesn't seem to mind the weight on her neck.

"Where's Ophelia?" I ask him, ignoring our audience.

"Dane!" Eric says, as if he's thrilled to see me. "What are you doing here?"

"Ophelia," I say, ignoring his question. "She came with you to the party. Where is she?"

"You tell me, man," Eric says with a laugh. "She's probably locked herself in a bathroom somewhere."

"Is she drunk?"

"No," Eric says with a shake of his head. "I wouldn't say she was drunk." Then he laughs again and the sound of it is so irritating to me, but everyone else with him is laughing now, exchanging looks, like they're all in on a big joke. I just wait, saying nothing, and let him deliver his punch line. "I'd say she was wasted."

"You know, he sleeps with a different girl just about every weekend," I say to the girl on his arm.

"What's your deal, bro?" Eric asks, but I'm already walking away.

Joe and I run into each other in the first-floor hallway and I tell him that I found Eric but not Ophelia.

"You think she left? Caught an Uber home or something?"

"I don't know. I've texted and called her. No answer."

"Where are Mark and Harry?" Joe asks.

"Man, fucking Harry is outside doing a keg stand. Useless."

"Maybe we should check upstairs," Joe says. "Just to be sure."

"We're here," I say with a shrug.

We climb the stairs together and start trying doors. Most of the rooms are occupied with people engaged in acts we have been strictly warned against in health class.

At the end of the hall I open the door onto a bedroom. I shut the door after a look, seeing only what I think is a pile of coats on the bed. A half second after I shut the door my brain is still interpreting the image and I open the door again for a second look. The pile of coats is actually a girl. The girl.

Ophelia is curled on her side, one arm trailing over the edge of the bed. I walk over for a closer look and put a hand on her shoulder. "Ophelia," I say quietly, trying not to startle her.

"What?" she says, startling me. I thought she was passed out but she's just lying still with her eyes shut.

"Uh, I got your messages."

"My phone is dead. It's dead because I texted you so many times and you didn't respond."

She's still critical of me, which means she's somewhat lucid. That's a good sign, at least.

"My friends and I came to get you. Take you home. You want to go?"

"I can't," she says. "Everything is spinning." Joe and I

exchange a look in the atmosphere of sobriety we share above her.

"I know," I say, sympathizing. "You might feel better if you throw up."

"You think so?"

"Maybe."

She pushes herself with one arm into a sitting position, but her eyes are still shut.

"You okay?" I ask.

She doesn't say anything, only clamps her lips together to stop her chin from quivering. She is trying not to cry and she's doing a pretty good job. But even though she screws her face down like a watertight hatch, tears leak from her eyes and cut a trail down her face.

Joe and I do the only reasonable thing we can think of, which is to stand there and watch her cry.

"I guess that's a no," Joe says after an awkward eternity of Ophelia crying and us watching her helplessly. Joe nudges my arm, trying to force me into action.

Ophelia is such a strong person it's hard to watch her losing it. Like somebody telling you the sky is actually green when you're standing under a dome of brilliant blue.

"You'll be okay" is all I can think of to say. I'm really useless in a crisis situation.

She shakes her head, then seems to realize that is a terrible idea and puts the palm of her hand against her forehead.

"I'd say you've got less than a minute to find a toilet," Joe says.

Ophelia frowns at that but doesn't seem to have the energy to tell Joe to shut the fuck up.

"It's okay," I say. "We can go find a bathroom." I don't dare touch Ophelia, even to put a comforting hand on her shoulder. It seems to me that if I do touch her, one of us will shatter like glass.

She reaches out a hand and places it flat on my chest, and when she leans her weight into me, my heart rate accelerates to a gallop. Her fingers are cold, I can feel, even through my shirt.

Ophelia puts her hand in mine and I pull her to her feet. The way she sways and stumbles makes me revise my estimate of her state from drunk to shit-faced and I lead her with some difficulty back the way Joe and I have just recently come. We find the bathroom—sleek white tile and fluffy towels. It doesn't look like a room where people are meant to go for shitting and puking.

"I'm going to go find the guys," Joe says as he keeps going past the bathroom door down the hall. "I don't need to see what's coming next."

Once we are in the bathroom with the door shut, Ophelia sinks into a seat on the edge of the tub, which is big enough to hold a few people. I lean against the sink and watch her, unsure what to do next.

"You want to throw up?" I ask, as if I can help her with that.

"Maybe."

"You want me to leave you alone?"

She shakes her head as she squeezes her hands together, fingers interlaced, and bounces her forearms against the tops of her thighs. When she speaks again her voice ripples on the tears she's holding back. "I feel sick, Dane," she says. "Really sick."

"What were you drinking?"

"Uch. I don't know. I think somebody was mixing rum into something." Now that she has managed to string more than a few words together in a sentence her slurred words make her sound even more drunk. In anyone else I would have found it annoying, but in Ophelia it just makes me disappointed that the person I like isn't really there to talk to.

"You're a lightweight," I say. "You shouldn't be touching that stuff."

"I don't care." Then she bursts into tears so suddenly it makes me jump with alarm. One minute she's fine. Wasted, and a little upset, but fine. The next minute her face is a faucet of tears, snot, and saliva. "I'm so stupid," she says, which is not what I was expecting.

A crying girl terrifies me because I have no idea how to handle it. With guys, if your friend starts to cry, you're supposed to ignore it, pretend like it isn't happening until he can pull his shit together. With girls it's a different story. You're supposed to say and do the right thing, but nobody knows what that right thing is.

"Hey, no worries," I say, my voice soothing. I move toward her and sink into a crouch so that we are at eye level. "We've all been there. Shit, I can tell you all about the time I puked my brains out at a party."

"No thanks," she says, putting her hand to her mouth. She takes a minute to compose herself, then, as if she's put aside all thoughts of puking, she says, "I'm not talking about that. I'm talking about Eric. You were right. He's not a nice guy."

"I never said he wasn't a nice guy. I said he was evil."

"Well, you were right." The gushing faucet has slowed to more of a trickle. Even with her face swollen and her eyes puffy and red, she still looks amazing. I try not to notice.

"What did he do?" I ask.

My question turns the faucet back to gush and it takes another minute for her to compose herself. After an audible gulp she says, "I can't talk about it."

"Okay."

"He told me . . ." she says, I guess deciding she really can talk about it. "He said I was acting like a little kid. You know, that we know each other well enough and we're at a party having a good time. It's just what people do. He said I was being a bitch."

"Because you didn't want to sleep with him." It wasn't a question. I was just finishing her sentence for her. This is who Eric is. People don't see it because of the gilded veneer, but his insides are rotten.

"I'm such an idiot," she says again.

"You're not an idiot. Eric is the idiot. He's too stupid to even know why he should want you."

"Oh my God, that's not what I mean. I mean I was only going out with him to make you jealous, because you never pay any attention to me."

"What are you talking about? I'm always paying attention to you. We live right next door to each other."

She closes her eyes and shakes her head, and then seems to think better of it because it probably makes the spinning worse.

"I don't even like smoking. Most of the time I'm sneaking out just so I can get a chance to see you. And you've never once shown any interest in me."

She's drunk, so I'm not going to put a whole lot of faith into anything she says. Some people think that the way a person acts when they're drunk, that's like the real person, without filters. But I don't believe that.

"Eric asked me to the party and I said yes only because I thought I might get to see you here. But you didn't care. You didn't even show up. Why didn't you show up?"

"I didn't come to the party because I wasn't interested in seeing you with Eric," I say. She looks like she's getting ready to cry again and I want to stop the flow before it starts.

"Why don't you like me?" she asks with a sniffle.

"Of course I like you. You're the coolest girl I know," I say, figuring it's okay to be honest. Chances are good she isn't going to remember any of this conversation tomorrow morning. "You know, guys are terrified of you. Because you're smart, Ophelia. And you're funny. And . . . well, you're beautiful. That scares guys, too. And when guys are scared, they act like total idiots."

"That's really dumb."

"Yeah, well. It's dumb, but that's the way it is."

Ophelia's eyes are shut against the glare of the constipation-inducing white tile, and the aggressive fluffiness of the bath mats. And I'm glad her eyes are shut. Because that way she can't see in my expression what has to be obvious to anyone when they see me looking at her.

I am already in love with her. But in that moment, I love her in a way that can only be understood by the great lovers of history—Romeo, Cyrano, Heathcliff. This is the perfect moment to unleash all of the love for her that there is in my heart.

Which is why it's probably for the best, that in this exact moment, she vomits into my lap.

I am crouched in front of her, balanced on my heels. The force of her gag reflex makes her lurch forward as she vomits, so most of it goes onto me instead of onto the floor between us.

Her vomit is bright pink and chunky, but mostly liquid. It covers the legs of my pants and the pockets of my hoodie and I feel the warmth and wetness of it spreading through my crotch, as if I have peed myself.

The white bath mat is pink now and the chunks of her vomit cling to the bath mat fluff. There is so much vomit it's hard to believe that it has all come from inside one person. The ceiling is the only safe place to look because the sight of someone else's vomit always makes me want to vomit. Just the smell of it activates my gag reflex.

"Oh, God." Ophelia sounds almost hysterical. "Why is it red? Is that blood? Am I bleeding inside?"

"I don't think so." My voice is tight from my gag reflex. "It smells like fruit punch."

"Oh, God," she says again. And then she starts to sob.

"Don't cry," I say. I pat her gently on the back and I notice a bit of the pink vomit on the heel of my hand. I wipe it on the shower curtain as my esophagus lurches again.

She stops crying then but not because I told her to. She sways in her seat, her eyes closed, then slides down the side of the tub into the vomit-soaked bath mat, groans once, and goes still.

"Shit." I crouch down again and put a hand in front of her mouth to make sure she is breathing and after a few seconds of carefully watching, I can see her chest rising and falling in a sleeping rhythm.

I clean my clothes as best I can without taking them off, shaking the front of my hoodie over the pedestal sink and flinging pink chunks everywhere. At first I just smell the fruit punch and think maybe girl vomit doesn't stink the way a guy's vomit does. But now that it has soaked into my clothes completely, it smells like regular vomit.

Joe knocks on the door and calls out to me as I am scrubbing the white hand towel against the crotch of my jeans.

When I let him in he looks around and lets out a whistle. "It looks like somebody murdered a Care Bear in here."

"Dude, I'm covered in it."

"She still alive?" he asks as he gestures toward Ophelia's crumpled frame. She looks taller than five feet eight lying there on the bathroom floor. I have no idea what she weighs but I know it is more than I can carry.

"I think she might have fainted at the sight of her own vomit."

Just then Eric shows up in the doorway and peers over Joe's shoulder. "Holy shit," he says, and laughs.

"It's not funny, fuck nut," I say, glowering at him in the mirror. "What the hell did you give her?"

"Nothing, bro."

"I'm not your bro. Her curfew was probably hours ago. When were you supposed to take her home?"

"How the fuck should I know?" Eric asks with an impatient frown. "What the hell is a curfew?"

"How the hell are we supposed to get her home?" I ask, though why I'm asking Eric, I have no idea.

"What do you mean?" Eric asks with an incredulous frown. "Take her home? Just let her sleep it off. She'll be okay in a few hours."

"You want us to leave her lying on a bathroom floor in a puddle of her own vomit for a few hours?" Joe asks. "Is that your plan?"

"She'll be fine," Eric says. "She'd probably rather hang

out in her own vomit than face her dad right now. He's a fucking nightmare."

"No shit," I say.

"Just get her a blanket or something," Eric says, gesturing over his shoulder with his thumb.

"Dude, stop helping," Joe says. "You're fucking useless."

"She looks hilarious," Eric says as he pulls his phone out of his pocket and holds it up to take a picture of Ophelia, passed out on the bathroom floor. Without thinking, I slap Eric's hand and his phone clatters into the sink.

"What the hell?" Eric shouts at me.

"You're not taking a picture of her," I say as I take a menacing step toward him.

"Oh, what are you going to do?" Eric asks. He picks up his phone but instead of trying to take a picture again he just puts the phone back into his pocket.

I am so angry right then that I am almost able to forget that I have never been in a fight before. Not one where I threw any actual punches, anyway. I have never hit another person in the face. But Joe, who has been in plenty of fights to compensate for his size, steps between us and pushes Eric out the door.

Once Eric is out Joe pushes in the lock and leans his weight against the door. Eric hits the door once with his fist, but then we hear him move away down the hall.

Joe and I both look at Ophelia, unconscious on the bathroom floor, as we consider our next move. Only Eric would leave a person to fend for themselves in Ophelia's condition, but there is no way we can carry her to the car without damaging her body or her dignity, so we take turns patting her cheeks and calling her name until she is conscious again. Now she is awake, but there is still no way she is going to execute a clean entrance at home.

I run a washcloth under warm water and clean her up as best I can, wiping her face and hands. "You'll be okay," I say, maybe trying to reassure both of us.

Joe and Harry help me get Ophelia to the Mercedes and I am grateful that they are the kind of friends who don't complain about helping her even though it means touching her puke. I drop the guys off at Joe's house.

On the drive home I keep looking at Ophelia in the passenger seat, wishing I could make conversation, but she is completely out of it.

I park the Mercedes on the street at the end of the driveway and switch off the engine. Ophelia is snoring softly but at least she seems to just be sleeping instead of in a coma.

"Shit," I say to myself, and wish Joe was still with me.

Getting Ophelia up the length of the driveway is, as predicted, a nightmare. She keeps stopping and sinking down to the ground, as if she wants to curl up and sleep in the mulched beds.

"Please walk," I keep saying, begging her. "It's bad enough that your dad has probably heard us and has my head in a rifle scope right now."

"I'm cool," she keeps saying, in that way that drunk people do when they are anything but cool.

When we finally reach the front porch I still haven't decided what to do. I debate whether I should just put her on the porch swing, ring the doorbell, and run, or if I should ring the doorbell, wait for her dad, and pretend like I just found her at the end of the driveway.

Either way, truth or not, I am the hero of this story. Though maybe that isn't the way Ophelia's dad will see it.

In the end I am denied the choice. Just as we reach the porch, the front door flies open and Colonel Marcus stands in the open doorway in a blue velour bathrobe and white athletic socks. I am grateful to not be staring down the barrel of a rifle, but even in a robe and socks, Colonel Marcus is a terrifying figure. He's four inches taller and can probably bench press my body weight.

"You have exactly three seconds to explain what the hell is going on here," Colonel Marcus says.

"Uh . . ." Three seconds. I can't decide what is the most important point to make if I only have three seconds. "I just found her and brought her home," I say quickly.

"Hi, Dad," Ophelia says. So useless. And her drunk speak makes Colonel Marcus even angrier. He's staring at her arm, which is draped around my neck.

"Ophelia," he says, "get yourself up to your room. I'll be up there to talk to you in a minute."

"Dad, listen, it's not Dane's fault," Ophelia says. "Don't be mad at him, okay?"

"What are you still doing here?" he asks her, and the way he says it, a chill slithers from my scalp to my scrotum, and I feel suddenly like I have to pee. "I said"—his voice slows to a crawl, each letter its own syllable—"get up to your room."

Ophelia shoves off me in her first effort to stand under her own power and tries to walk through the doorway past her dad, but she is still so drunk that she bounces like a pinball off of him and the doorframe and then the table just inside the front door. Colonel Marcus and I both watch, I in horror, he in anger, as she staggers her way to the stairs and hangs onto the bannister like a life preserver. Her skirt is so short that it rides up in the back as she's climbing the stairs, and her underwear is practically visible. Colonel Marcus's head snaps around as he looks at me to see if I'm noticing Ophelia's short skirt. It's like a scene from a horror movie, and he's just discovered that I am the killer.

"If I find out you were up to any funny business, I'll be calling the police," Colonel Marcus says. "At the very least I'll be speaking to your mom tomorrow."

"Honestly, sir," I say quickly, "I just picked her up from a party and she was really drunk so I brought her home, to make sure nothing happened to her."

Colonel Marcus's eyes narrow to slits and he leans minutely, almost imperceptibly, toward me. "Boy, how stupid do you think I am?"

"I don't! I mean, not stupid at all. I'm telling you. I wasn't even at this party and—"

"What the hell is that smell?" he asks, ignoring my story, which isn't shaping up to make a whole lot of sense anyway.

"It's vomit, sir."

"Your vomit?"

"No, sir. I haven't been drinking. Honestly. It's . . . uh . . . it's Ophelia's vomit. She threw up on me."

"If I catch you around my daughter again, I will kill you. I will kill you and they will need your dental records to identify the body. You get me?"

"I totally get you, sir." I have more to say but he slams the door in my face before I can get the second syllable of "totally" out of my mouth.

Mom hardly ever ventures upstairs in our house, so when she knocks on my bedroom door the next morning, I know immediately that Colonel Marcus has followed through on his threat/promise to visit. The look on Mom's face isn't as angry as I'd expect it to be and when we get downstairs I am surprised to find both Colonel Marcus and Ophelia in the kitchen. Ophelia sits at the island counter in one of the tall stools. Her eyes are red and watery and a large bottle of Gatorade, half empty, sits on the counter in front of her. Her hair, still damp from a shower, is knotted haphazardly at the base of her neck. Even from six paces, I can smell the alcohol, rising with the heat from her pores. The fact that she is still beautiful in her hungover state is at once shocking and evidence that I will never be cured of loving her.

By contrast, you wouldn't know that Colonel Marcus was awake at 1:00 A.M. to look at him. His shoes are polished, his collar starched, and his judgment of me is cool as ice.

"Hey, Dane," Ophelia says.

"Uh . . . hi." I glance at Colonel Marcus to make sure I'm not violating some protocol.

"I explained to my dad about what happened last night," Ophelia says as she spins the tall stool to angle her body in my direction. "That I drank at that party and called you to come and get me."

"Oh?" It comes out sounding like a question, but I hope no one else notices that fact.

I keep my gaze locked on Ophelia's face, afraid that if I exchange a look with Mom or Colonel Marcus, they will plainly read the fear on my face and misinterpret it as a lie. "I just wanted to apologize for getting you mixed up in the whole mess," Ophelia says.

"It's cool," I say.

"Dane, where were you last night?" Mom asks. Her tone is hard, but Mom doesn't scare me. It's not as if I can be any more of a disappointment to her than I already am.

"Well, I was at work," I say, easing into it, "then I was just hanging out with the guys. We were skating in the park when Ophelia texted me."

"Do you still have the text in your phone?" Colonel Marcus asks.

"Do you have a warrant?" I speak without thinking, forgetting to be afraid.

Ophelia is still facing me so I am the only one who sees her eyes widen and a smile lift the corners of her mouth.

"I apologize for my son," Mom says to Colonel Marcus. "He has this idea that he's hilarious."

Mom is acting pretty cool right now, but as soon as Colonel Marcus and Ophelia are gone, I expect her to start threatening me with the usual punishments—take away phone privileges, or take the keys to the Mercedes.

Whatever. It's only a few weeks until graduation and my eighteenth birthday, and I already have a limited interest in being alive. I'm untouchable.

"Yeah," Colonel Marcus says. "I can see that."

"Dane didn't do anything," Ophelia says, "except help me out. He got me home safely." Ophelia is speaking to Mom and her dad, but she is looking at me as she says it. A warmth spreads from my toes all the way to my scalp. An inside warmth. The kind of warmth I only feel around Ophelia.

"Are you sure she didn't ride with you to that party?" Colonel Marcus asks me.

"Positive," I say, deciding then that if I'm going down, I'm taking Eric with me. "She went with Eric, but he wanted to leave her there to sleep it off."

Ophelia's eyes close as Chuck and Mom start to splutter.

"What are you talking about?" Chuck asks as Colonel Marcus turns his surprised anger in Chuck's direction.

"Eric was there," I say, and then I suggest helpfully, "you should ask him what happened. He drove Ophelia to the party. He left her there, so I brought her home."

"That doesn't sound like Eric," Chuck says weakly as we are all thinking the same thing—that it sounds exactly like Eric.

Mom's expression is apologetic. She knows what it's like to have a kid who is a disappointment.

"Well, I'm glad Ophelia got home safely," Mom says. "It sounds like all's well that ends well."

Colonel Marcus is clearly not appeased by Mom or her bank-teller smile.

"Do you know where your son was last night?" he asks Chuck.

"Well . . . no," Chuck says, and I enjoy watching him squirm under Colonel Marcus's accusing stare. Colonel Marcus can definitely take Chuck in a fight, and I would pay money to see it. "Eric lives with his mother. He only stays here occasionally."

"It sounds like you should keep better tabs on him," Colonel Marcus says. I'm really enjoying the scene now that the focus has shifted away from me and it's Eric and Chuck who are the bad guys.

"Eric has always been something of a . . . free spirit," Chuck says. If Eric was poor, he'd be a juvenile delinquent. Rich, he's a free spirit.

"Well," Colonel Marcus says, "Ophelia can't be hanging around people who are attending parties where there is alcohol. I appreciate that Dane brought her home. At the very least he had the courage to do the right thing, which it sounds like this Eric hasn't been raised to do."

"Now, wait a minute. . . ." Chuck says, but Colonel Marcus is taking Ophelia's arm and tugging her off the kitchen stool.

Thanks a lot, Ophelia mouths in my direction.

"Ophelia, you will be grounded until graduation," Colonel Marcus says.

"That's not fair!" Ophelia says, raising her voice for the first time. "Prom is in two weeks. And the senior class trip."

"I guess you should have thought of that before you decided to go out drinking."

"Sir," I say, "last night was a fluke. Everybody at school knows Ophelia is a total nerd. She's a really good student. Grounding her until graduation seems harsh."

"And I'll be taking away her phone," Colonel Marcus says, as if I haven't said a word, "so you don't have to worry about any more midnight calls from her in a drunken state. You don't have to worry about any calls or messages . . . at all." His last words are weighted for Ophelia's benefit as he keeps his hand on her arm and pulls her to the door.

Mom and Chuck are both staring at me as we listen to the front door shut firmly. "What?" I ask. "For once, I'm not the bad guy. I only did what was right." I exit before they can say another word.

When I get home from work that evening Eric's car is in the driveway and lights are burning in every window of the house.

"Shit," I say out loud to myself on a sigh and rest my forehead against the steering wheel. I want to leave. I want to have someplace to go that is mine and where no one can bother me. As I make my way up the front walk all I can think about is leaving. Just get back in the Mercedes and drive. Somewhere. I have contemplated running away as many times as I've contemplated killing myself. And, as with death, my main worry is that there's really no place to go.

From just inside the front door I can hear raised voices coming from the kitchen. Eric's voice is the loudest but Chuck's voice is unnaturally deep as he tries to command the conversation.

When I walk into the kitchen they both go silent and turn to look at me. Eric's eyes burn with hatred, but Chuck just looks tired.

"What the hell?" Eric says, glowering at me. "Goddamn crybaby tattletale."

"What are you? Five?" I ask.

"What did you tell people that I did?" Eric asks.

"Eric," Chuck says, "that's enough."

"I told them the truth," I say, ignoring Chuck. "I told Ophelia's dad you drove her to the party. I showed up later to clean up your mess."

"Like you're some kind of saint," Eric says. "You drink, get high, hang out with your ghetto friends."

"Get out of my house," I say quietly, but it's a dangerous kind of quiet. I can feel the anger building, like the coyote's funeral pyre. The anger is there and it's ready to burn out of control.

"Dane, it's okay," Chuck says, dismissing me, as if I am nothing. To Eric he says, "Do you deny that you took that girl to that party? Deny that you were going to leave her there when she was drunk and insensible and couldn't take care of herself?"

"It's not okay," I say, but my voice is still quiet and they don't even hear me. They just keep arguing and aren't really paying attention to me. I'm a ghost in my own house.

"I gave her a ride," Eric says. "So what? I barely even know her. It's not like she was my responsibility."

"Get out of my house," I say again, testing my voice at a new volume. Not quite a shout, but louder and deeper than it usually sounds.

They are still arguing, their voices raised with their meaningless irritation.

"Get *out!*" There. I am shouting now and they both turn to look at me, their faces masks of surprise. Everyone is accustomed to the Dane who mopes through life. The Dane who is pathetic and sad and hopeless. But I can't stand another moment of them, treading on my life, my privacy, my sanity.

"Get out of my house! This is my house. My dad's house. It's not your fucking house! If you want to scream at each other, do it someplace else."

Mom comes running out of the first-floor bedroom at the sound of my voice.

"Dane, I'm sorry," Chuck says. "You're right. I'm sorry." He looks as if he's ready to cry, an antelope caught between a lion and a hyena.

"Dane," Mom says, coming to put her hands on my arms,

as if to keep me from flying into a million pieces. "That's enough, Dane. Stop shouting."

"You're nothing to me," I say, spittle shooting onto my lower lip as I scream at Chuck and Eric, even as Mom holds my arms. "Both of you. Do you hear me? You're nothing. Get the fuck out!"

"Please calm down," Chuck says. He's holding his hands up as if to ward off a blow.

"Out!" The single syllable stretches to eternity as I squeeze my eyes shut and I can feel the scream travel through every molecule of my body.

I am surprised to find that after that scream, I feel better. From the looks on everyone else's faces, they feel worse. But I feel better.

Chuck leaves the room without another word but he is back in a moment with his laptop bag and another larger bag.

"You don't have to leave," Mom is saying to Chuck, but he puts a hand on her arm and speaks quietly to her, reassuring her.

Then Chuck is turning to Eric and gestures for him to follow. "You're leaving your car here," Chuck says to Eric. "Let's go."

"I need my car," Eric says. "I have school tomorrow."

"It's my car," Chuck says. "I make the payments. You can have it back next week. Maybe." Then Chuck turns to me and says, "I'm sorry."

I only nod in response and am careful not to look at Eric again.

When they are gone I breathe a long, slow sigh of relief.

"Chuck is on your side, Dane," Mom says.

"There's no sides to this, Mom. This is still my house, isn't it?"

Mom sighs and goes back to her room, shutting the door quietly behind her.

Monday morning I am awake early and waiting outside when I hear Colonel Marcus and Ophelia come out of the house. Their voices are raised in anger and I am straining to hear.

"I will drop you at school," Colonel Marcus is saying. "No more riding with your friends."

"I'd rather walk," Ophelia says.

"Suit yourself," Colonel Marcus says, then throws a bag into the back seat of his car and climbs in.

I wait, figuring she's lying to her dad, because that's exactly what I would do, and any minute one of her friends will pull around the curve in the road to come and get her.

There isn't a car in sight once Colonel Marcus is gone. I watch as Ophelia starts down the driveway, her head held low, her shoulders bent under the weight of her backpack. That's some serious stubbornness, choosing to walk instead of riding with her dad. School must be at least a couple of miles away.

After a few minutes, I get in my car and drive the same way, catching up with her about a quarter mile from our houses.

I'm guessing I'll have to take a little bit of hell from her for what I told her dad about Eric. I'm not sure what she remembers about our conversation when she was drunk. There's no way I'm going to be the one to mention it, but maybe she will.

"You want a ride?" I call to her from the car window.

She keeps walking so I have to coast along beside her at three miles per hour. She's mad, I can tell, and won't even acknowledge me.

"You should have kept your mouth shut about Eric," she says after about a tenth of a mile of silence.

"Why?" I ask, testing out my newfound bravado on her. I might have been screaming at Chuck and Eric fewer than twelve hours ago, but with Ophelia I am less certain. "Eric didn't give a shit about you when you were passed out on the bathroom floor Saturday night. He wanted to leave you there."

"No shit. As if the whole thing isn't humiliating enough, you have to rub it in by telling everyone. Make me look like an idiot."

"I'm sorry," I say, and I'm not sorry at all. "You were going to get grounded either way. Getting Eric in trouble was just a bonus."

She stops suddenly and turns to look at me through the

half-open window. "Is that why you told them? Because you wanted to get Eric in trouble?"

I put the car into park and sit there for a minute, thinking. I want to tell her the truth. I just lack the courage. But maybe the truth is the only thing that will make her not angry with me.

"I told them because I figured it was the best way to guarantee you never see Eric again. If he comes within fifty yards of your house now, your dad will shoot him. He's a total loser and he doesn't deserve you."

She nods at that, just once. And I can feel her forgiving me by degrees. The fact that I admitted I wanted to keep Eric away from her is enough to make her happy. For now.

I wait, patiently, for her to finish thinking it through.

"My dad will kill me if he sees me talking to you," she says, looking up and down the street for signs of anyone.

"No, he won't. He must have already paid the deposit on your tuition for next year. I'm pretty sure it's nonrefundable if you kill your kid."

"I don't think he'll care at this point."

Finally, she concedes and reaches for the door handle. I wait while she gets herself settled, putting her books on the floor and buckling her seat belt.

Ophelia and I don't say much on the ride to school, partly because I've got the music turned up.

"You listen to the Smiths a lot," Ophelia says.

"I identify with Morrissey's existential angst."

"I'm sure you do."

"What's wrong with The Smiths?"

"Morrissey is a racist."

"He is?" I ask, genuinely surprised.

"Yes."

"Damn. First plastic straws, now Morrissey," I say as I reach for my phone and switch to another playlist.

"All of our heroes die in the light," Ophelia says to the window.

We're in the parking lot at school now and I cut the engine but neither one of us makes a move to get out of the car. The first bell hasn't rung yet and there are plenty of people still milling around in the student parking lot.

"I've never skipped school before," Ophelia says suddenly, like she's blurting a confession.

"Seriously?" I ask.

"Nah. I actually like school."

"Weird."

"I like school, but I kind of can't wait for the whole thing to be over. I can't wait to have the freedom to do what I want, when I want."

"And what do you want to do, Ophelia?" I ask her. We're still just sitting. She hasn't even unbuckled her seat belt.

"Right now? Or with the rest of my life?"

"Pretend like right now *is* the rest of your life. One day left on earth. What do you do with it?"

"Dane, are you asking me to spend my last day on earth with you?" she asks me with just the hint of a smile.

"Sure. Yeah. I guess that's what I'm asking you."

"Well, if you put it that way . . ."

As it turns out, Ophelia and I aren't very creative about how we would use our last hours on earth. First, we hit the Starbucks drive-through for provisions. It's not as if I would plan my last day on earth that way if I had any advance warning, but not everybody gets the luxury to plan their last day.

"The school is probably going to call my dad," Ophelia says around a mouthful of muffin as I drive away from the Starbucks.

"I doubt it," I say. I'm driving aimlessly, heading away from McLean, wondering how far we can get and if never coming back is a viable option.

"I suppose it's not as if I can get in any more trouble than I am already."

"Exactly," I say. "So what are you worried about?"

She doesn't even hesitate before she says, "Having a psychotic break during my freshman year at college. I worry about that."

"Wow," I say. "That's a really specific worry."

"It's not my only worry. Maybe just the most likely."

"Why do you say that?" As the Mercedes glides to a stop at a red light I take the opportunity to turn and look at her. Really look at her. And maybe see something other than the fact that she's pretty and fierce.

She shakes her head. "I'm already stressed out about the

school calling my dad, and me getting in even more trouble than I already am. I don't want to talk about it right now."

"Fair enough. You want a Klonopin?" I ask. "Take the edge off a little?"

"No, thanks," she says, and then, with a wry glance in my direction, "My family isn't rich. We actually have to feel things."

"Whatever. You live in McLean."

"My dad only has that house because he knows the owners. They're stationed overseas for a few years so they agreed to rent it to us cheaply. My dad wanted to live in McLean because the schools are good."

"Well, either way, you aren't exactly living in poverty."

"We used to, my mom and me," Ophelia says. Her face clouds with a thought outside of our conversation.

"It makes sense that you grew up without money," I say, "why you seem so normal."

"I guess. Whatever normal is."

"Were you happier living with your mom?" I ask, wondering if maybe my family would be happier if we had less money.

"I'm not sure," she says, seriously considering my question. "My mom can be great. Really great. But she can also be really terrible." There's more there, under the surface, that she isn't saying, but I don't push her.

We're approaching a light when it turns yellow and I decide not to risk getting pulled over. I brake suddenly and put my hand out instinctively to stop her from pitching forward in her seat.

Ophelia looks at me, looks at my hand on her arm. "Thanks," she says.

"*De nada,*" I say, keeping my hand on her arm longer than is probably necessary but it doesn't seem to make her uncomfortable. "Anyway, you're practically eighteen. You'll be on your own soon. Gone."

"Gone," she says with almost a sigh, like the idea really appeals to her. "Mentally I'm already gone from my dad's house. Have been for a while."

I pull onto the George Washington Parkway, a road that's fun to drive because of the curves, both sides of the road flanked by thick forest. We ride in silence as I take the bridge into DC and then loop back along the tidal basin to pick up the parkway headed back the way we came. The tidal basin is surrounded by hundreds of cherry trees that explode into pink clouds every year. Even though it's only late spring, the cherry blossoms have already come and gone. The blooms last only a few weeks, which is supposed to be like a metaphor for life—enjoy the little pleasures while you can, because life is going to suck and then be over. It probably sounds better in haiku.

I pull off the parkway into Fort Marcy park. I've come to this park dozens of times and never run into any other people here. Only occasionally do I see another car in the parking lot.

"I've never been here," Ophelia says as I pop the trunk to the Mercedes and take out Chuck's golf clubs.

"Yeah? I come here sometimes when I want to be alone. Which is often, I guess."

"What are the golf clubs for?" she asks.

"Practice."

"I didn't know you golfed."

"I don't, usually. My dad liked to play."

The park is an old Civil War fort, which you'd never know by looking at it. There's an open green space and a steep hill that climbs to a bluff overlooking the Potomac River. Ophelia walks beside me as we follow the trail up to the open green space above the parking lot. At the top of the hill we leave the trees behind and here the landscape is shaped like a large bowl, with grass and a few picnic tables and, on top of the hill, a single cannon, a reproduction of the cannons that would have lined the top of the hill during the Civil War. We walk down, then up to the other side of the grass bowl, to the ridge that overlooks the river.

We stand silently watching the river, slow and wide at this point. "There was a famous guy, he was a politician or something—he killed himself here," I tell her. Today the sun is shining and it's warm away from the shade. It's easier to forget you are sad when the weather is good. When you live through winter in sadness, it's easy to imagine spring will never arrive. But somehow it does, and even if you are sad, you have to notice the earth warming and the birds singing and the flowers blooming. "I always wonder where he did it," I say, looking around.

"Stop it," Ophelia says, and her shoulders shake, as if she's caught a chill.

"It was a long time ago. Like, in the nineties. The articles about it don't say how he did it. But I always wonder, you know, if this, or that," I say as I point first where I'm standing, then over by the tree line, "is where he died."

Chuck's golf bag will balance upright on a kickstand. I set it on a flat patch of turf, then take out two clubs, one for me, one for Ophelia.

I put a tee from the bag into the turf, then balance a ball on the head of it and hand Ophelia a club. I nod at the golf ball but she takes a step back and says, "You first."

My swing catches some of the turf but the ball sails high and away and we both watch it disappear into the river. Then I lift the golf club high over my head, in a two-handed grip, and bring it down hard against packed earth and jagged rocks. The head of the golf club breaks off and skitters across the ground for a few feet before falling off the edge of the overlook. I drop the shaft of the club on the ground and reset the tee and a new ball for Ophelia.

"Whoa," she says under her breath. "Okay."

"Sometimes I like to break shit when I'm mad," I say.

"Whose clubs are these?"

"Chuck's."

"Oh. You mad at him? Because he's with your mom?"

"I'm mad because it was so easy for everybody to forget

my dad. I'm mad because I'm the only thing left to remind people that he ever existed. And I'm utterly forgettable."

"You're not forgettable, Dane," she says, and her voice is as soothing as a fuzzy blanket. "I'm sure there are people who think about you all the time."

"Like who?" I ask.

She sighs, impatient with me, which is our natural state together. "Girls at school, I guess."

"What are you talking about?" I ask. "I'm not good-looking. I'm terrible at sports, except for skateboarding, I guess."

"Girls like you. Because you are good-looking. And mysterious. And sad."

"Like Morrissey?" I ask, trying to make a joke.

"Morrissey is old enough to be my dad. My grandad," she says after a moment's consideration.

"Some people are into that."

"Gross. Anyway, a lot of girls at school have asked me about you."

"What girls?" I ask.

"What do you care?" she asks, and she sounds irritated.

"I'm just curious. Anyway, it doesn't matter. Like you said, you can never be in a relationship because you don't know how. That's me, too. I'm pretty sure something's seriously wrong with me. I go to therapy, take meds."

"I think you're just sad. But not in a bad way," she's quick to add. "Believe me, I've lived with crazy. My mom is a nutjob. There's nothing wrong with you."

In the two years I have lived next door to Ophelia and her dad, she's never given her mom more than a passing mention. I'm curious about Ophelia's family, mostly because it's always comforting to hear about a family that is more screwed up than your own.

She works her hands around the grip of the club as she settles back into a golfer's stance. I watch in silence, appreciating the curve of her hip, the length of her leg, as she shifts her weight into position.

Her swing is better than mine, catching only the ball with a resounding *thwack*. The ball sails like a rocket and is out of sight, flying too far for us to even see it land in the river.

Instead of hitting the club on the rocky ground, she swings it hard against the trunk of a tree. The shaft bends at an alarming angle, but does not break in half.

She laughs as she brushes the hair back from her face, then tosses the twisted golf club aside and resets the tee with another ball.

The snick of a new club being drawn from the bag. *Thwack,* as another ball sails high. Then a gust of breath as I put all of my strength into swinging the third club against another tree. Ophelia ducks instinctively as the club head breaks free and spins across the clearing.

I watch her silently as she takes out another club and sets up to tee off.

"Is your mom white?" I ask.

The look Ophelia gives me is hard to read, but I get the

sense I have, once again, met her expectations, and they weren't that high. "Yes," she says. "My mother is white."

"I didn't mean to offend you."

"You didn't. It's just that the color of my parents is more important to other people than it is to me."

"Where is she?" I ask. "I mean, why isn't she around? You're a great kid. You work hard in school. You do sports and sing and do the school play. If I was like you, my mom would think I was the greatest."

"She lives in Ohio with her parents. She went back home after her most recent failed marriage." She pauses then, and the weight of her feelings fills the silence before she speaks again. "She was in the hospital for a while."

"Yeah? What's wrong with her?"

"She's crazy," Ophelia says. Just a statement, without emotion. I wonder how many times she practiced saying that before it came out so easily.

"Like, legit crazy?" I ask.

"Define 'legitimately crazy.'"

"I don't know. There's depressed, and mixed up, and then there's crazy," I say as I use my hand to chop out the lines along the sad to deranged spectrum. "Does she hear voices? Does she wear a tinfoil hat?"

"Maybe. To both. I haven't seen her in a while. Her official diagnosis is bipolar. But not the celebrity kind. She doesn't like to take her medication. When she's up, she meets a guy, falls in love, sometimes she ends up married.

When she's down, she's usually in the hospital or staying with my grandparents."

"Your dad seems like a pretty stable guy," I say, though thinking his universal soldier persona is maybe a little less than stable.

"He is, I guess. Other than the fact that he was once married to my mom. They were only married for a couple of years. He won't say it, but I think they just got married because my mom was pregnant with me."

"She was already pregnant when they got married?"

"Yes. He's never told me that, either, but I figured it out when I was old enough to do basic arithmetic." Her smile is kind of quirky as she says this, and I feel sorry for her. I know she probably feels like there was a time when she was unwanted. Maybe she still does.

"Anyway," she says, shrugging it off, the way people learn to do, "I used to live with my mom, but my dad sued for custody after she left me home alone one weekend to go to the beach with her girlfriends."

"How old were you?" I ask, fascinated now by her story. Even if my mom is a morally bankrupt adulteress, she would never have left me home alone when I was little.

"I was eight," Ophelia says.

"Seriously? She left you alone for a weekend when you were eight?"

"I was fine," she says with a dismissive wave of her hand, though somewhere inside there must be an eight-year-old who still can't quite believe it. As if to make it all seem socially acceptable, and failing to, she adds, "I was doing all the cooking and cleaning by then, anyway."

"So, what happened?" I ask, now able to picture it in my mind—eight-year-old Ophelia, home alone eating microwave mac and cheese, when the phone rings and it's the Colonel, wanting to know how she's doing. "Your dad called the house and found out you were there alone?"

"Basically. So, he sued for custody, saying my mom was unfit. The judge agreed, obviously, and I've lived with my dad ever since. We move every couple of years, but he said we'd stay here long enough for me to finish high school. I didn't want to start at a new school senior year."

"Like me," I said.

"Right," she says with a sympathetic nod. "I forgot."

"I don't really care. I mean, I don't have any friends at school, and I'm not a great student, and I don't do any sports or anything—" I stop, realizing I sound like I really do care.

"When you said that earlier, about your mom and her boyfriend wanting to forget about you because you are the only reminder that your dad ever existed, I feel that way about my mom. My dad pretends like she doesn't exist. And I feel like if I talk about her, I'm just reminding him that half of me is her."

"Yes. That," I say, and that's all I have to say. Ophelia gets it.

"We should go visit him," Ophelia says.

"Who?"

"Your dad. You ever go see him? At his grave?"

"Never."

"Well, maybe you should."

We sit in the grass, which from a distance looks lush and thick and perfect, like a carpet, but up close is crawling with life and dotted with clover and twigs and other elements of non-perfection.

We sit through a long period of silence. People always talk about awkward silences, when we are thinking the things that we aren't supposed to say out loud. It isn't that kind of silence. It's the kind when you have something to say, but you can't decide what it is. Or you haven't figured out how best to say it yet.

"Some cemeteries are really nice places," Ophelia says, the first to break the silence. "You know? This place is kind of beautiful, if you don't think about it too much."

We spend a few minutes looking around, taking in the scenery. Ophelia's right. The cemetery where my dad is buried is quiet, and peaceful, and there are lots of trees and birds chirping and flowers everywhere.

"I was thinking, some dead people live in a nicer place than a lot of living people." She's been leaning back on her hands, but now she sits up and dusts her hands together, then tucks her legs under her skirt and starts picking idly at the tips of the grass.

"Most living people aren't really happy about being

alive," I counter. "And you'll never know if being dead is worse, until you get there."

"I don't think about it that way," Ophelia says. "I think about death as just another stage of life. Maybe our consciousness leaves our bodies and travels someplace new and exciting."

"Like Mars?"

"Like heaven," Ophelia says, brushing off my Mars comment.

"If I tell you something crazy," I say, "you promise not to laugh?"

"I promise not to laugh . . . out loud."

"You know that coyote that lives in our neighborhood? The one that was howling that night, when we were sitting on the porch?"

"I've never heard it."

"Well, I didn't just hear it. I saw it a few times. And then a couple of weeks ago, I found it, dead, by the side of the road."

"That's sad. But what's so crazy about that?"

"Not that. It was about the coyote when it was alive. I guess I kind of got this idea . . . You know, the coyote showed up right after my dad died."

"Uh-huh."

"And so I was thinking, you know, what if the coyote was, like, my dad. Reincarnated."

"So, you think that your dad died," Ophelia says, speaking

so slowly it's like she's trying to stall for sanity to intervene, "and came back as a coyote?"

As we sit there talking, it's as if I can see myself standing on the edge of a cliff. I can stay on the cliff, safe, and keep the truth about the coyote and the coyote funeral pyre and everything that is crazy and wrong about me on the inside. Or I can step off the cliff, tell Ophelia the truth, and watch her quickly slip away from my grasp as I fall. Once you show someone who you are, there is no coming back from it. I don't have the courage to step off the cliff, so I retreat to the firm footing of just talking bullshit.

"I don't know. It just got me thinking. There are so many squirrels in our neighborhood. And my dad hated squirrels. If he was going to come back as an animal, it would definitely be something that ate squirrels. If he came back as a squirrel, that would be like his own personal version of hell. And if you really think about it, with so many people on the planet, if reincarnation is real, then most people would have to be something lame, like a squirrel. Sometimes I'm talking to people at a party, or I'm watching them at school, and all I can think is . . . fucking squirrels. You know?"

"I get it," Ophelia says, taking the little bit of crazy I share with her in stride. "It's comforting to think your dad would be a coyote. Like his life had some meaning."

"I guess."

"I think people misinterpret the idea of reincarnation. I suppose it's nice to think that way when you've lost someone close to you. But if you're reincarnated, it doesn't mean you come back as a house cat, or a barnacle, with the same personality and memories. It means that the earth reabsorbs your matter and turns it into something else. Once you become compost, you just revert back to the elements that make a tree from an acorn. And now you're an oak tree," she says, waving at the tree that shades Dad's final resting spot.

"That's a maple tree," I say. "This conversation is really starting to creep me out. I don't like thinking about my dad in that way."

"Sorry," she says. "So, if your theory about reincarnation is correct, and you died and were reincarnated, what animal do you think you'd be?" Ophelia asks me.

"I'm not going to lie. I think I'd probably be a squirrel, or an oyster, or something lame. But I don't want to believe that about my dad. Because he was awesome. He was funny, and smart, and he didn't give a shit what anybody thought about him."

"So, kind of like you?"

"No. God, not at all. I'm nothing like my dad."

"If you say so. I guess you're right about most people being squirrels, but you can't think that way. If you think that way you may as well just lie down and die. I don't want to be a squirrel, Dane. I can't. I can't have survived my shitty childhood with my mom and all of her shitty boyfriends just to grow up and be a squirrel the rest of my life."

"You won't," I say with confidence. "You're too cool for that."

Ophelia takes a moment to think about what I've said. I appreciate that she doesn't laugh, or try to make a joke about it. She just thinks about it.

"You know how sometimes people will survive a plane crash or a suicide attempt, and suddenly they're a changed person?" I ask. "Like, there's this guy who tried to commit suicide jumping from the Golden Gate Bridge but survived, and now he thinks that it was some kind of miracle, like God actually gave enough of a crap about his life to spare it."

"How do you know about that? Do you just spend all of your time reading about suicide online? You've really got to find a hobby, Dane."

I ignore her comment and keep talking, because I still have more to say. "People who go through experiences like that, they suddenly believe that they have some purpose in life. Like, their life must have meaning, or why else would God let them live?"

"I don't think God has anything to do with it," Ophelia says.

"Agreed. I'm not saying that. What I mean is, people go through these near-death experiences and it changes them, makes them feel like life—their life—has a purpose."

"Sure, I get it," she says. "Like Owen Meany."

"Who?" I ask with a frown.

"It's a book. About this kid, Owen Meany, who spends his whole life preparing for this one moment when he saves the lives of other people. His life didn't have any meaning other than to save the lives of other people whose lives may or may not have any meaning."

"That's really confusing."

Ophelia waves her hand to tell me to keep talking.

"Anyway," I say, "my point is that I can't help but feeling the opposite."

"You mean you feel as if your life has no meaning?"

"Yes."

"Is that what you're worried about?" she asks with some surprise. "Of course your life has no meaning. Unless you do something meaningful, life is meaningless."

"That's depressing."

"You're the one who's looking for a reason to live," she says with a shrug. "But I don't think you're a squirrel, Dane."

"I appreciate you saying that, even if it isn't really true."

"I'm serious. I mean, a squirrel doesn't sit around contemplating the meaning of life, or reincarnation. A squirrel just is. It collects nuts, and climbs trees, and maybe has baby squirrels, but it doesn't ever stop to wonder if it has some higher purpose."

"Like Eric. He's a squirrel. He's only motivated by the most basic physical wants and desires—the shit he's been programmed to think is important. He's a designer-label squirrel. An Instagram influencer squirrel."

"That's hilarious," Ophelia says, staring off into the middle distance. "The squirrels of Instagram. I'm not going to be able to look at most people without thinking about squirrels now."

"Sometimes I think it would be easier to be a squirrel," I say. "To not have to wonder. To not have to figure anything out. To not have to feel as if I need some purpose in my life. I mean, right now I'm not planning on college. I'm not planning on anything."

"You could join the military. My dad left home when he was seventeen to join the army."

"That's a horrible idea. I don't get to do anything I want to now. If I join the military I'd just do what someone else wants me to do all the time."

"Then what do you want to do?" she asks.

"I used to want to kill myself. I still think about it sometimes. Not because I'm so sad that I want to die, but because it's exhausting trying to figure out what I should be living for."

"This conversation is kind of insulting, you know?" Ophelia says. She's giving me the side-eye, her gaze weighted with some deeper meaning that I am too dense to understand. "Like, I'm sitting right here, and you're telling me there's nothing in this world worth living for. I mean, I'm in this world. It's kind of a dickish outlook."

"I never said I wasn't a dick. I just said I was less of a dick than Eric. There's a difference."

"That's fair. You know what I like about you, Dane? You don't go through life like everybody else. Most people never stop to wonder about the bigger picture, the meaning of life. They think clothes or a car or social media can define them."

"It's actually a pretty hard way to be."

"Sure, yeah. But most people act like they've already got everything figured out. You don't do that. You're genuinely lost. I like that about you."

"Thanks," I say, because there doesn't seem to be anything else I can say.

"You know, my mom was the one who picked out my name."

"Yeah?" I ask, unsure where this part of the conversation is going.

"Yeah, she named me after the character in *Hamlet*."

I shake my head, my eyebrows raised with question.

"You know, Shakespeare? In the play Ophelia goes crazy—kills herself."

"Really? That's messed up. I guess that explains why it isn't a common name. It's like naming your kid Adolf or something. Bad associations."

"Right. Sometimes I think, maybe my mom identified with Ophelia so much, identified with her just going completely bonkers and drowning herself in a river. Seems like kind of a shitty thing to do, though. Give your kid a name like that."

"Maybe not. Maybe there were other things about Ophelia that your mom thought were important. Because she was smart or beautiful or emotionally intelligent. I don't know. I haven't read *Hamlet*. You should ask her."

"I don't like to ask questions like that, unless I think I already know the answer. It's safer that way."

"I get that. Don't ask the question if you might not like the answer. That's how we got into the whole mess of having world religions, you know?"

Ophelia laughs at that. "And now we've come full circle."

We decide that it will be best for Ophelia if she's home when her dad gets there. I pull the Mercedes into the driveway about the same time that we would normally get home from school.

Ophelia takes her time getting her books and jacket out of the car and we stand in the driveway talking for a few minutes.

"I hope you don't get in more trouble," I say, just to have something to say.

"I don't care so much anymore. A few more weeks and we're done. I leave the first week of July to visit my grandparents in Ohio before I start college. This is it, you know?"

My heart hurts at her mention of leaving, but I try hard not to show it. "We did a terrible job of living today like it was our last."

"I don't know," she says, and her smile is soft and warm. "I can think of worse ways to spend my last day on earth than to spend it with you."

It's a good thing I can't think of a cool response to that because while I'm still trying to think of something clever to say, she leans toward me and kisses me. Just on the cheek, but it's definitely one of those moments, the kind that will never leave.

"I'm glad I went to that party with Eric," Ophelia says. "It was worth getting into trouble for you to finally think about me in some way other than the annoying girl next door."

I'm not sure what I would have said if I'd had a chance. Before I can even finish taking a breath to respond, she is gone and, once again, I'm standing there wondering why I can't ever say what I should.

You would think that after Ophelia and I spent our last day on earth together I would be in a hurry to see her again, to spend more time with her. I can't help feeling like the whole thing was just a fluke. Like she wanted to get to know me better and now that she does, she regrets it.

Since I've started going to school at McLean I always eat lunch alone. It's hard to find a place on campus where I can avoid people entirely. There are worse things than being alone.

Most teachers lock their classrooms when they leave for lunch, but sometimes I find one open where I can hang out until just before the bell rings. Today, when I test the doorknob to Ms. Guinn's room, I find the door unlocked, and her spending the lunch period alone at her desk.

Instead of making up an excuse for being there, I ask her if she would mind if I spent my lunch period in the classroom. She doesn't ask me why, which I take to mean either she doesn't care, or she understands my desire to be alone. Either way, she just nods her head toward the empty rows of seats in a silent invitation.

Even though I am the only one in the room besides Ms. Guinn, I take the same desk where I usually sit for class, toward the back of the room.

Ms. Guinn is reading from a tattered paperback book while I stare out the window. Her classroom overlooks the back of the school, above the locker rooms on the lower level, near the maintenance entrance and dumpsters. That's where the Heads and Skaters congregate during their lunch periods. They are the kids who don't fit in among the more polished students. Their long hair and vintage clothes look dirty and out of place in the pristine halls of McLean High School.

Though they are as rich and privileged as anyone else who attends the school, they do their best not to look the part. And I understand that. On the inside they bear scars and wounds that make them feel ugly and out of place. And so, they make themselves ugly and out of place and relegate themselves to the ugliest part of the campus. If I had a crowd at school, the Heads and Skaters would be it. But I just float somewhere around the edges.

Ms. Guinn is sitting behind her desk to eat lunch, which I find somewhat sad. She's tied to the same desk all day. You would think she'd want to do something else with her thirty minutes to eat. It seems crazy to me that adults only grant themselves a thirty-minute lunch, the same lunch period given to us from kindergarten to graduation. The people who set the school schedule are adults with free will. So why don't they exercise that power and give themselves a longer lunch period? The only reason I can see is that they want to use that power to make life hell for kids, which is sad if you think about it.

I sit silently, preoccupied with thinking about Ophelia and Eric, the two trains of thought making head-on collisions in my brain. When Ms. Guinn breaks the silence it makes me jerk with surprise.

"We missed you in class yesterday."

"I seriously doubt that," I say.

"Well, I missed you. You're every teacher's worst nightmare and greatest hope. You always think, 'Here's a smart kid who could really excel in school. Maybe I'll be the one to reach him, to make him realize his potential.'"

"That's sad. I'm probably not worth you getting disappointed about anything."

"Why are you here to eat lunch instead of spending time with people your own age? It's your senior year. You should be enjoying yourself."

"Why do you eat in the classroom?" I ask her. "Teachers can go anywhere they want."

"Honestly, I'm trying to avoid people. I spend all day repeating the same thing to six groups of people. I'd rather not have a dull and pointless conversation with one of my fellow teachers during lunch."

"You don't have any friends you work with?"

"Friends?" she asks, and seems to be asking herself. "No,

I wouldn't say I have friends here. Acquaintances, really. I don't have a lot of friends."

"Are you trying to make me feel sorry for you?"

"Do you?"

"I suppose not. At the end of the day you get to go home to your own place. You do what you want, when you want."

"You'll have that soon, too," says Ms. Guinn. And then, after a thoughtful smile, "Probably sooner than you'd like."

"What do you mean?"

"I mean you'll graduate soon. You said yourself that you aren't going to college. So, I guess you'll get a job and your own apartment. I'm sure your mother isn't planning to let you sit at home and be a freeloader for the rest of your adult life."

"I was reading this article online. It was by some scientist. He was saying how humans are really nothing more than an ecosystem for bacteria. We can't live without them in and on our bodies. There are trillions of them in our body, and most of them don't do us any harm. Most of them we need to digest our food or keep our skin healthy. That was his whole theory, that our only purpose is to provide habitat for bacteria, and when we die they just move on to another habitat."

"I'm not sure if that's an interesting existential argument, or just depressing."

"That's the point. The ultimate meaning of life is just to be a host for these bacteria. It got me thinking. He could be right. It could be that all of this"—I pause and gesture at my body, moving my hands in circles as if washing myself—"is just an ecosystem for bacteria. Nothing more. Which would mean that everything we do is ultimately meaningless."

Ms. Guinn sits still, her plastic spoon poised above the cottage cheese container as she looks critically at the curds within. "Dane, as your adult role model, I have to tell you that if you are using recreational drugs, you should stop. It isn't good for your brain development."

"I am on drugs, but not for recreation. Off-brand Prozac. And Klonopin for acute anxiety attacks. But my therapist has been reducing the amount of antidepressants I take. I'm practically normal."

"So, what are you trying to tell me?" she wants to know. "Everything is meaningless because we're all just ultimately hosts for flesh-eating bacteria?"

"It's something to think about."

"I suppose. But even if that's true, so what? You still have to have a job. You still have to get out of bed in the morning and eat to stay alive. If life is truly meaningless, well, we're here anyway. Might as well enjoy ourselves."

"Is that why you're eating cottage cheese for lunch?" I ask her. "Because you love it so much and you're just trying to enjoy yourself?"

"I eat cottage cheese because it's low-fat and high-protein and a couple of months ago I saw a picture my niece posted of me on Facebook in which I had three chins."

"You're a slave," I say as I cross my arms over my chest

and shake my head. "Just like everyone else. I thought you were different."

She tosses the cottage cheese container into the trash along with her plastic spoon. Then she places her hands flat on the desk in front of her and sighs. "No, Dane. No. I'm not different from anybody else. Maybe you think you're special. That your life has to have some special meaning the rest of us don't have. But I know that life is just what you make it. Nothing more. Nothing less."

I sit forward suddenly and put my elbows on my knees. I want to make her understand. No one seems to ever be able to understand what I'm saying. It's so frustrating. "What I'm thinking is if we're just hosts for bacteria, then maybe Earth is just a host for us. And the earth is floating out in space among all these other planets that are just hosts for other life-forms. Always and forever without end. Do you see what that would mean? It would mean that the entire universe is meaningless."

Ms. Guinn holds my gaze for a long minute—she doesn't say anything, but doesn't break the connection, either. Maybe she really is thinking about what I'm saying.

Finally, she says, "I've noticed that you seem to have an interest in Ophelia Marcus."

I appreciate the fact that she says "an interest" instead of "an infatuation," or "a crazy dream that a girl like Ophelia might want you, when she could have any guy she wants."

"Is it that obvious?" I ask.

"Mm. Painfully," Ms. Guinn says, then quickly adds,

"though probably only to me because of my perspective at the front of the room."

"We skipped school together yesterday. We spent the whole day together. Now I'm hiding in here hanging out with you because I'm too embarrassed to see her again. I'm afraid that after she spent a whole day getting to know me, she regrets ever leading me on."

"Jesus, what's wrong with you?"

"It's crazy, I know. I know she's too good for me."

"That's not what I meant. A girl like Ophelia doesn't skip school to spend the day with you if she doesn't like you. I mean, I don't know her that well, but I know she's never skipped school before. She did it just so she could be with you."

"You think?" I ask, refusing to be convinced.

"I know. And maybe that could be your meaning of life for you. At least for right now."

"What do you mean?" I ask.

"I mean that maybe endeavoring to be good enough to deserve Ophelia, that could be your *raison d'être*."

"Impossible," I say, irritated by how little Ms. Guinn seems to understand the situation. It's too late. I've already pissed away high school on skateboarding and smoking weed.

"Well, God, if there's no use in even trying to make up for lost time at eighteen, then I am absolutely and truly screwed. I might as well give up right now."

"I don't blame you," I say.

"Get out," Ms. Guinn says, pointing toward the class-room door. "Get out and go find Ophelia. You don't have to tell her you're in love with her—in fact, definitely don't tell her that. Or at least don't lead with that."

I still have half of a lunch period to find Ophelia.

There are vending machines in one corner of the cafete-ria, so my plan is to get a drink, casually survey the room, and if I see Ophelia on the first pass, I'll go talk to her. If I don't, well, I won't have made a fool out of myself, and I can exit with my tail between my legs and no one will know I almost made a fool out of myself.

The vending machine steals my money without deliver-ing my drink and now I'm worrying about whether I should try to pay again or just give up on the drink. I'm hoping that no one has noticed that the vending machine, like life, has tricked me into a false sense of optimism. As I'm standing there, deciding what to do, I see Eric enter the cafeteria with an entourage of guys wearing khakis and collared shirts. Rich guys can get away with wearing all kinds of things that would get you beaten up anyplace else—pants with some kind of embroidered animal on them, like ducks or whales, sometimes with a canvas belt. It's almost as if they're mak-ing a statement with it. Like, *I'm so rich I can wear this absolutely ridiculous article of clothing and nobody will challenge my right to do so.* I mean, my family is rich, too, but if I showed up any-where dressed the way Eric and his friends do, Joe, Mark, and Harry would beat me up just on principle.

Eric and his entourage come into the cafeteria while I am still managing my anxiety about the vending machine. He is looking around, searching for something. And I think, son of a bitch, he's looking for Ophelia. That fucking squirrel is looking for Ophelia.

And then he finds her.

I follow Eric's gaze as it locks on to Ophelia's curls, somehow more beautiful now than ever before. She is sitting at a table with a couple of the girls from the field hockey team.

Eric is making his way toward Ophelia and my heart starts to beat hard in parts of my body where you don't usually feel a heartbeat—the tips of my fingers, the backs of my eyelids. I head toward Ophelia, the prey, who is still unaware that she has been singled out as a victim, like a newborn wildebeest with a false sense of security within the herd.

I hurry to be the first to arrive at Ophelia, and Eric and I arrive at the table at the same time.

Ophelia's expression is deadpan as all conversation at her lunch table stops. You wouldn't know she has any particular feeling about either one of us by the look on her face.

"Hey, Ophelia," Eric says, doing his best to ignore my presence.

"Hey," Ophelia says. It comes out like a question as she looks up at Eric, then casts her eyes in my direction.

"What the fuck, man?" Eric says to me. "Can I help you?"

"You're evil and need to be stopped."

Eric takes a deep breath and lets out a sigh, as if dealing with me is the biggest inconvenience he's ever had to face. "I'm talking to Ophelia," he says, his condescension rich enough to make a meal out of it. "It's none of your business."

That's fair. Technically, Ophelia is none of my business. After all, she isn't my girlfriend.

I appeal to her with my eyes, waiting—asking—for her to tell Eric he is a piece of shit and to leave her alone.

But she doesn't. I mean—what the hell? Ophelia doesn't take shit from anyone. Or, to be more precise, she doesn't take any shit from me. But I assume that means she doesn't take shit from anyone else, either. But here she is, waiting to hear Eric out, to listen to what he has to say. She doesn't give him a *Drop dead* look and put him in his place, which is what Ophelia does best.

It's disturbing. As if the universe as I understand it is suddenly turned upside down.

"You should leave her alone," I say.

"What the fuck are you talking about?" Eric asks. He looks at Ophelia and her friends, making sure his audience is paying attention. "Look, Dane, you were out of line the other night, but I'm willing to let it go."

"Let it go?" I ask, incredulous.

"Ophelia," Eric says, ignoring my comment and turning his full attention to her, "can I talk to you? Alone?"

"Don't do it," I say to Ophelia.

"I don't need your permission to do something," Ophelia says, directing her gaze at me, as if Eric doesn't exist, as if the entire cafeteria doesn't exist.

The steady stream of adrenaline slows to a trickle, then a drip, as Ophelia waits for me to acknowledge what she has said. "I know," I say. "I'm not telling you what to do."

She turns her attention to Eric then and says, "I don't want to talk to you, Eric. I want you to leave me alone."

Eric's eyes go wide and he makes a sound that is a mixture of surprise and disgust, as if he's choking on his disbelief. Instead of being embarrassed or disappointed in himself, he's indignant. And then the thin veil of his public face vanishes and the evil within is naked to the world.

"You're not hot enough to act like you're some kind of prize," Eric says to Ophelia.

If his words inflict any wounds, they are invisible on Ophelia. Her eyebrows twist in silent judgment, then she dismisses Eric by breaking eye contact and turning back to her friends.

I am amazed by her restraint. If she feels anything about Eric, anything at all, then it is hidden from the rest of us.

"You're a bitch," Eric says.

Ophelia's blush is obvious, but she doesn't lose her shit. She turns back to look at Eric and says, "You have to take advantage of girls who are drunk to get any action. So, looks like you're the bitch."

Ophelia's friends laugh and so do a couple of Eric's friends. I'm sure this moment is confusing for him, because

Eric is used to being treated like a god. But Ophelia doesn't believe in gods. His hands ball into fists and when he opens his mouth, the words that come out are so hate-filled and filthy that at least one person gasps. I might be the one who gasps.

Without conscious thought, I pick up the hard-plastic lunch tray in front of one of Ophelia's friends, gripping two corners on the long end of it, then swing the edge of it into Eric's face. In what seems like slow motion, green beans and macaroni and cheese and half a dozen fish sticks that are pressed into the shapes of gaily leaping dolphins fly into the air, then fall like rain onto Ophelia and her friends. There's tartar sauce, too, and ketchup, and it falls in fat drops into their hair and onto their clothes.

The girls scream with disgust while Eric screams with rage and pain, though it sounds like more pain. I wasn't thinking as I swung the tray, and when it connects with his face I instinctively let go of it. I drop the tray so I can hold up my fists to ward off the punch I think is coming, but it doesn't arrive.

Eric's hands are covering his face and there's blood seeping through his fingers. He reminds me of an abstract painting, the kind my mom prefers to decorate our house. His friends are stunned and can't seem to decide if they should comfort their friend, or avert their eyes and try not to notice him as he sobs.

Ophelia and her friends are looking at the USDA-approved lunch items that dot their clothes and hair and the tabletop. The scene reminds me of a movie I saw once, about these kids who had the ability to stop time. They could move through the world as everyone around them were rendered statues. We are now all quiet and motionless. Except for Eric.

My attack on Eric is so sudden and savage that no one knows how to react. Even though Eric has used the forbidden and universally reprehensible C-word, people in the cafeteria are looking at me like I am a murderer.

The silence is broken as one of the vice principals storms into the fray. Our school has three vice principals, which is excessive, and they rotate the unlucky assignment of cafeteria monitor. Today it is Vice Principal Maples, who totters around school on high-heeled shoes and wears pencil skirts. She doesn't stand a chance in a footrace with a student. Her face is a mask of alarm, as McLean High School is definitely not a place where students fight in the lunchroom. "What is happening?" she shouts as she waves her arms for Eric's friends to step away.

"Oh, God!" Eric is saying over and over. If there is a God, I hope he isn't the kind that would answer Eric's prayers.

"What is your name?" Vice Principal Maples shouts at me. I ignore her and turn to walk away. "Hey. Hey!" she shouts at my retreating back, but I think she isn't sure whether to come after me or help Eric, who is still moaning and carrying on about his pain. I feel two hundred pairs of eyes follow me through the cafeteria and out the fire doors into the main corridor.

I am halfway down the hall when Ophelia catches up to me at a run and puts a hand on my arm. "Dane! Where are you going?"

"I don't know," I say. "Are you okay?"

"Me? Yeah, I'm fine. That was crazy. You're going to be in big trouble."

I shrug and it isn't just for show. I really don't care. "I don't care all that much."

"Well, you should. What were you thinking?"

"I guess I wasn't. Or," I say as I think about it, "I guess I was thinking that Eric shouldn't be talking to you that way."

"That's . . . sweet," she says, her voice rising as if it is a question. "I guess. But I can take care of myself, you know. I'm worried they're going to expel you."

"It doesn't matter. I don't need their piece of paper. They can keep it."

"You don't mean that," she says. I do mean it, though I don't correct her. "Where are you going?"

"I don't know. I guess I'm running away."

"They'll catch you."

"You're helping them," I say, and she laughs at that.

I start to leave her then but she says my name again and it stops me. When I turn back she puts her arm around my shoulders and pulls me into a kiss. Everything falls away, the universe collapsing back into the nothingness it was before the Big Bang. The school hallway speeds past us like a train moving along the track and we are transported to our own place in time, where nothing can touch us. With sudden clarity I can see that the universe has no beginning or end. There is nothing except for this moment. This kiss. This girl.

I pull away first, overwhelmed by the moment. "Listen, I've been thinking," I say, and before even a second goes by, the cafeteria door at the end of the long corridor bangs open and I hear the click of Vice Principal Maples's shoes on the stone tile. "There's not much time before graduation. And, you know, maybe for the next few weeks we could just be together. Like yesterday, only all the time. We can be together for as long as it's good."

"What are you saying?"

"I mean, like you said, you set a date to break up from the beginning. Just be boyfriend and girlfriend during the functional part of the relationship."

"The first couple of months," Ophelia says, and her face softens with understanding and what looks like happiness, and her voice sounds kind of thick, like maybe she's going to cry.

"Yeah, the golden time," I say with a nod.

"Sure. Yeah. Okay. You want to . . . pick a date, I guess?"

"I—uh—I gotta go," I say. "Tonight. Maybe tonight we can talk."

"Okay," she says, still grinning. I figure she's my girlfriend now so it's okay if I lean in to give her another kiss before I run.

I don't stay a fugitive for very long.

It turns out that Eric's front teeth are knocked loose, his

face split open, which is going to make him look a lot less like an Abercrombie model if they can't fix it. An ambulance is called, which triggers a lockdown for the school. Everyone has to stay put until the paramedics have come and gone.

There is no reluctance on the part of my schoolmates to rat me out. I am an outsider, after all—a new kid even though I have lived in McLean for most of my life. Our audience all wants their turn to tell the story, but Ophelia, Eric, and I are the only ones who know what prompted the fight.

At least no one had a chance to capture it on video. I hit Eric without warning and that first blow was the beginning and end of the fight.

The school security officer finds me just outside the front entrance. It occurs to me that if Ophelia had not stopped me to talk then I could have made a clean getaway. Really there is no place to get away to. No matter what, they're going to catch me eventually. Which is why I don't even bother to protest as the security officer escorts me to the office.

The school calls my mom about the attack on Eric, and I wait for her to arrive in the reception area of the office. There is nothing I can say to defend myself, so I remain silent when Mom and the principal ask me why I attacked Eric.

Mom tries to make excuses for me. She says that I have been troubled since the death of my father, which is true, but irrelevant.

Eric's injuries aren't life threatening, but they are face

threatening. He might have to go the rest of his life without being devastatingly handsome.

In the end I am suspended for three days without ever opening my mouth to defend myself. I wonder if Eric will end up suing Mom and me for his medical costs as well as pain and suffering. Though I am pretty sure you have to prove human suffering to get an award from a judge and jury and, as a non-human, Eric doesn't qualify.

As Mom and I leave school she's on the phone with Dr. Lineberger to schedule an emergency meeting. Dr. Lineberger agrees to see us and we drive straight to her office.

"Dane," Mom says. "What is going on with you?"

"What do you want me to say?" I ask without looking away from the window.

"This is serious," Mom says. "It's a miracle you weren't expelled right before graduation."

"Oh, enough with the graduation," I say, irritated now that she is interrupting my thoughts about Ophelia. "Who cares about graduating high school?"

This time Mom and Dr. Lineberger both sit in the chairs while I stand at the window looking out at the parking lot. There is nothing interesting to look at, but I don't want to see their faces as they talk about me. I am too busy replaying my conversation with Ophelia over in my mind and wondering where she is now and if she's thinking about me.

"Dane," Dr. Lineberger says, "would you like to explain your side of things?"

"Eric is evil and he needed to be stopped. He thinks he can act any way he wants just because he's rich and good-looking. I'm sick of it."

"That's no reason to attack him," Mom says.

"I was protecting Ophelia. He took her to that party, tried to take advantage of her."

"Well, that's something for her father to worry about," Mom says, the volume of her voice rising to fill the office. "You can't just go attacking people because you've got a crush on some girl."

"She's not just some girl. She's the love of my life."

Mom laughs, just a short burst, like she can't stop herself, but she immediately looks apologetic. "I'm sorry. I know you like her. This is what I'm talking about, though. You let your emotions control everything. You don't think."

"Oh, what do you know about it? All you care about is your new life with your new boyfriend and I'm just a major inconvenience for everyone."

"That's so unfair," Mom says. "I have every right to be worried about you. You're going out to parties and doing God only knows what, drinking and getting high. Now you're fighting at school. At some point you have to become a functioning member of society. You're eighteen. Not a kid. What am I supposed to do?"

"Nothing," I say as I look out the window again, the only way to get any privacy with both of them staring at me.

Dr. Lineberger encourages Mom to go sit in the reception

area so she and I can have a chance to talk privately. Once Mom is gone, Dr. Lineberger sits back in her chair and waits for me to talk.

I end up telling Dr. Lineberger the whole story about what caused my fight with Eric. I explain to her about Ophelia's theory of romantic relationships. Dr. Lineberger is skeptical of the plan.

"So, you set the date to break up ahead of time?" she asks.

"Yeah," I say with a nod. "It's pretty brilliant, if you think about it."

"I'm not sure," Dr. Lineberger says. "It's kind of . . . lazy."

"How so?"

"Well, it's like saying that you can have a relationship, you just agree that you aren't going to do anything to make it work. And that's what relationships are. Work. Like your relationship with your mom. You have to keep talking, keep communicating, keep trying to see things from the other person's perspective."

"Your kind of relationship doesn't sound very appealing."

She smiles at that. "I'm afraid that's the only kind of relationships there are. Everything else is just for movies. They're make-believe."

"I guess," I say, noncommittal. "But it's not as if a girl like Ophelia is going to want to be in a relationship with me long-term. I've got nothing to offer."

"What things do you like about Ophelia?"

"She's smart. And she's funny, when she's not making fun of me. And I don't think she cares what anyone thinks of her. I mean, she started a coed a cappella group at our school. They're called Unaccompanied Minors and she's really into it. You couldn't really come up with anything dorkier than that if you were actually trying to be dorky. But that doesn't bother her. I don't know. She's just fierce."

"That's interesting," Dr. Lineberger says, putting a finger to her lower lip. I imagine she usually does it with her pen, but since the time I told her to stop writing during our sessions she has left the notebook and pen untouched on her desk. "You didn't even mention how she looks."

"Oh, well, she's beautiful. But with Ophelia it's almost beside the point. I think I would love her no matter what."

"I suppose that's easy to say when someone is beautiful," Dr. Lineberger says, and arches her eyebrows wryly.

"True."

"And what do you think she likes about you?"

"Honestly, I have no idea."

"Maybe you should ask her."

"That's a terrible idea," I say.

"So, you love her, and you want her to be your girlfriend, but you can't ask her a simple question like that?"

"Exactly."

"Do you see why that could be a problem for a long-term relationship?"

"Of course," I say with a nod. "That's what I'm telling you. We're intentionally planning to not have a long-term relationship. Why does that seem so crazy? Other people who get together and say, 'This is it, we're in this until the day we die'—now that's crazy."

"I suppose," Dr. Lineberger says, though she's noncommittal. "But is it terrible to want that?"

"I just don't want Ophelia, or any girl, to feel like I expect too much out of her. I can't ask someone to make that kind of commitment to me."

"To you, in particular? You can't ask anyone to make that commitment to you, but it would be okay for someone else to ask a girl for that kind of commitment?"

"I'm not speaking generally. I mean I can't ask Ophelia for that kind of commitment. I have nothing to offer her. And her parents are both a disaster, in their own way. She's had it rough."

"You've had it rough, too."

"Not really. I mean, I lost my dad. Yeah. That's hard. But I've never been poor, never had to worry about where my next meal is coming from. Ophelia's mom is crazy. Bipolar, I mean."

"That is tough," Dr. Lineberger says with an eager nod. "It's hard for a child not to associate their parents' shortcomings with their own behavior. Somehow make it their own fault."

"I don't do that," I say with certainty. "I don't think I caused any of my mom's failings."

"And what do you see as your mom's failings?"

"She's shallow. Disloyal. Selfish. You heard her. She said that if my dad hadn't died they'd probably have gotten divorced. Him dying saved her a whole lot of trouble."

"Do you really believe that?"

I think about her question. Really think about it. "Maybe" is the only answer I have.

"Did you ever think, Dane, that maybe the reason you have such a problem with your mom being with Chuck isn't because she's being disloyal to your dad, or to his memory, but that you see it as her being somehow disloyal to you?"

"I don't know what you mean." And honestly, I really don't.

"I mean, when you're still growing emotionally and intellectually, and learning to be independent, it's hard to think of your parents as their own people, with feelings of their own. And, I think, if you see your mom moving forward in her own life after the death of your father, and you hear her say things like your parents' marriage was in trouble even before your father died, then that's not just disloyal to your dad, it's disloyal to you. Because half of you is your dad. And, maybe, by her taking up a relationship with Chuck, she's rejecting not just her marriage to your dad, but also being your mother."

"I do fear rejection. It's true."

"And it's hard for you to articulate why anyone should love you. I ask you why you think this girl, Ophelia, likes you, and you can't give me a single reason."

That one stings, because it's true, and I turn my head to the side and stare hard out the window as I feel the pinprick of hot tears behind my eyelids.

Dr. Lineberger seems to sense that I can't talk at the moment, because if I do, I'll start to cry. She gives me some time and space by talking, so I don't have to. "It's normal for your mom to want to have a companion. Just because Chuck is part of her life, that will never replace what you are to her. You're her only child. She loves you. She only wants you to be happy. And as long as you remain unhappy, you are able to deny her any happiness for herself."

"I never tried to make her unhappy," I say, and my voice is tight with the tears I'm holding back.

"Maybe not intentionally," Dr. Lineberger says, "but as long as you stay angry with her, as long as you aren't willing to accept her relationship with Chuck, or her right to be her own person, you're both going to be miserable. Her relationship with Chuck, it doesn't take anything away from how she feels about you. Do you see that?"

I nod, because now I'm really crying and there's no way to open my mouth without a big sob filling the space between us.

When it becomes obvious that I won't, can't, say anything else, Dr. Lineberger takes pity on me and cuts our session short. "Why don't we stop for now, give you some time to think about this conversation. We can pick it up again next week."

I nod again, still not trusting my ability to speak, and leave without saying goodbye.

On the drive home Mom asks if I'm hungry and if I want to stop at the Lebanese Taverna. We haven't eaten at the Taverna since my dad died, but when he was alive we ate there whenever we went out for a meal as a family. I agree, thinking maybe it will be nice to spend some time in a place where Dad was so familiar, even if I have to be with Mom to be there.

The owner of the Lebanese Taverna is sitting at the bar in the small dining room reading the paper when we arrive. He recognizes Mom right away and comes to greet us and personally show us to a table near the window.

Mom and the owner spend a few minutes chatting, catching up, and he doesn't ask why he hasn't seen us in a while. He knows about Dad, catered his funeral, which is a pretty high compliment, I guess.

He doesn't leave us with menus, instead insisting that he will serve us a sample of our favorites. Once he's gone from the table Mom starts talking to me. Just idle chitchat, gossiping about friends and people in the neighborhood who don't matter to me.

I'm not really listening to her, and I'm not even sure what she's saying when I interrupt her to say, "Where are all of my toys from when I was little? The ones you made me pack away?"

"Wh-what?" Mom asks. My question is unexpected and I can see her trying to connect the dots.

"You made me pack away my old toys when I was a kid," I remind her. "You said they were going into the attic to save until I had kids of my own."

"Oh, Dane," Mom says with a half-hearted smile. "You got so upset when I wanted to clean out your room. You always wanted to hold on to everything, but you never played with half of your toys. I said that so we could get rid of them without you getting so upset."

"So, there are no toys in the attic? What did you do with them?"

"I—I think I dropped them at the Goodwill or something. I don't really remember."

"But you lied? You lied to me about what was going to happen to them?" I'm stating it like a question, forcing her to admit the truth.

"It's not really lying. It's the kind of thing a parent tells a child to protect their feelings. Like telling a kid that the family dog that has to be put to sleep is going to live on a farm in the country."

"I don't know what you're talking about."

Mom's smile is wistful now. "When I was a kid, my family had this dog. He was a stray we had taken in. He was fine with everyone in the family but he could be really aggressive toward strangers. My parents thought it was too much of a risk to keep him, so they had the animal shelter come and take him away. I was really upset, so my mom told me that they were taking the dog to the country to live on a farm, where he could run free and be much happier."

"What happened to the dog?" I ask.

Mom's smile fades as she realizes that I am not prepared for the ending of this story. "Well, I don't know for sure. Maybe he did find a good home. Or maybe he had to be put to sleep. The point is, my mom said what she needed to say to protect my feelings. I didn't realize, probably until I was about your age, that the dog might not have gone to live on a farm."

"That's really sad," I say.

"I suppose it is," Mom says, and she actually does seem sad about the dog. For once she seems human to me, no longer heartless and cruel, just somebody, like everybody, trying to make sense of the world.

"Do you ever think about that?" I ask her. "Think maybe it would have been better if your parents had told you the truth? You could have been sad for the dog. But they took that away from you."

"I mean—no, not really. I think my parents were just trying to protect me."

"You think so?" I ask. "It sounds like they were protecting themselves. You know? Maybe they couldn't deal with you being upset or hating them for what they did. They did what was easiest for them at the time."

"I suppose you could think of it that way," she says, sounding unsure again. "As a parent you just want your kid to be happy. When your kid is unhappy, then you're unhappy. You do what you can to make your kid happy in the moment, to spare them. And I guess, to spare yourself."

"Maybe that's why Dad didn't want me to know he was sick. You think?"

"Sure. Yeah, of course. He wanted to delay you being unhappy about anything. I guess he figured, if he got better, then he would have made you unhappy for no reason. We knew, we both knew, that you weren't really happy at Brandywine. I guess that was a mistake, too. We were unhappy in our marriage and as long as you were away at Brandywine we wouldn't have to see all of the fighting, the anger, making you unhappy all of the time." She laughs a little but it's the kind of laugh you make right when you are about to start crying. "You were unhappy but we didn't have to look at it."

"There's nothing wrong with me," I tell her, confident about it.

"Oh, Dane . . ." she says, and her eyes are full of tears.

"I'm serious. There's nothing wrong with me. I needed to be sad and you wouldn't let me. You aren't mad at me for being sad. You're mad at yourself for making me that way and you took it out on me."

Her hands are clasped on the table, curled in a tight ball, as one fat tear escapes her cheek and falls onto the first joint of her thumb.

"You could be right about that," she says after she's taken a moment to pull herself together.

"I want you to know, Mom, that I'm not mad at you anymore. I've been mad at you and Chuck for months and it's making me sick. So, whatever you need to do, just do it. I'm not going to be mad anymore."

"I appreciate that, Dane, but I'd really like for us to get to a place where we feel like we are a family. I know it's just the two of us now, really, because long-term I don't know what Chuck and I are planning. I don't really want to be married again. I was married for over twenty years and I'm not sure that I want that again. I like having Chuck as a partner, someone I can rely on, but I'm not sure what the future holds."

"You don't have to tell me all of this," I say, wishing she wouldn't.

"I know, I don't. Talking about it with Dr. Lineberger, I realize that maybe I was a bit insensitive to you and the way you have been feeling. It's not like I've ever been through something like this before. I've just been dealing with it the best way I knew how. Dad's illness was so hard on me—you have to remember, that whole time you were away at school, I was here. I was watching him decline every day, going through it by myself. I guess once he was gone, I was ready to feel something else. Something better. You didn't have the same amount of time to adjust like I did."

We're both quiet as the server comes to the table with our food and asks if we need anything else. Mom says no and smiles and, as soon as the server is gone, picks up the conversation.

"It's funny, you know, though you'll probably get mad at me for saying this, but even though you remind me of your dad sometimes, in some ways you and Chuck are so alike. You're both so sentimental and worry about everyone's feelings. I mean," she says, laughing suddenly through her tears, "I was just going to cancel your dad's phone number after he died, but Chuck insisted we hold on to it. He was so worried that some old friend would try to get in touch with Craig and he wanted to be able to respond. He didn't want people finding out about Craig being gone the hard way."

I have been focused on my food, serving myself from the small platters that were delivered to the table, kind of lost in my own thoughts, but when Mom mentions Dad's phone number I freeze, the spoon halfway between a platter and my plate.

"What did you just say?" I ask.

"About what?"

"Dad's phone number."

"Oh, just that Chuck wanted to hold on to Craig's number so we didn't lose touch with any of Dad's old friends, people who he hadn't spoken to in a while, who might not know that Craig was gone."

"So, who has Dad's phone now?" I ask, though I already know the answer, and it's making my head spin and my vison blur.

Mom shrugs as she surveys the food and takes some for her own plate. "I guess Chuck keeps it at the office or something. I gave it to him to keep since he thought it was so important."

"And Chuck has had Dad's phone this whole time?" I ask, carefully portioning out my words to keep my voice from giving anything away. "Since Dad's been gone?"

"Yes," she says, now almost hesitant, as if she's worried she has said something to destroy the truce we have established. "Does that bother you?"

Yeah. It bothers me. It bothers me a lot. I think back to all of the messages I have sent to Dad over the past year, trying to remember all of the things I have said. The whole time I thought I was unloading to a stranger, but, really, I've been telling Chuck. Telling him every intimate thought, maybe telling him how much I hated Mom. And him. Telling him what traitors they are.

My face burns hot with a blush and I'm not sure if I want to scream, or cry, or jump up and run out of the restaurant.

"Dane, what is it?" Mom asks. "You look as if you've seen a ghost."

Three days' suspension from school gives me a good glimpse into what life would be like for me without a job after high school, without some purpose to fill my days. The first day I'm off from school I spend the whole day in my room, watching TV and my phone at the same time, with periodic naps. By bedtime I am so bored it makes me anxious and restless. At night, after the sounds of the house have quieted to a sleeping rhythm, I climb out onto the low roof outside my bedroom window and watch for signs of Ophelia.

But she doesn't come.

With no way to reach her, I'm left to experience what life was like for the Pilgrims, or the westward pioneers of the nineteenth century—the only parts of American history that are left over in my brain after all my years of school. Back then people couldn't just call each other. It could take weeks before someone knew how you felt because the only way to tell them was by letter. I wonder if Ophelia is thinking about me, and if what she's thinking is that it was a major mistake to kiss me or to agree to be my soon-to-be ex-girlfriend.

On the second night of my suspension from the world there is a tap on my window. This time, I am prepared. I know it is Ophelia.

I open the window and stand ready to help her as she climbs through the window. She doesn't need my help, but I offer her my hand anyway.

"Thanks," she says, taking it, and she doesn't let go even after she is safely inside.

"I was hoping you'd come," I say honestly.

"Everybody at school is talking about you," Ophelia says. "What you did to Eric's face."

"Great. Before today I don't think anyone knew I existed. Now I'm the guy who messed up Eric Feint's face."

"I wouldn't worry about what anyone thinks. How much trouble are you in?"

"Three days' suspension."

"And?"

"And nothing. Eric had it coming." I say this with a lot more courage than I feel. I'm already worried about returning to school. I've been trying to figure out a way to never go back.

"Well, I thought it was kind of romantic. Dumb, but romantic."

"I'd rather not talk about it."

"Which part?"

"The whole thing is humiliating, and when I come back to school Eric is going to kill me."

"Maybe."

She relaxes onto my bed and pats the mattress beside her, telling me to come and sit.

"Tell me about what your mom said."

"She made me go see my therapist. I told my therapist about you. About our plan to have a relationship with an end date established."

"Seriously? You told her about that?"

"Yes. She said it was lazy, to plan to not work at a relationship."

"What is she, some kind of expert on relationships?"

"I don't know. She's a family therapist, so I guess."

"Well, I think it's perfectly sane," Ophelia says.

"I thought you didn't know anything about sanity, or functional relationships."

"Obviously, I don't. I'm dating you, right?"

My hand is over my eyes as I laugh, so when she kisses me, it comes completely out of nowhere. One minute I am laughing and the next minute her hand is on the side of my face and . . . I don't know. Her hand tugs at my chin as she turns my face so her lips can reach mine. Our lips find each other with our eyes closed and then my hand ends up on her hip and then, suddenly, I do know.

I pull back to look at her face, to read from her expression if this is really happening or if she had just—maybe—fallen into my face and it is all a mistake.

But then we are making out and it feels strange, like a plot twist in a movie that you didn't see coming.

"What's wrong?" she asks in a whisper, her eyes wide, an adorable furrow in the smooth skin of her forehead, just above the bridge of her nose.

Wrong? So many things. So. Many. Things. "Nothing's wrong," I say. "I just . . . I wasn't expecting this."

"Well, I'm your girlfriend now. Right?"

"Yeah, that whole thing is a little weird."

"I thought you had a huge crush on me."

"Who said that?" I ask too quickly, and feel the heat rushing to my face.

"Nobody. I'm just kidding."

This is ridiculous. This girl is lying in my bed with her

arms wrapped around me and we just spent ten minutes exchanging saliva and God only knows what kind of bodily bacteria, but I can't bring myself to admit that I like her.

Correction, that I love her.

"We're not having sex," she says.

I roll away, lying on my side and folding one arm under my head.

"Who says I want to have sex with you?" I ask, and her face falls with surprise.

"Very funny," she says, recovering quickly.

We share a smile and she leans in to kiss me again. On the outside I'm perfectly cool. At least, I think I am. The inside is a different story. For maybe the first time in my life I am aware of exactly how alive I am. I am conscious of every sound my digestive tract makes and the thump of each squeeze of my heart as it pumps at an alarming rate for a person at rest. I hear my saliva, loud in my ears as I swallow and wonder if I usually swallow saliva this often and just don't notice it.

"I guess we need to set a date," she says.

"A date for what?"

"The date we're going to break up. We can't just leave it open-ended. That's how people end up in unhappy marriages."

"I don't know. What's a good date to break up?" I say just to go along with her crazy.

"I was thinking, maybe graduation day. It's an ending— the end of high school, the end of childhood . . ."

"The end of homework," I add. "Thank God."

"So, graduation day. That will be our last day."

"If you think so," I say, though I'm thinking graduation is still weeks away and I'm not sure there is enough about me to hold her interest for even that long.

"I mean," she says, pulling back a little, "I'm not leaving for school until July. I go to stay with my grandparents for a couple of weeks before I move into my dorm. So, do we pick some arbitrary milestone like graduation? We break up then? Or do we just decide to do it when I leave?"

"I hadn't really thought it through that far," I say.

"Ending on graduation day is probably too cliché," she says. "But ending because I'm leaving for school seems wrong, too. It goes against everything. Then we're not really choosing the date to end. We're giving up control."

"Maybe we should end it the night before graduation. That way after commencement is over we just keep going, except in opposite directions."

"How opposite? We'll still live next door to each other for a month."

"I'm speaking metaphorically. You'll be getting ready to go off to Ohio and college and I'll . . . well, I'm not sure what I'll be doing, but it will just be a drag if you feel like you have to keep talking to me after graduation. We end it the night before, and then you don't have to feel bad or obligated or anything that will hold you back from starting a new life."

"I guess," Ophelia says, sounding noncommittal. "I can't stay," she says, whispering it into my ear.

"I know," I whisper back, and I'm not talking about this moment, or even tonight. I know that nothing good can stay. I know it better than anybody. "This is the right thing, knowing ahead of time when to break up."

"I mean I can't stay right now," she says. "I have to get back before my dad notices I'm gone."

"Oh, right. Yeah. You'd better go. I don't want you to get in trouble again."

"I'm not worried about it. But I worry about you."

I worry about me, too, I think, but don't say it.

By the third day of my suspension I've got cabin fever and decide to go into work a couple of hours early. As I leave the house to go to my car, the sound of footsteps crunching on gravel startles me, and I look up to see Colonel Marcus just leaving his house. He stops when he sees me and raises one hand in greeting. He's dressed in his dull green uniform, though with all the colored ribbons and glinting silver insignia his olive jacket isn't going to blend into any forest. At first I think that's all the interaction we're going to have, but then he tosses the briefcase he is holding into the passenger seat of his car and comes to the edge of the driveway to talk.

"Hello, son," he says. The way he says "son" doesn't offend me the way it does when other adult males say it. Colonel Marcus is saying it in a way that makes me feel like one of the young men under his command.

"Hello, sir." As a rule, I never call anyone "sir," not even my own father, who could be terrifying in his own right. With Colonel Marcus I always call him "sir." I can't help myself.

"Home from school again, huh?"

"I got suspended for fighting."

"I know. Ophelia told me."

"She did?"

"Yes. She told me you got suspended for hitting that boy with a lunch tray, the one who took her to the party."

"I'm surprised she told you about it," I say.

"Well, I'd say she had an ulterior motive. I think she wants me to like you."

"It wasn't much of a fight. I just hit him out of nowhere with a lunch tray. I knocked his front teeth loose."

"Better you than me. If I got my hands on him I'd end up breaking his neck."

"You'd probably get a worse punishment than three days' suspension."

Colonel Marcus nods and rocks back on his heels. "For sure. How'd your mom react? You're in big trouble, I assume."

"Yeah, she freaked out a little."

"It's hard to be a single parent," Colonel Marcus says, taking Mom's side. "Always having to be both the good guy and the bad guy."

"It's hard to be a single kid, too," I say, before I actually think about whether it's a good idea to say anything.

"I wouldn't know."

"Well, it is. Whatever's wrong with your parents, you're the only one who knows about it." I stop and bite off the rest of what I was going to say as I realize I might be insulting him. But he seems to understand where I'm coming from and nods once in acknowledgment.

"And now your dad's business partner is with your mom," he says, not a question, and I can tell from his tone that Colonel Marcus understands our domestic situation perfectly.

"I guess so." My cheeks flame red at his mention of Mom and Chuck dating. Even if he can't read my mind, he makes me feel as if he can, and that's almost as bad.

He grunts in understanding and I get the sense, for sure now, that he must be a professional interrogator.

For most of the time we have been talking he has been casually glancing around at the street, the branches of the trees above us, his watch. He hasn't really been looking me right in the eye. But now he does, and it makes me distinctly uncomfortable. "Ophelia's very focused on her studies. And she's going to a great school next year. She's got the opportunity to really make something of herself. She doesn't need any distractions, or to be risking her future on childish things. Understand?"

"I guess so," I say. "Don't worry. I know I'm not good enough for her."

He doesn't even seem to digest what I say, but I know with Ophelia and her dad, looks can be deceiving.

"You going to be okay?" Colonel Marcus asks.

"Yeah," I say, too late for it to sound true. "Uh—yes. Sir. I'm fine."

He turns then to get into his car and I feel as if I should salute him. Instead I say, "Bye," weakly.

"Dane, you're early," Mr. Edgar says when I arrive for work that afternoon. "Employee of the month!" He will never—ever—get tired of that joke.

"I just couldn't wait to get here and start mopping, Mr. E.," I say as I walk through the store to see where I need to start my work.

Mr. Edgar and I keep up occasional banter back and forth as I work the aisles, dusting and mopping and polishing the cooler doors.

There's something about the work at the store that calms me, as if the only thing in the world that matters is the stain on the floor, the dust on the shelves. My brain is still working, worrying and imagining, but the focus of my energy on my menial tasks relaxes me and quiets the throbbing in my brain.

It is almost time to close the store when I finish the last of my chores, and I go to sit behind the counter to wait while Mr. Edgar goes through the business of closing his register for the day. We sit in companionable silence for a few minutes. My shift is done, but I always wait to make sure he gets to his car safely.

"Mr. Edgar," I say.

"Mm." He's still counting cash but does his best to seem like he's listening to me.

"What religion is your family?"

"The easiest kind," he says, smiling to himself. "No religion. I mean, we do Christmas, obviously, so we can get the presents. But I didn't grow up going to church or anything. Why?"

"I'm just wondering. Do you believe in reincarnation?"

Up until now he has been looking at the cash drawer as he counts his money and runs the daily report, but now he looks at me over the top of his glasses. "I'm going to say . . . no. It seems to me like any god who would go to the trouble to manage reincarnation would probably do better to spend their time preventing war or famine."

"But some religions believe in reincarnation, right?"

"I'm no expert, but I think Buddhists believe in some form of reincarnation."

"If you died and were reincarnated, what would you want to come back as?"

"Human."

"I mean like, what kind of animal?"

"A human is an animal. But I'd only want to come back if I could return with all the knowledge I've gained through being alive for fifty years. Because if I had to start all over again, what's the point?"

"Most people say a lion or a wolf or something."

"And live outside and possibly starve or get shot by some

big-game hunter? No thanks. What's wrong with human? That's it. I'd want to come back as a fully evolved human."

"Nothing, I guess," I say. "Nobody has ever given me that answer before. But it's a pretty good one."

When I park my car on the street that evening, I look up the long driveway to my house, lights burning in almost every window. I'm not ready to go home, to see Mom and Chuck. I have avoided Chuck since finding out that he knows every intimate thought I've had since Dad died. He probably still doesn't realize that I know, but I am too embarrassed to be in his company now. The only person I can really stand to see right now is Ophelia. Before I can talk myself out of it, I crunch down the gravel drive to Ophelia's front door. I knock and wait. After a few minutes nothing happens so I knock again.

I sense rather than see someone look out the small panes of glass that flank the front door, and a series of locks click before the door whooshes open. Colonel Marcus is holding his phone to his ear and only thrusts his chin at me in greeting as he makes an *mm-hmm* sound into the phone, clearly listening to the person on the other end. He steps back and holds the door open to let me enter, then waves his hand in the direction of the living room, gesturing for me to move inside.

Ophelia is studying, no surprise, open books spread around her on the couch and coffee table. Colonel Marcus doesn't follow me into the room. I hear his voice as he moves into the kitchen to continue his conversation and I head toward Ophelia as she looks up and turns to see who is coming inside.

She smiles when she sees me and I make the effort at smiling back, though the corners of my mouth tug downward involuntarily. Her expression changes as she sees something in my eyes that makes her stay silent.

I barely make it to the couch, sit down several feet from her, and hide my head in her lap before the tears come. I press my face into her thighs and wrap my arms awkwardly around her waist as one of her books digs painfully into my chest. My tears are hot against my skin as they seep out from my eyes and into her clothes.

I need to sniffle as snot threatens to run out onto her clothes, but I know that when I do take a breath in to abate the snot, what's going to come back out is a sob.

"Oh, Dane," she says, her voice just a coo when the sob can't be held inside any longer. "It's going to be okay."

I hear the sound of footsteps as Colonel Marcus comes into the room, and I feel Ophelia as she gestures him away. I cry for a while, for what feels like forever, as the tears keep coming. Ophelia keeps her hand on my back, rubbing it in a circle of warmth that waxes and wanes.

Finally, I sit up and Ophelia says, "You want some juice or something?"

I laugh at that, just a hiccup, and shake my head no.

"You want to talk about it?" she asks.

"There's nothing to talk about. Not really," I say. But then I do talk. I tell her about the conversations I've been having with Mom and Dr. Lineberger, and about the way I felt when I found the coyote dead on the side of the road, and how I'm angry, so angry, all the time, and it makes me exhausted. I just don't feel like I belong in the world anymore. Or, maybe, that I never did.

"I feel like that sometimes," she says as she gathers her books and stacks them on the coffee table. "You know, the other day, when you were talking about your mom and how mad you are at her, it reminded me of something that happened when I was younger. It's hard because you don't know my mom, and I can't really explain her to anybody who doesn't know her. She can be so charming, and funny, and she's really smart. She comes up with the craziest stories, makes every experience more interesting because of her imagination. I could never be as creative as she is. But most of the time, she's unreliable, and unpredictable, and . . . confusing." She pauses as her forehead creases at some thought she doesn't articulate. "Anyway, the house where we lived when I was little was really small. Her bedroom was on the first floor, where the only bathroom was, and upstairs there were just two small bedrooms. One time I was upset with her and she came upstairs to talk to me. And I started yelling at her, really screaming. I don't even remember what she did to make me so mad. Probably she spent all of our grocery money on wine, or she'd left me home alone all night to go out with some random guy. I don't remember. But I was so angry, I was yelling at her. And then she turned around to go back downstairs and, somehow, she tripped on one of the top steps and she fell, all the way down the stairs. It was so horrible. I can still see it if I close my eyes." As if to illustrate, Ophelia closes her eyes and faces the horrible memory of her mother falling. "And I was a kid, you know? Though I don't think I ever got to be a little kid. Not really. I was always taking care of her. But when she fell, it felt like I had caused it. Like my anger with her had made her fall down the stairs. I imagined that the fall could have killed her, or seriously injured her."

"Was she okay?" I ask.

"Yeah. Yeah, she was okay. But I wasn't," Ophelia says with a small, humorless laugh. "It felt like because I had let my anger out, had said all of these terrible things to her, it was as if I had pushed her down those stairs."

"I get it," I say with a nod.

Ophelia looks up and across the room and I follow her gaze to see Colonel Marcus standing there, his hands folded in front of him, resting in the at-ease posture. I hadn't even heard him come back into the room, have no idea how long he's been standing there listening. His face holds no expression, but he and Ophelia lock eyes, communicating without speaking.

"It made me feel," Ophelia says, her eyes still on her dad, "as if it is never okay to say what you feel, to tell anyone what you truly thought of them if you were angry or upset. If you say what you feel, it hurts people in ways that you can't take back. Somehow, I knew that from then on, and I could never tell my mom that I hated the person that she was. I've felt sorry for her from that very minute, and I've never been able to feel anger toward her without feeling terrible about it since then."

A quiet descends on the three of us and I realize the room has gotten dark as we have sat.

"Your mother loves you," Colonel Marcus says to Ophelia. "Sometimes people can't help themselves, the way they are. And we're all afraid, all the time, that we're going to disappoint the people we love." He's speaking to Ophelia, but his words feel like they are meant for me, too.

Ophelia nods at this and takes in a deep breath before she sighs. The feeling in the room is powerful in its confusion. So many emotions mixed up in the same space. It hasn't occurred to me before the kind of struggles that go on behind the windows of my neighbors' houses. But inside this space I feel safe, and like it's okay to say off-the-wall shit about how I feel.

"Anybody hungry?" Colonel Marcus asks. "I think I might run out to get a pizza."

"Sure," Ophelia says with a smile.

We are left alone in the house as Colonel Marcus goes out for a pizza, which surprises me, but doing anything other than talking with Ophelia is the farthest thing from my mind. Late into the night we sit on the couch talking and eating pizza and Colonel Marcus leaves us to go upstairs to his room at some point. The way we talk to each other, Ophelia and me, it's the same rhythm as it's always been, but there's something different now. Instead of talking about the world around us, we talk about us and how we feel and who we are. And it feels good. The way you would want it to feel if you could really open up and say the true things to a therapist, or to your parents.

I hang out at Ophelia's house until Colonel Marcus comes to tell us it's time for me to go home. Ophelia tells him she's going to walk me to the driveway and he gives her a look but doesn't object. I suppose her grounding extends to at least the property line.

We stand in the driveway of my house and I lean against Chuck's car as Ophelia slides her arms into my hoodie and rests the weight of her body on mine.

"I'm glad you came over," she says. "See? My dad isn't nearly as frightening as you think."

I put my hand under her hair, against the warmth of her neck, and she kisses me. I'm glad she takes the lead because I don't really know how. Her arms around my waist feels good and I feel like I'll never be able to get as close to her as I want to be.

I suppose I am thinking about sex as we are making out. It would be a lie to say I wasn't. But the way I feel as we're kissing and our hands are moving over each other it's more than that. I feel as if I could drink her, take her in like a tall cold bottle of Gatorade and feel her make the trip down my esophagus and settle into my stomach.

Now we are just standing, me still leaning against the side of the car, the length of her body pressed against mine. She buries her face in my neck and her breath warms me.

"What time will we break up?"

"How do you mean?" I ask with a frown she can't see because her face is still buried in the warmth of my neck.

"I mean," she says, pulling back a little, "we're going to break up the day before graduation; does that mean it ends at midnight on that day? Because if you leave it at all ambiguous it would be hard to know. Do I just wake up that morning and I never hear from you again?"

"Instead of setting a time, which would be weird, we should just end at whatever point we go to sleep that night."

"Even if it stretches into the next day?" she asks. "So, say I fall asleep at one in the morning, that would be our end point?"

"Yes. Exactly."

"Okay," she says with a nod. "So, the night before graduation. Whenever we fall asleep that night, that's it. No talking or seeing each other after that."

"Okay," I say, thinking somehow we have just resolved something, but it sure doesn't feel that way.

The senior prom is being held at a private club that overlooks the Potomac River. Against my wishes and better judgment, I agree to go. By some miracle, Colonel Marcus has agreed to let Ophelia go and to ride in my car. I guess even Colonel Marcus has to accept that at a certain point,

Ophelia is going to be grown-up and not under his control anymore.

Of course, he's probably only letting us go together because he has signed up to chaperone. I didn't even know that was a thing.

I leave the house when it is still light outside, trying not to feel self-conscious about wearing a tuxedo, which makes me feel like a kid playing dress-up. To make things worse, Mom is walking over with me to pick up Ophelia so she can get a picture of us together before we leave. I explain to her that Ophelia and I will probably get a formal portrait taken at the dance, but Mom insists that it isn't the same thing.

Colonel Marcus answers the door. He's wearing a suit and tie, his shoes shined to a mirror finish. He offers Mom a glass of wine while we wait for Ophelia to make her entrance.

Mom and Colonel Marcus are sitting in the living room talking as they drink their wine. Colonel Marcus has great manners, is on his best behavior for Mom. They talk and laugh and I think about what it would be like to have Colonel Marcus as a stepfather. Not so terrible, I decide. And then I entertain thoughts of Mom and Colonel Marcus dating, and him giving surprise inspections of my room. And it doesn't all seem so terrible because at least Colonel Marcus doesn't know all of the gory, horrible details of how the inside of my mind works the way Chuck does. But if Mom and Colonel Marcus got married, then Ophelia and I would be stepsiblings, and even though we have already set a date and time to break up, I am still hopeful we might have sex before that time. I'm not sure I would be cool with having Ophelia as a stepsister, even though our breakup would definitely happen well before Mom and Colonel Marcus got married. Ophelia would be eternally out of my grasp, so pretty much the way things are right now.

I am standing at the back of the couch, trying to find something to do with my arms that doesn't feel awkward, when Ophelia walks into the room.

Her dress is light purple, a color that would look terrible on anyone else, but against her black hair and complexion it is perfect. Her hair is loose and falls in perfect ringlets. If I'm being honest, I prefer the way she usually looks, in jeans and a T-shirt, her hair tamed into a braid. I prefer it because when she looks like she normally does, even though she is still beautiful, it's easier for me to look at her. The way she looks right now, it almost hurts to look at her. The weight of her beauty is like an ache so deep inside you can't rub it.

"Wow," Mom says, breaking the silence, which is a good thing, because I don't have it in me to speak.

"You look beautiful, sweetheart," Colonel Marcus says with the casual manner of someone who gets to look at her whenever they want.

Then everyone turns to me, waiting for me to say the right thing.

"It's good you don't usually look like that," I say. "No one would be able to do anything else but stare at you."

From the look on Ophelia's face, I know I've said the right thing. Maybe for the first time ever.

Then Mom is posing us by the fireplace and on the front porch for pictures and my collar is starting to itch.

We hold hands on the drive to the prom, and on the walk from the car to the entrance, where a committee of people waits to check everyone's ticket. We stop to pose for a formal picture and I'm sure that the camera has captured only a goofy smile from me that looks more like a grimace under the harsh lights. I'm sure everyone must be thinking what I am . . . what is that gorgeous, insanely smart and talented woman doing with that complete tool?

Ophelia has to make the rounds among her friends. She is so confident and comfortable among people. And I am not. Eventually, feeling unnecessary, I drift from her side and walk out onto the terrace, to contemplate the lights of Washington, D.C., shimmering on the river. For other people I think that the size of the world represents experiences and possibilities and for me it just seems too large and too frightening to ever make sense of one person, one squirrel, one coyote. I realize I have never felt more like a squirrel than I do right now, with the din of my classmates behind me, ready to take on that horizon that will always feel too distant and huge to be considered a destination.

I am surprised when Ophelia comes to find me and slips her hand into mine.

"Here you are," she says, and her words feel important because of the way I have been thinking.

"Here I am," I say. She laughs at the seriousness of my tone.

"I figured I'd find you out here, away from people."

Ophelia steps in to me for a hug. She puts her arms around my neck and, for once, I don't mind that she is as tall as I am in her high-heeled shoes. Her face is even with mine and she kisses me deeply. Every nerve in my body feels a spark as she presses herself into me. After our kiss, she puts her face in the side of my neck, her breath tickling me.

"You didn't have to leave your friends to come and talk to me," I say.

"I'm not here tonight because I want to be with them. I want to be with you."

"For at least a few days," I say.

She laughs at that. "They're all fucking squirrels, Dane. All of them, except for you and me."

"You've always been the only one," I say, because I feel safe saying it with her so close that she can't see my face, and maybe she can't even hear me over the sound of my heart.

"Took you long enough to say it," she says.

"Maybe it will be the only time I can."

She pulls her head back and looks me in the eye and I have to fight the urge to look away in embarrassment. "Once is enough," she says.

"Hello, Dane," Dr. Lineberger says, gesturing to the seats in her office.

"Hello."

"So, your mom says you've stopped taking your antide-pressants completely. Is that right?"

I hadn't really thought about it until that moment, but Dr. Lineberger is right. I haven't taken any of my antide-pressants in over a week. No, maybe two weeks. "I guess you're right."

"What about the Klonopin? Have you taken any for anxiety lately?"

"Maybe here and there. Habit, I guess. I took one before I went to the prom. I didn't expect to be that nervous about it, you know? It was my first time going to a dance."

"How was it?" Dr. Lineberger asks.

"Pretty lame."

"That sounds about right," she says with a knowing smile.

"At least there wasn't a whole lot of dancing. That part worried me the most. Did you go to your prom?" I ask.

"Oh, yes," she says as she nods. "That was a very long time ago."

I tell Dr. Lineberger about how Colonel Marcus was at the dance as a chaperone and she laughs as I imitate him strolling along the edge of the dance floor like a soldier in parade formation.

For all my worry about being forced to dance at the prom, we really didn't do much dancing. We went on the dance floor during slow songs and stood as close together as we dared under Colonel Marcus's watchful eye.

"So," Dr. Lineberger says, clasping her hands and placing

them on her knee, "have you had a chance to think about our conversation from last time?"

"Ye-es," I say, easing in slowly.

"And, do you think maybe you are in a place where you can start to forgive your mother for being human?"

"I suppose. I've been trying to be nicer to her, to not say the mean things that I think."

"Well, that's a start."

"I want to forgive her. I do. It's just hard. Every time I think I can just forgive her and move on, she does or says something that sets me off."

"Well," Dr. Lineberger says, holding up her hands in supplication, "being irritated with your parents when you're a teenager is just normal. Nature has its own way of encouraging you to leave the nest. If it was easy for grown children to get along with their parents then nobody would ever move out or get a job or start a family of their own. It's totally normal."

"It's nice to hear that something about me is normal."

"It's nice for anyone to hear that," Dr. Lineberger says. "We all go through life thinking that our problems or our feelings are unique. But I sit in this chair every day listening to people talk about their family challenges. There's no such thing as normal. There's a famous Russian author, a dead one, named Leo Tolstoy. Have you heard of him?"

"I think I was supposed to read a book by him last year and didn't."

"You should give him a try. Russian literature is probably pretty relatable for someone as in tune with your feelings as you are. Anyway, in one of his books Tolstoy says that happy families are all the same, but each unhappy family is unhappy in its own way. I find that to be very true. At least the part about unhappy families. Though I can't say if it's true that all happy families are the same. In my work, I don't meet a lot of happy families." Her eyes roll back in her head a little as she says this last part and I think that maybe not only would I be qualified to be a therapist at this point, but also maybe it would be kind of interesting. Like watching a reality show.

"You know what I think?" I ask her, because I really want her to know what I think. "Sometimes I think there's nothing wrong with me. I think there's something wrong with everybody else. I think about how sad I am to have lost my dad—all the time I'm sad. But I think that's normal. I have this kick-ass girlfriend, and, I mean, she's not going to be my girlfriend for very long, only until graduation, but she's the best. I totally dig her. And there's nothing wrong with that. Like, why shouldn't I be crazy about her? Why should I feel ashamed to say that I'm crazy about her? Everyone around me, they think I should take pills so that I don't feel too this or too that. That's what's crazy. All this time I've been looking for a reason to live, and it's right here. Just . . . feeling something."

"Being sad isn't the problem," Dr. Lineberger says. "Being crippled by sadness is what's the problem. You have to find something that makes you want to get out of bed in the morning. For some people, they have to search for that thing every day."

"It's just a lot easier to find things to be unhappy about," I say. "There's so many things that can make you unhappy, if you think about it."

"And so many things that can make you happy, too."

"I guess."

It's lunch period and I'm headed to Ms. Guinn's classroom. This time, she actually asked me to come. I can't imagine why. I've been staying on top of my work lately, showing up for class. Maybe she wants to congratulate me for doing the bare minimum that is expected, but I doubt it.

She sets aside the book she's reading when I walk into the classroom. "Hello, Dane. Thanks for coming."

"Am I in some kind of trouble?" I ask.

"No. Take a seat."

I obey, taking a seat right in front of her desk.

"I wanted to talk to you about your final grade. What grade do you think you should get for the year?"

"If I'm being honest? Maybe a D."

She nods. "I agree with you."

"Is that it? That's why you wanted me to come by?" I ask.

"No. I agree with you that based on your work and effort, you deserve a D for the year. Do you know what that would mean?"

I'm unsure if this is a trick question, so I just shake my head.

"It would mean that you don't graduate. You need at least a C in Civics and English to graduate. It would mean summer school. That is, if you want to graduate. Do you?"

"I don't know. This whole time, I thought I didn't really care about school. Didn't care about my future. But lately, I've been thinking, I'm pretty sure I didn't believe I could graduate. And, even if I did, what's the point? I can't decide what I want to do, where to go."

"You don't have to figure that out right away. You could start by taking a few classes at the community college. Find out if anything interests you. Or maybe study a skilled trade. Maybe you'd like a job that involves working with your hands. The point is, you don't have to know right now."

"Okay."

"The reason I wanted to talk to you is because I figured your performance in your other classes was about the same as it was in my class." Her smile is almost apologetic as she says, "After talking to your other teachers, I know that assumption was correct."

"Yeah," I say, and blow out a sigh, "I'm pretty much a straight-D student."

"I was a lot like you in high school. Actually, I was a Goth—wore a lot of black clothes and makeup, smoked clove cigarettes, listened to the Cure a lot. . . ." She kind of drifts off then, looking into the middle distance as she's lost in her memories of a misspent youth.

"I'm not really into the Cure," I say. "I used to like the

Smiths but I don't listen to them anymore. Did you know Morrissey is a racist?"

"I had no idea. That's disappointing. Anyway, I didn't bring you here to talk about eighties music. I asked you to come see me today so I could tell you that I'm going to give you a B as your final grade for the semester."

"Really? Why would you do that?"

"Because I think once you leave this place, get out into the world, you'll find something to make you happy and productive. I think keeping you here, for summer school or to repeat the senior year, would be a mistake. I've spoken to some of your other teachers—most important, your Civics teacher—and I've asked them to consider giving you the same chance. I can't make any promises, but . . . we'll see."

"That's nice of you, I guess. I don't understand why, though."

"You don't have to understand. Just say thank you and don't screw up the chance I'm giving you."

"Thank you," I say obediently.

"Now, get out of here before you say something to make me change my mind."

The Parent Teacher Student Association is hosting a graduation event, a fact I hadn't cared about before today. I never had plans to attend my own graduation. The event is supposed to include parents and teachers for the early part of the evening, then switch to a students-only party that will go until dawn.

I think the theory is that if parents provided an all-night party, it would minimize the potential for students to engage in risky behavior. This theory is, of course, ridiculous. Anyone looking for opportunities to destroy their future will find a way.

Ophelia is going to the graduation party and asked me if I would be there. I said maybe, while thinking no.

In my imagination I am crashing the graduation party. I'll walk into the room and the needle will scratch off the record and everyone will stop and stare at me, standing in the entrance, all of them thinking I'm a madman. But that isn't what happens.

When I get to the party it's early enough that there is still a big crowd of people, parents and teachers and the entire graduating class. No one really seems to notice my arrival. The principal is up on the stage, talking into a microphone, and there's occasional applause as the principal hands out some awards to people—parents for their volunteer contributions and a teacher who was voted everybody's favorite. I see Ms. Guinn, standing off in a corner watching the presentation, and I see Eric, hanging out with his posse of douchebags. Mom and Chuck are here, too, chaperoning the event, and Eric is only allowed to stay as late as they do.

Now it's Eric's turn to be angry and resentful toward Mom and Chuck as they have put restrictions on his freedoms. I know from what I have overheard around school that Eric's friends all have hotel rooms for tonight, where they will go to drink and party until dawn.

Eric is angry about having to miss all of the fun, and he blames me for the trouble he is in.

I walk through the crowd, looking for Ophelia. Finally, I find her. I hadn't seen her before because she's standing next to the steps that lead to the stage, waiting for the principal to call her up to accept an award. I don't hear the principal's words or what award Ophelia is getting.

I reach the front of the room right as Ophelia climbs onto the stage and walks over to the podium to accept her award. The principal gives her a hug, which surprises me. I never could have imagined having a relationship like that with an authority figure, especially an authority figure from school.

Just as Ophelia takes her award and gives a wave to the applauding crowd, she looks down and sees me near the front of the room. Her expression shifts from surprise to a smile and she hurries to leave the spotlight. She arrives at my side slightly out of breath, a question in her gaze. She hugs me, and the people around us are watching with interest.

"Where have you been?" Ophelia asks me as she takes my hand and pulls me to the edge of the room.

"I was going to stay away. Let you have your night. This might be the last time you see most of these people."

"I don't care about any of these people. The only person I care about is you."

"Okay," I say. "You want to get out of here? Maybe talk about it someplace else?"

"Yes. Definitely," Ophelia says. "It's our last night."

"I know," I say. "I wouldn't have missed it for anything."

We decide to go down to the park. At our age, there is no other place we can be alone, be completely free to say and do what we want.

Down at the park we pull a picnic table out to the edge of the pavilion, as far as the chain that holds it in place will allow us, as if there was a real risk someone might come down to the park to steal a five-hundred-pound picnic table with a steel base. We stand on the table so we can climb onto the roof of the pavilion and stretch out under the stars. We are lying on asphalt shingle, and it feels like sandpaper catching against our clothes. The roof of the pavilion has a low pitch, so that lying on our backs the surface feels almost flat, like lying on a mattress covered in fine gravel.

No one would choose a mattress covered in gravel, but it is the bed I share with the girl I want to hold, so it's okay.

Ophelia takes up a comfort position, her head resting on my chest, her weight pressing my arm into the rough surface beneath us. I don't mind. The softness of her body against mine outweighs the discomfort of the asphalt shingle, and I open my mind to the expanse of the universe that blankets us.

The moon is half lit, and I contemplate the dark half, dimly visible if I focus on it.

"My dad," I say, "used to tell me, 'I love you the way the moon loves the sun.' He said that all the time."

"That's lovely," Ophelia says. Her voice sounds sleepy, but, as if to reassure me she is really listening, she shifts her head against my shoulder. "What does that mean?"

"My dad always said the moon is just a rock. Cold and dark, no light of its own. The moon loves the sun because the sun makes the moon beautiful. Shines on it to give it warmth. Lights it up so that the people on earth worship its beauty. He always said I was his sun. I mean, sun, like S-U-N. I was his son, his boy, but I was also his sun. Because I was the thing that made him shine, made him something other than a cold, dark rock." My voice catches on this last part and there is no way Ophelia doesn't notice. I am close to crying, the way I always am when I think about my dad. The two biggest objects known to man, the moon and the sun, and I can't think about either one of them without thinking about my dad, without wanting to cry. "I haven't been anybody's sun since my dad died," I say, and my throat aches with restrained sobs.

"I'm sorry I didn't really know him," Ophelia says. "Sounds like he was really romantic."

I appreciate that she has something to say like that. That she was sorry not to have known my dad. Rather than just saying she was sorry for me that he is gone.

"I guess. Yeah, I suppose he was romantic. A lot more romantic than my mom. She doesn't believe in true love."

"Well, you can be my sun. I mean, like the star at the center of our galaxy. Not my kid. That would be creepy and weird. You know, I remember when I just accepted the fact that my mom was never going to really be there for me. She was never going to live up to my expectations for what a mom should be. It was like a gut punch—took everything right out of me."

"And now?"

"And now I'm used to it. I won't say I've accepted it. Maybe I never will. But I've stopped hoping for a different outcome. No expectations means no disappointments, right?"

"Right. But someone like you—you should be allowed to have expectations. You're smart and you're going to do awesome things with your life. It must be exciting for you, leaving to go away to school," I say, testing how much it hurts to think about her being gone.

"Exciting. Scary. The great big 'what if.' I don't think I'm so smart. I just work hard."

"You are smart," I say as I turn my head to deposit a kiss somewhere on her head and getting a big mouthful of hair. "Smartest person I know."

"You're pretty smart, too," Ophelia says, "when you aren't saying something dumb."

"I've been thinking a lot about tonight," I say.

"Oh?"

"Yeah. I've been thinking I'm going to miss having you as my girlfriend."

"I suppose we didn't really think it through, deciding to just end it at graduation. It seemed so far away when we started talking about it."

"And now it's here. But, I've been thinking, you know, can I really love you? Love you the way someone should love you, when I have this giant hole in my heart? Being in love, it's like . . . standing at the edge of a cliff, deciding to jump off holding hands. Like that movie with those two women who drive off the cliff together."

"*Thelma and Louise.*"

"That's their names?"

"That's the name of the movie. And their names."

"Yeah. Like Thelma and Louise. You stare off into the abyss and decide, 'I'm going to do it, I'm going to jump.'"

"And it's going to hurt a lot when you land," Ophelia says, finishing my thought.

"Yeah."

We're both quiet for a minute, maybe thinking about what Thelma and Louise ended up with at the bottom of the cliff.

"Is that what you think?" Ophelia asks me. She props herself up on one elbow to look right into my face. "You think you're in love with me?"

I study the side of her face that is illuminated by the streetlight from the parking lot. I look at the lines of her cheekbone and the side of her nose.

"I think you're like a goddess," I say. "I don't believe in a god, but I worship you. I could be the founder of a religion with you as the goddess. That's how amazing I think you are."

"I suppose it's easier to say 'I love you' than to say that,"

Ophelia says as she puts her head back on my shoulder, flipping her hair out of the way as she lands. "I wish we had a blanket. I could go to sleep out here."

"Yeah," I say as I take a deep breath and push out a lungful of air. "Let's pretend like we can just stay here forever. We never need a job, or money, or a roof over our heads. We can just stay here and be comfortable forever."

"Until we have to go to the bathroom," Ophelia says.

Maybe she's not as romantic as she likes to think she is.

"Until then, I guess," I agree.

"I don't want to go to sleep. Once we go to sleep, that's it. Tomorrow is graduation."

"Let's go back to my house," I say. "We can hang out in my room where it's more comfortable."

"I think we should go out to a twenty-four-hour place to eat first. Our last night ends when we go to sleep. I want to stay up for as long as possible."

"I want to stay up all night," I say. "I want to hold you for as long as I can."

ACT V

WE KNOW WHAT WE ARE, BUT KNOW
NOT WHAT WE MAY BE

If you knew you were going to die at the age of seventeen, it would impact every decision you made—who you dated; if you tried to be a better person; whether you told the people you loved that they are important. Probably you wouldn't worry about whether you were popular or not, and you wouldn't care about tools like Eric. People like that would be insignificant.

You definitely wouldn't worry about grades, or whether you were going to college.

But if you didn't have the luxury of knowing ahead of time when you were going to die, maybe you'd keep a part-time job in a grocery store and go to classes at the local community college until you figured out what you wanted to do. And if you never figured it out, well, that's fine, too. There's lot of people who live to be forty-seven or sixty-seven and they haven't figured it out, either.

The sun is shining and I am uncomfortably warm in my graduation gown. The gown and hat are black. The girls are dressed in red, making the graduating class of McLean High School look like a checkerboard of chaos.

The commencement speech, by some politician whose kid goes to McLean High School, is probably only about fifteen minutes long, but it feels like forever. I'm not the only one who feels that way. People are shifting in their seats, murmuring to each other.

Now, as class valedictorian, it's Ophelia's turn to get up and speak. I have given up many golden hours of time with Ophelia over the past few weeks as she has prepared her speech for graduation. I resented it at the time, but now I am glad she is the kind of person who takes time to prepare. I feel my face flush in sympathetic embarrassment for her, every molecule of my body hoping that she doesn't make a fool of herself onstage.

Ophelia is tall, her back erect, and her black hair is stunning against the dark red of her graduation robe. Her hair is loose, hanging in a perfect halo of ringlets under her graduation cap. Even from my seat in the sixth row, the softness of her brown eyes gets to me the way it always does. She's not awkward or scared, and just pauses for a moment, using the same tactic teachers do to get a restless class to settle.

As I look at her up at the podium, I feel the same sense of reverent awe that I always feel when I look at her. But now I feel a sense of pride, too. I'm proud that this girl was my girlfriend, if only for a little while. It means that there is something worth liking about me. Even, maybe, something worth loving.

"I had a speech prepared for today." Ophelia's voice is strong, the first words of her speech perfectly clear. Her mouth twists into a conspiratorial smile as she gives the impression, like she always does, that maybe she's in on some kind of joke the rest of us just don't get. "I spent a lot of time writing it, and rewriting it, and I had it just the way I wanted it. I always like to be prepared, to know exactly what the outcome of anything will be, so I had planned my speech carefully for today. And then, a few days ago, I threw out that speech and wrote something else.

"It was hard for me, because I don't like surprise endings. I want movies to end with a kiss, the heroine riding off into the sunset, the good guys winning the fight, and the bad guys getting what they have coming to them. I want only happy endings." From the corner of my eye I catch Eric, seated a few rows ahead with others who have names earlier in the alphabet, chuckling, turning in his seat to give a couple of his friends a knowing look at Ophelia's use of the phrase "happy endings," but Ophelia is oblivious to it. It is a reminder that education, even the most privileged kind, does not necessarily lead to enlightenment.

"A friend of mine once said to me," Ophelia continues, her eyes searching for me in the crowd, "that everything ends—and usually things end badly. At the time I agreed with that. When we think about endings, often it is something bad—the end of a fun experience; the end of a relationship; the end of a life."

Ophelia's gaze leaves mine as she moves on to captivate other people with her direct stare. "But I feel differently now. I think I've figured out the secret to a happy life," she says, and she says it in a way that makes everyone want to be in on the secret with her. "Maybe tomorrow the idea will seem trite, but today, I know the meaning of life." She leans back from the podium a little and looks around the audience. Then she comes back into the microphone to say, "Do you want me to tell you the meaning of life?" She waits again, waits to see that her audience is engaged, that they really are waiting to hear the meaning of life. I know I am.

"The secret is, you can't think of life as a series of beginnings and endings. We think about it that way because we begin with birth, and end with death. But life isn't about beginnings and endings. Today, our graduation day, can be looked at as an ending. The end of high school, the end of important friendships, the end of relationships with some teachers we love, and some we don't. For some it is the end of incarceration in the halls and classrooms of our school. It's the end of a lot of things.

"Graduation is also a beginning. It's the beginning of adult life, the beginning of college, the beginning of the real world.

"But I think, when we look at life as a series of beginnings and endings, we miss the things that are really worth commemorating. We forget to care that all of those parts are important. We celebrate graduations and retirements and births and deaths, and we forget to celebrate all of the parts in between. And that's really sad.

"So, that's all I wanted to say to you today. By all means, celebrate graduation as an ending, or as a beginning.

Celebrate it as whatever you want. But don't forget to celebrate the moments in between, because those are the moments that really matter.

"Goodbye, graduating class of ___ , and Godspeed."

Ophelia takes off her graduation cap and, with a whoop, throws it high into the air. The sun catches her cap as it sails through the air, and leaves the perfect outline of the tassel and board etched in my mind like a memory that just might stay there.